THE NORTON L

Selected Ta

NIKOLAI GOGOL was born on March 20, 1809, in the Ukrainian town of Sorochyntsi, on the periphery of the Russian Empire. He attended the Nizhyn School of Higher Art, now Nizhyn Gogol State University, where he first began writing. On leaving school in 1828, Gogol moved to St. Petersburg to pursue his literary ambitions, and his first collection of short stories, *Evenings on a Farm Near Dikanka*, was published in 1831 to general acclaim. While his early stories were written in the tradition of Ukrainian folklore, his later stories, known as the Petersburg tales, established his reputation as a great surrealist and satirist of life under the Russian Empire. In his later years, Gogol lived abroad throughout Europe, particularly Italy, where he developed a great appreciation for Rome, and wrote the first part of his unfinished masterpiece *Dead Souls* (1842). He died in Moscow, Russia, on February 21, 1852.

MICHAEL R. KATZ was born in New York and educated at the Horace Mann School, Williams College, and the University of Oxford. He taught Russian language and literature at Williams College, the University of Texas at Austin, and Middlebury College, where he is the C. V. Starr Professor Emeritus of Russian and East European Studies. He is the author of two monographs—*The Literary Ballad in Early Nineteenth-Century Russian Literature* and *Dreams and the Unconscious in Nineteenth-Century Russian Fiction*—and the translator of over fifteen Russian novels into English, including works by Turgenev, Dostoevsky, and Tolstoy. He lives in Cornwall, Vermont.

KATE HOLLAND is Associate Professor of Russian literature in the Department of Slavic Languages and Literatures at the University of Toronto. She is the author of *The Novel in the Age of Disintegration: Dostoevsky and the Problem of Genre in the 1870s*, and co-editor of *A Dostoevskii Companion: Texts and Contexts* and *Dostoevsky at 200: The Novel in Modernity*, as well as articles on Dostoevsky, Herzen, Saltykov-Shchedrin, Tolstoy, and historical poetics. She is President of the North American Dostoevsky Society.

For a complete list of titles in the Norton Library, visit
wwnorton.com/norton-library

THE NORTON LIBRARY

Nikolai Gogol
Selected Tales

Translated by

Michael R. Katz

Introduction by

Kate Holland

W. W. NORTON & COMPANY
Celebrating a Century of Independent Publishing

W. W. Norton & Company has been independent since its founding in 1923, when William Warder Norton and Mary D. Herter Norton first published lectures delivered at the People's Institute, the adult education division of New York City's Cooper Union. The firm soon expanded its program beyond the Institute, publishing books by celebrated academics from America and abroad. By midcentury, the two major pillars of Norton's publishing program—trade books and college texts—were firmly established. In the 1950s, the Norton family transferred control of the company to its employees, and today—with a staff of five hundred and hundreds of trade, college, and professional titles published each year—W. W. Norton & Company stands as the largest and oldest publishing house owned wholly by its employees.

Introduction copyright © 2023 by Kate Holland
Translation, Note on the Translation, and Annotations copyright © 2023 by Michael R. Katz

Associate Editor: Katie Pak
Assistant Editor: Olivia Atmore
Project Editor: Maura Gaughan
Associate Project Editor: Selin Tekgurler
Manufacturing by LSC Communications
Compositor: Westchester Publishing Services
Book design by Marisa Nakasone and Justin Rose
Production Manager: Karen Romano

Library of Congress Cataloging-in-Publication Data

ISBN: 978-0-393-42792-9 (pbk.)

W. W. Norton & Company, Inc., 500 Fifth Avenue, New York, N.Y. 10110
www.wwnorton.com

W. W. Norton & Company Ltd., 15 Carlisle Street, London W1D 3BS

1 2 3 4 5 6 7 8 9 0

Contents

Introduction

It is clear from the beginning of Nikolai Gogol's "The Nose" (1836), when a barber finds a nose in his breakfast loaf of bread, that the tale is the product of an extraordinary imagination. As the story continues, and the nose turns out to belong to a pompous civil servant, and it begins to walk around the streets of the Russian imperial capital, St. Petersburg, wearing clothes that indicate its position as superior to that of its former owner in the all-important state hierarchy, that initial impression is only reinforced. Finally, when neither the story's narrator nor any of the characters express any surprise at the inconceivability of the nose's shenanigans, but are concerned only with social propriety, it becomes clear that this startlingly original imaginary universe has a distinctly satirical edge. The other stories in this collection also reflect this vision, their strange perspectives forcing us to reassess how we see the world.

Gogol's rich artistic vision was shaped by the linguistically and culturally mixed region of his birth on the left (or east) bank of the Dnieper River in Ukraine, then part of the Russian Empire; the social stimulation of time spent in the glittering literary circles of St. Petersburg; and finally the aesthetic draw of Rome, one of Europe's most artistically and architecturally inspiring cities. His life is one of dramatic contrasts and often frustrated rebellion against the perspectival limits and expectations imposed by social and cultural authorities which could not countenance the contradictions of his character and imagination. His works too, straddle the boundary between Romanticism and Realism, providing inspiration for the later big names of Russian literature such as Fyodor Dostoevsky, whose own first work, *Poor Folk* (1846), could not have been written without Gogol's tales.

Gogol's Life

Nikolai Vasilevich Gogol, or Mykola Vasylovych Hohol, as he is known in Ukrainian, was born in 1809 in the town of Velyki Sorochyntsi in the Poltava governorate, in the socially, culturally, and linguistically diverse area known as left-bank Ukraine.[1] Part of the Russian Empire since the seventeenth century, this area had enjoyed some autonomy at the beginning of the eighteenth century under the Cossack Hetmanate but was under more direct Russian imperial control by the end. Gogol's original last name, inherited from his father, the playwright Vasily Afanasyevich Gogol-Yanovsky, reveals both his Ukrainian Cossack noble ancestry (Gogol) and his Polish noble ancestry (Yanovsky) and reflects the long historical influence of the Polish-Lithuanian Commonwealth, the state to which Poltava belonged prior to its incorporation into the Russian Empire. That Gogol chose to remove the Polish part of his name testifies to his own deep understanding of the complex linguistic and cultural intermingling that held sway in the region of his birth. Ukraine, known at the time as "Little Russia," held a paradoxical position in the Russian cultural imagination, representing both the imperial periphery—the quintessential boondocks—and an attractive source of well-defined folkloric tradition and bewitching tales which were fashionable in the literary circles of St. Petersburg,

---

1. While until recently most English language treatments of Gogol have discussed him as a Russian writer, current scholarship is beginning to focus more on his complex identity as a Ukrainian writer on the periphery of the Russian Empire. For a comprehensive discussion of Gogol as a colonial writer as well as an analysis of the importance of the literary and linguistic context of left-bank Ukraine, see Yuliya Ilchuk, *Nikolai Gogol: Performing Hybridic Identity* (Toronto: University of Toronto Press, 2021).

where Gogol moved following his graduation from the Nizhyn School of Higher Art in 1828. From his arrival at the imperial capital in 1831 to his first publication, the story collection *Evenings on a Farm Near Dikanka*, in 1832, Gogol was keenly aware of the benefits and drawbacks of his identity as an imperial subject from the periphery and learned how to use national stereotypes to his advantage.

Gogol arrived in St. Petersburg three years after the Decembrist revolt, an uprising of liberal gentry who, following the death of Alexander I and the private refusal of succession by his younger brother and heir apparent Konstantin, attempted a coup against the next in line, the Tsar's next younger brother, Nikolai, in favor of Konstantin. These years saw Tsar Nikolai I's repressive consolidation of power and the rise of conservative nationalist ideology in court circles and beyond. While Gogol's Ukrainian identity was a potential vulnerability and made him the occasional butt of ridicule and national stereotypes, recent scholarship has revealed his agile negotiation of the perils of language and identity within the high literary circles he occupied.[2] Accounts of contemporaries testify to Gogol's keen fashion sense and attunement to issues of social self-representation, and his ability to shapeshift in linguistic and cultural terms clearly emerges in his Petersburg tales of the 1830s. These stories, as well as his famous play *The Government Inspector* (1836), in which a provincial town is bamboozled by a corrupt civil servant impersonating a government inspector, reveal the gap between the self-mythologizing of the Russian imperial state and the chaotic reality beneath.

Following mixed criticism of *The Government Inspector,* Gogol traveled to Rome in 1836, where he experienced a period of great creativity that peaked in 1842 with the publication of the first part of *Dead Souls*, his novel-epic. Though the work was envisioned in three parts, as a Russian *Divine Comedy*, only the first part, the "Inferno," was ever published in full. Following Dante, Gogol conceived the first part as a savage indictment of Russian society and its foibles, while the other two parts would represent an attempt to find redemption in contemporary Russian life. The story of a

2. Ilchuk, *Nikolai Gogol,* 42–66.

civil servant who buys up dead serfs to work his land in a money-making scheme, the novel straddles the uneasy ideological position of satirizing the bureaucratic and economic corruption of the Russian Empire, as did *The Government Inspector,* while suggesting an imminent great national spiritual rebirth represented in its final image of a speeding carriage, or *troika.* Gogol, a conservative and a traditionalist in many ways, and becoming even more so with age, saw the representation of Russia in *Dead Souls* in religious and ethical rather than political terms. But if the critique of society came easily to the author of *The Government Inspector,* he had more difficulties with the positive elements. Frustrated with the second part, he burned it, leaving only fragments. In the last part of the 1840s, Gogol became very religious and experienced a depressive spiritual crisis. He had always been attracted to the more mystical aspects of Russian Orthodoxy, and at the end of his life he was haunted by demonic visions. He died in 1852, possibly of starvation from fasting, a central part of the ascetic practices surrounding Russian Orthodoxy. Already in Gogol's lifetime, critics were divided over the question of how to read his stories: as satirical attacks on the Russian state and its institutions, or as pathbreaking aesthetic experiments in the art of storytelling? The stories in this collection testify to the persuasive nature of both of these interpretations.

Ukrainian Tales

The first story of this selection, "Ivan Fyodorovich Shponka and His Auntie" (1832), belongs to the second volume of *Evenings on a Farm Near Dikanka.* This two-volume collection of stories of Ukrainian peasant life reflects the complex social, cultural, and linguistic context of the Poltava governorate where Gogol grew up. It is structured around a frame narrator—a Ukrainian beekeeper, Rudy Panko, who relates to the reader a series of wondrous tales he has heard against the backdrop of lavish descriptions of feasts and celebrations which cater to Russian readers' interest in the culture of the Ukrainian periphery. Published in St. Petersburg, the collection, with its avuncular narrator, showcases the storytelling central to all of Gogol's tales. It is written in a mixture of literary Russian and Ukrainian colloquialisms which would have provided

"local color" to the Russian readers but served as a familiar refer-
ence for those who, like Gogol himself, had grown up in the bilin-
gual environment of left-bank Ukraine.

"Shponka," like many of the other stories in the collection, is
presented as having been narrated to Panko by another character, in
this case a certain Stepan Ivanovich Kurochka from the village of
Gadyach. Panko prefaces the story by commenting on Kurochka's
storytelling style (he tells the whole story from beginning to end), as
well as telling us where he lives (near the church) and where he can
be found every morning (choosing fish and vegetables at the
market and chatting to the priest or a Jewish farmer). This preface
emphasizes the social and cultural texture of the tale as well as
the shape of the narration. It is the form of these stories which is
important in the context of Gogol's literary trajectory, rather than
the events they represent. "Shponka" recounts the life of the titular
hero from his school days, where his exemplary behavior meets
with the teacher's approval, through his army service, to his sudden
summons to his estate following his mother's death, when he meets
his larger-than-life "Auntie," Vasilisa Tsupchevska, a strong-willed
unmarried woman of immense size and strength who is taken right
out of Ukrainian or Russian folklore. Ivan himself is passive in the
face of such forceful personalities as Vasilisa and Grigory Grigorevich Storchenko, a nearby landowner whose pillow-like cheeks Ivan
kisses with a great deal of enjoyment, reflecting an undercurrent of
homosexual and homosocial desire throughout Gogol's writing.
Such motifs have led more than one critic to argue that Gogol's literary imagination at least suggests his possible homosexuality, though
his strong religious beliefs throughout his life may well have pre-
vented him from acting on his desires.[3] Sensual pleasure is a significant driver of narrative within the story: the magnificent feast
Storchenko offers Ivan at his house serves as the story's centerpiece,
and the melons Ivan's father grew remain bright in the memory of
Storchenko's neighbor, serving as a reminder of the rich fertility of
the land. The story's material, the social fabric of Ukrainian peasant
life, differs markedly from the material of the Petersburg tales that

3. On the question of Gogol's sexuality, see Simon Karlinsky, *The Sexual Labyrinth of Nikolai
Gogol* (Chicago: University of Chicago Press, 1976).

follow, which deal with the urban psychosocial reverberations of the state bureaucracy. But its organization and vision, as well as its emphasis on storytelling and use of Romantic tropes such as dreams, foreshadow the later stories.

The Petersburg Text and "Notes of a Madman"

All the other tales in this collection are inspired by St. Petersburg, the city that was Gogol's home from 1828, and belong to a group that has become known as Gogol's "Petersburg Tales," though they were not originally published under that title. These stories, perhaps most notably "Nevsky Prospect" (1835), reflect Gogol's move from Ukraine to St. Petersburg, a move that involved a change in perspective on the Empire and its meanings. The imperial capital, founded in 1703 by Peter the Great, came to stand for both the achievements of absolute power and the extraordinary sacrifices required by such power. Dostoevsky would later call St. Petersburg "the most abstract and premeditated city on earth."[4] Gogol's Petersburg tales play a crucial role in the establishment of the so-called "Petersburg text."

"The Petersburg text" is the name given by scholars of Russian literature to a body of work that mythologizes the paradoxical nature of St. Petersburg as at once an Enlightenment city and a place constantly subject to existential threats of falling back into the chaos out of which it was built. The genre came to fruition with the poem *The Bronze Horseman* (1833), by Alexander Pushkin, a poetry and prose writer generally regarded as the founder of modern Russian literature and with whom Gogol was frequently compared during his lifetime. Subtitled "A Petersburg Tale," *The Bronze Horseman* juxtaposes a mythologized vision of the founding of St. Petersburg with the reality of its location on a swamp beset by regular flooding. Pushkin's poem contrasts the surfaces of the city, the Italianate palaces and grand bridges and boulevards, and what lies beneath, the threadbare huts and swirling floodwaters. This contrast maps onto a broader tension between

---

4. F. M. Dostoevskii, *Polnoe Sobranie sochinenii v tritstati tomakh*, ed. V. G. Bazanov et al. 30 vols. (Leningrad: Nauka, 1972–90) 5:101.

order and chaos that looms about the geometrically precise lines and angles of Peter the Great's city.

The protagonist of *The Bronze Horseman* is a clerk (*chinovnik*), defined by his low rank (*chin*) on the Table of Ranks, the system of classification of service roles in the bureaucracy introduced by Peter the Great, a reproduction of which can be found in this volume. One of the main institutions of the Petrine order, the Table of Ranks was intended to define the duties and positions of those working in the imperial bureaucracy and was meritocratic in theory; those who achieved certain ranks were granted individual noble status, and those higher could be granted hereditary nobility. However, it became increasingly viewed as an inflexible system that kept those in the lower ranks in their place, offering very little possibility of promotion to the ranks that granted nobility. Like Pushkin's protagonist, Gogol's heroes are pen-pushers, copying clerks; those whose primary function is to transcribe the words of others. The protagonists of "Notes of a Madman," "The Nose," and "The Overcoat" are all lower-level clerks whose entire social lives are defined by their rank. Their working lives are portrayed as tedious days of drudgery in which individual needs and desires are subsumed by the all-consuming bureaucratic machine.

In *The Bronze Horseman*, Pushkin juxtaposes the themes of madness and subjection to power, as his clerk protagonist's mind is warped by the loss of his fiancée and the absolute nature of Peter's power over the city and its inhabitants. In "Notes of a Madman" (1834), Gogol also brings together themes of madness and subordination, but his protagonist, Poprishchin, is even more constrained by the limits of his professional and social status—his rank is that of titular councilor, grade 9 on the Table of Ranks, just below the level at which hereditary nobility is granted, and his main responsibilities consist of sharpening quills in the director's office and copying documents. Poprishchin, though, is liberated by a madness that makes all things possible. Stymied in his romantic ambition to marry the director's daughter by his rank and his failure to be promoted, he takes refuge in a shift in perspective where he identifies with her dog and imagines its correspondence with another dog, before then identifying with a news story about an interregnum caused by the Carlist Wars in Spain. His desire to escape a world in which he is slighted by footmen helps to create an alternative, and far richer, universe in which he ultimately imagines himself as the rightful heir to the Spanish throne. The escapism of Poprishchin's fantasy is a dominant strain throughout Gogol's tales.

Poprishchin's fantasy is also an act of mutiny that echoes the Petersburg theme, introduced in *The Bronze Horseman*, of the clerk's rebellion against the system—his insistence on following his desires against the all-powerful machinery of the state. Such acts of rebellion are always punished; if not by the literal ghost of Peter the Great, then by other mysterious and powerful forces at work in the city. Poprishchin's punishment hardly emerges, because "Notes of a Madman" is narrated entirely in the form of his own diary entries (it is one of very few of Gogol's stories with a narrator-protagonist). Poprishchin's narration increasingly narrows on his fantasy world, and his fate remains unclear. Other Petersburg tales such as "Nevsky Prospect," "The Portrait," "The Nose," "The Carriage," and "The Overcoat" have a first-person narrator who is outside of the main action of the plot and provides often-satirical commentary on the plot developments. In each of these stories, rebellion leads to punishment. In "The Nose" and "The Overcoat," the hubris of bureaucrats in believing themselves able to rise above their positions appears to be punished by supernatural or inexplicable events.

"Nevsky Prospect"

"Nevsky Prospect" is structured around the revelation of these mysterious forces. The story takes its name and setting from the city's main boulevard, the most potent symbol of man's supposed triumph over nature. Nevsky Prospect is St. Petersburg's main artery, leading from the religious heart of the city, the Alexander Nevsky Monastery, to its naval heart, the Admiralty. All other main streets lead out of that central boulevard. As a main thoroughfare, Nevsky Prospect was a space where people from all walks of life mixed and collided. It was the hub of commerce, where all the foreign merchants and department stores offered their wares, and was thus the center both of the city's foreignness and of its consumerism. It was also a stage upon which different classes of society appeared to present an image. In the famous opening of "Nevsky

Prospect," in which Gogol's narrator follows the different groups of people who appear on the boulevard over a twenty-four-hour-long period, the street seems to carry no secrets—these lie beyond, on the side streets and back alleys of the city's interior.

"Nevsky Prospect" begins with the narrator claiming that "there is nothing finer than Nevsky Prospect," a hyperbole deflated somewhat by the qualification "at least not in Petersburg" (p. 28). This combination of hyperbole and deflation sets the tone for the story's complex rhetorical balance between paeans to the splendor of its subject and the suggestion that all will not be as it seems. The following paragraphs focus on the people passing through the street at different times of day, from different classes and different professions. In the morning servants go about their business, while by noon their place is taken by students. They are then replaced by dandies and civil servants later in the afternoon. The plot begins in the evening, when Gogol picks his two protagonists out from the crowd.

The opening of "Nevsky Prospect" is influenced by the genre of the physiological sketch. This genre applies the concept of physiology—the science of functions of living organisms—to a metaphorical study of the city as a kind of living organism. It is an attempt to sketch out the anatomy of the city, to classify it. The story also reflects the influence of the *feuilleton*. This genre, imported from the French press, was frequently employed on the front pages of the few newspapers that existed in Gogol's day. It constituted a description of a city and its inhabitants from the perspective of someone walking through the streets, a perspective that saw the city broken down into its constituent parts, the different professions, different social classes that the walker observed. The profusion of detail and the classification that Gogol's narrator provides seem, at first sight, to provide a rational explanatory framework according to which the reader can process the city and its complexity. However, upon closer observation, this framework breaks down before the complexity, multiplicity, and unity of reality. At the end of the very first paragraph, the narrator describes life on Nevsky Prospect as a phantasmagoria, invoking the horror theater of magic lanterns and its spectral subjects. Under the scrutiny of the observer, the city ceases to become a subject for realism and can only be described in the terms of the fantastic.

Physiology gives way to more creative modes of observation such as anthropomorphism, as Gogol's narrator takes on the perspective of the sidewalk, and the extended use of metaphor, metonymy, and synecdoche, as men with side whiskers become the whiskers themselves, and hats and dresses come to stand for those wearing them. The profusion of detail means that the vision of the whole disintegrates before the eye of the viewer. Gogol shows how the modern city, built by humans, reflects the deeper contradictions of human consciousness in manifold ways; such contradictions are incorporated into its design. Born of a utopian sense of triumph over nature, Petersburg is the intentional city par excellence, and encourages a sense of disorientation before it and alienation from it. Gogol's use of metaphor, metonymy, and synecdoche also serves to achieve this effect, performing what Russian Formalist critic Viktor Shklovsky referred to as *estrangement* or "making something strange."[5] By taking the everyday image of the mustache and making it represent the man, and then describing a parade of mustaches, Gogol makes the mustache deeply unfamiliar, jolting us into understanding and causing us to revisit an everyday phenomenon with a sense of wonder and thus reengage creatively with the world through his story—which is what Shklovsky argues is the purpose of such estrangement.

The allusion to phantasmagoria invites the suggestion that all is not as it seems on the street and in the city. The structure of the story is paratactic: it takes its form from the rhetorical figure of parataxis, of two images juxtaposed with each other that differ in content and meaning. Drama emerges from the contrast between the two images. Having picked out two young men from the nocturnal Nevsky crowds, Pirogov and Piskarev, Gogol's narrator observes them as they follow two different women, one blond and one brunette, through the city. The women set the heroes on two very different trajectories, one tragic and the other comic. Despite, or perhaps because of, their paratactical connection, the two characters are very different: Piskarev is an artist, who exists primarily on the spiritual and aesthetic plane, and who is taken in by Petersburg's world of

5. Viktor Shklovsky, "Art as Device," in *Viktor Shklovsky: A Reader* (London: Bloomsbury, 2017), 73–96.

dream and illusion, while Pirogov, whose name derives from the Russian word for "pie," is a figure of comic burlesque. Piskarev follows the brunette, whom he takes for some distinguished lady. We can soon guess that the truth of her identity is much more mundane, but the narrator presents her through Piskarev's eyes, which adds to the story's mystification and delusion. The artist follows her away from Nevsky Prospect, into the hidden corners of the world beyond Petersburg's main artery, into the backstreets and dark interiors fraught with danger. As he follows her into an apartment building, Piskarev wonders if this could be a dream. What he doesn't guess is the truth of who the woman actually is: a prostitute who has brought him back to a brothel for a squalid night. Piskarev has been taken in because of his artistic temperament—his romantic desires cast a false layer of meaning to an ordinary St. Petersburg phenomenon. Dream and reality collide in the story's tragic ending.

Pirogov is Piskarev's opposite, in social status, in temperament, and in tastes. The woman he pursues, the blond, turns out to be the wife of a German craftsman.[6] The Germans, drunk, send Pirogov away. He returns in pursuit of the blond but is unceremoniously turfed out. He is outraged, raving that he will inform his general and the Tsar himself about the insult to his person, but is mollified by eating a cake and strolling along the street and forgets all about the incident.

The ending of "Nevsky Prospect" performs a rhetorical revelation that is parallel to the revelation of the story's plot, providing a series of images that are not what they seem: a man with a splendid frock coat is not rich, rather that is all he owns; while two men looking at a church are talking about crows, and another waving his arms is talking about Lafayette. Nothing, the narrator argues, can be trusted, least of all ladies. Undercutting the possibility of any easy reading of the city or his story, he suggests that the beguiling quality of the city and its inhabitants is tinged with the demonic, and that

6. Gogol uses the Germans to mock and parody Romanticism. The German characters, Schiller and Hoffmann, are named after two of the most celebrated and influential German Romantic authors, Friedrich Schiller and E. T. A. Hoffmann, and the narrator does not hesitate to milk all the possible misunderstandings and jokes from their names, while at the same time giving a clue to the intelligent reader about the significant influence played by the real Hoffmann on Gogol's writing.

the rationally created St. Petersburg is far closer to the Ukrainian folkloric landscape of "Shponka" than might ever be expected.

"The Nose"

"Nevsky Prospect" provides the raw materials for two other Petersburg tales, "The Nose" and "The Overcoat." Picking up on the synecdoche from the beginning of "Nevsky Prospect," "The Nose" tells of how the collegiate assessor Major Kovalyov's nose detaches itself from his face and begins living its own independent life. While "The Nose" was mostly read in its own time as an amusing but trivial story, as time went on critics begin to read more subtextual messages into its strange plot, seeing it as, variously, a commentary on storytelling, a satire on Russian society, a Marxist critique of socioeconomic class, and even a psychosexual fantasy.[7] The strange, dreamlike, psychosexual undercurrent to the tale was even picked up by a few of its original readers. The first publication to which Gogol submitted "The Nose" rejected it on the grounds of vulgarity. Early drafts of the story were titled "The Dream," and ended with the revelation that the whole thing was a dream; the title in Russian, "Nos," spelled backwards is *son,* the Russian word for "dream."

When it was first published, "The Nose" was part of a general trend for "nosology," for stories dealing with noses.[8] This trend came in part from the popularity in Russia of Irish novelist Laurence Sterne's *Tristram Shandy* (1759–67). In that novel, a nose (referred to as an organ) plays an important part in one of the work's many digressions. The novel's narrator spends so much time reminding his reader that he's referring to the nose and not a certain other organ, that, in the manner of a Freudian slip *avant la lettre*, the reader can't help but think about that other organ.

Thus the first generation of the story's readers would not have found it strange to read a tale where the protagonist is a nose, and one of its most shocking elements is the way its characters take the nose's appearance in stride. When the barber, Ivan Yakovlevich,

---

7. Robert A. Maguire, introduction to *Gogol from the Twentieth Century: Eleven Essays* (Princeton: Princeton University Press, 1974), 3–55.

8. V. V. Vinogradov, "Naturalisticheskii grotesk: Siuzhet i kompozitsiia povesti Gogolia 'Nos,'" *Evoliutsiia russkogo naturalizma. Gogol' i Dostoevskii* (Leningrad: Academia, 1921), 7–88.

discovers the nose in his morning bread, and recognizes it as belonging to Kovalyov, a regular client, his horror is overshadowed by the irritation of his wife, who adds it to her long list of grievances against her husband. This pattern of the surreal eclipsed by the banal continues throughout the story. Ivan Yakovlevich's main concern is that the police might find him with the nose, and he tries to get rid of it as quickly as possible. His plan to throw it in the river is foiled by the attentions of a police officer. In this way, from the story's very beginning, any concerns over the nose's newly independent status are subsumed into the anxieties of daily life and power struggles in the socially and bureaucratically stratified city.

When the narrator turns his attention to Major Kovalyov, the nose serves as pretext for the satirical portrayal of the systems of prestige accorded by the hierarchies of the Table of Ranks. When Kovalyov sees his nose emerging out of a carriage, he focuses first not on the shock of its loss or its autonomy, but rather on the fact of its outranking him in bureaucratic status; while he is a collegiate assessor, the nose is a state councilor. Acknowledging the difference in their ranks, the nose insists that "there can't be any close relations between us" (p. 90). Throughout the story, the appearance of the nose is treated as a lapse in propriety that reflects poorly on Major Kovalyov, rather than as a disruption of reality. The loss of the nose, an unprecedented and disruptive event, is placed into familiar frameworks of social prestige and reputation. The newspaper to which Major Kovalyov appeals in order to place an advertisement seeking the nose's return refuses out of fear for its reputation, even while its clerk offers him a pinch of snuff, apparently blind to the effect such an invitation might have on a would-be client deprived of his nose. The narrator's ironic humor at the expense of Kovalyov and other bumptious bureaucrats helps to distract and overcome any lingering horror at the story's plot. Searching for reasons for the nose's disappearance, Major Kovalyov remembers a staff officer's wife whom he suspects wants to marry him off to her daughter and begins to believe that she may have somehow engineered the disappearance. In the end, the situation is resolved as mysteriously as it began. As the narrator puts it, "The most *absurd* things occur in the world. Sometimes there's no semblance of truth whatsoever" (p. 105).

"The Carriage" and *Poshlost*

Vladimir Nabokov famously identified as central to the works of Gogol the force of *poshlost,* defining it as "not only the obviously trashy but also the falsely important, the falsely beautiful, the falsely clever, the falsely attractive. By describing something as *poshlost*, we pass not only an aesthetic but also a moral judgment. Everything that is true, honest, beautiful cannot be described as *poshlost*."[9] An untranslatable concept, *poshlost* is a powerful motivating energy for many of Gogol's stories, a force that is invariably punished, whether through the flogging Pirogov receives in "Nevsky Prospect" or the disappearance of Major Kovalyov's nose. Such punishments never reduce the boundless supply of *poshlost*. In "The Carriage" (1836), which is set not in St. Petersburg but in a provincial town, the *poshlost* of the pretentiously named landowner, Pifagor Pifagorov-ich Chertokutsky, is expressed in a fabulous act of alcoholic-fueled braggadocio as he first impresses his neighbors at a dinner with descriptions of his (imaginary) new carriage, then invites them all to dine with him the next day to see it. The boast is then punished the next day by a humiliating hangover as he awakens to news that his visitors have arrived, and he takes refuge in his quite ordinary carriage to escape them. After discovering him in his hiding place, his nonplussed guests depart. The story, admired by the master of the short story Anton Chekhov himself, is a perfect minimalist rev-elation of *poshlost*, an unmasking of pretention and envy. As is typi-cal of Gogol, the unmasking is never explained; there is no moral to the story. Instead, readers are invited to share only in the thrill of exposure.

"The Portrait"

Through Piskarev in "Nevsky Prospect," Gogol raises a constant theme in all the Petersburg tales: that of the artist's place in a society obsessed with appearances and with rank. "The Portrait" (1835), the tale of a painting and the supernatural events that accompany

9. Vladimir Nabokov, "Nikolai Gogol," in *Lectures on Russian Literature* (New York: Har-court Brace Jovanovich, 1981), 70.

its creation and display, takes place in that same liminal dream-world as Piskarev's story, a world in which the boundary between dream and reality is never clear. The story begins in an art shop where the impoverished young Chertkov buys a painting of an old man that catches his eye. While starting at the painting, Chertkov notices that the figure seems to stare back at him: "The dark eyes of the old man gazed in so life-like, yet such a deathly manner that it was impossible not to experience fear. A part of real life seemed to have been preserved in them by some inexplicable force. The eyes had not been merely painted; they were alive; they were human. They were immobile, but could not have been more frightening if they'd moved" (p. 125). Unthinkingly, Chertkov brings the painting home, and later that night, the old man seems to emerge from the painting and take gold coins from its frame, terrifying Chertkov, until he wakes up from what has apparently been a dream. Upon waking, he wishes the money had been real. The landlord, to whom he is indebted, calls for a policeman, who cracks open the frame of the painting and reveals a bag of gold coins. Chertkov uses the money to advertise himself as an artist and becomes successful by ignoring his own creative inspiration and giving the clients what they want. Realizing his unhappiness, he traces it to the painting of the old man and understands its demonic force.

Both "Nevsky Prospect" and "The Portrait" raise the Romantic theme of art as divine inspiration, a realm almost universally misunderstood by the masses. Piskarev's imprisonment in dreams and addiction is presented as a central facet of his identity as an artist. In "The Portrait," artistic genius is shown to exact a terrible price. While Gogol's own art flirts with the concept of pleasing the crowd, he is also insistent upon the nature of creativity as belonging to a higher realm, one that lies at the intersection of the demonic and the divine. His storytelling runs the gamut from a social enterprise that draws upon folk tradition to the product of an imagination so idiosyncratic and transformational that it seems to suggest something demonic, even to the author himself. That Gogol was sometimes tortured by his own creative processes is suggested by the fiery end of Part Two of *Dead Souls* and the ascetic fanaticism of his final days. The Romantic trope of creativity as a power that must be paid for by some demonic pact that emerges in "The Portrait" constitutes the dark side of Gogol's creative genius.

"The Overcoat"

An expansion on the poor man with the rich frock coat pointed out by the narrator at the end of "Nevsky Prospect," "The Overcoat" (1842) relates the story of Akaky Akakievich Bashmachkin, a clerk who uses all his savings to buy a magnificent overcoat which is then stolen, leading to a demise which can be interpreted as either tragic or ironic. Probably the best-known of Gogol's Petersburg tales, "The Overcoat" is regarded as a masterwork by later writers. The clerk-protagonist of Dostoevsky's *Poor Folk*, Makar Devushkin, is lent the book by the object of his affections, Varvara Dobroselova, and reacts with outrage at the author's treatment of his fellow clerk. He demands a happier ending for the novel, casting light on the central interpretative bone of contention of the story since its first publication: is Gogol sympathetic towards Akaky Akakievich and his plight, or is the clerk the victim of the satirical arsenal of his narrator just like Major Kovalyov?

The continually obfuscating and undercutting narration of "The Overcoat" keeps the reader at a distance from Akaky Akakievich and his fate. Refusing, as convention dictates, to name the department at which the clerk works, the narrator seemingly explains that refusal by making the generalization that "now every private individual considers a personal insult an insult against society" before telling a generalized story conveyed through hearsay as proof (p. 162). He proceeds to give a very precise physical description of Akaky Akakievich and a baroque and far-fetched account of how he came by his name. This dismissive tone of the narrator confirms the dehumanizing impulse conveyed in the name itself, with the absurd and repetitive quality of the first name and patronymic and the modest nature of the last name, Bashmachkin, which means "bast shoe." Each subsequent utterance of the narrator seems to undermine that which came before, and we find ourselves stumbling in the rhetorical swamp of the narrator's vague, syntactically contorted, and self-contradictory prose. While most of the story is marked by this narrative distancing, the end of the third paragraph offers a glimpse into an alternative perspective on Akaky Akakievich.

In spite of merciless mocking from his fellow clerks, Bashmachkin makes not one single copying error, and only remarks, when the joking is over, "Leave me alone. Why are you treating me like this?" (p. 164). Here the narrator abandons his distancing strategies and seems to offer compassion, noting "something strange" in his words and tone. He observes that one young man "stopped suddenly, as if stabbed through the heart" by the words, and something changed in him. "Some sort of unnatural force" pushed him away from the colleagues he had previously thought polite and distant. And long afterwards, we are told, the figure of the clerk would appear before that young man uttering those same words, and in those words, he would hear the message, "I am your brother." And then, the narrator adds, "the poor young man would cover his face and many times later in his life would shudder at seeing how much inhumanity there was in man, how much fierce boorishness was hidden behind refined, cultured good manners." This passage seems to provide both Akaky Akakievich and the young man with a genuine moral and psychological agency of the kind that Kovalyov and Pirogov do not possess.

The abandonment of the satirical tone in favor of a more direct moral and social criticism is all the more puzzling in that it is never repeated. In fact, the narrator seems to remain steadfastly outside of Akaky Akakievich's head, even at one point commenting on his response to a man and a woman on the street in the following manner: "Akaky Akakievich shook his head, grinned, and then continued on his way. Why did he grin? Was it because he had encountered something totally unfamiliar, but about which everyone retains a certain feeling, or was it that he thought as follows, like many other civil servants: 'Oh, those Frenchmen! What can I say, if they want something like that, exactly like that. . . .' But perhaps he didn't think that at all—after all, it's impossible to delve into another man's soul and to know everything he's thinking" (p. 178). Here the narrator explicitly refuses to grant Bashmachkin consciousness. This refusal to grant his protagonist internal perspective allows the narrator to present Akaky's subsequent fate, the robbery of his coat, and his appeal, first to his Superintendent, and then to the Important Person, followed by his death and haunting of his superiors, as a series of curiosities akin to the events that take place in "The Nose" and "Nevsky Prospect." Ultimately, as with "Shponka," it is the verbal and tonal texture of the storytelling that hold the work together, and with the exception of that early passage, neither narrator nor reader is ever permitted to sympathize with Akaky's fate. Rather, we are invited to laugh at both the foibles of Akaky and his superiors, and the absurdity of the byzantine power structures of the Russian state.

In the originality and idiosyncrasy of their vision, Gogol's tales seem to have hardly aged after almost two centuries and continue to hold the power to jolt us out of our conventional perspective on the world. Though the Russian imperial and historical context of their creation is significant in shaping the spaces within which the narrative unfolds, and in inspiring the themes and preoccupations of the tales, Gogol's short stories seem to anticipate many of the dilemmas and experiences of modernity and even postmodernity, such as the individual stories that lie beyond the daily routines of city streets, the dark fantasies that undergird workplace and social power dynamics, and the fine line between sympathy and mockery in our own observations of the differences of others. Gogol's mastery at once enlightens and obscures the ancient art of storytelling and remakes it for the modern age.

A Note on the Translation

Gogol's works are less known in the West than the novels of Turgenev, Dostoevsky, Tolstoy, and the plays of Chekhov. Although his characters are no less universal, Gogol's style is imaginative and inventive—as the critic Philip Rahv once wrote, "[Gogol] is so a great master of style and verbal orchestration that his power to move us is virtually indissoluble from his language."[1]

Gogol's style was originally considered to be "too Russian" for Western readers. The Vicomte de Vogüé, a nineteenth-century popularizer of Russian literature in the West, wrote in his influential study of the Russian novel: "[The reader] must not expect the attractive style or class of subjects of Tolstoi or Dostoevski. . . . Gogol wrote of more remote times, and, besides, he and his work are thoroughly and exclusively Russian."[2] Nevertheless, translations of Gogol's works first appeared in English very soon after their publication in Russian. Versions of "The Overcoat," "The Nose," and "The Carriage" appeared in 1835–36. "The Portrait" followed in

---

1. Philip Rahv, "Gogol as a Modern Instance," in *Russian Literature and Modern English Fiction*, ed. Donald Davie (Chicago: University of Chicago Press, 1965), 239.
2. Quoted in Rachel May, *The Translator in the Text: On Reading Russian Literature in English* (Evanston, IL: Northwestern University Press, 1994), 22.

1842. An entire collection called *The St. Petersburg Stories* was published by the American writer and translator Isabel Florence Hapgood in 1886.

The indefatigable Constance Garnett translated most of Gogol's works into English during the 1920s. One astute critic wrote that her versions have "undeniable grace and elegance . . . but they fail to do justice to the sometimes tortured and always vigorous language of the original and her imperfect knowledge of Russian resulted in a large number of inaccuracies."[3] Her translations were subsequently revised and republished by Leonard Kent in 1964 and revised again in 1985. Other English translations, such as those by David Magarshack in 1949, Ronald Wilks in 1972, and Christopher English in 1995, endeavored to preserve the stylistic variety of the author, but their British English can still strike American readers as stilted and old-fashioned.

My translation is into standard American English: I try to strike a balance between faithfulness to the author's language and readability for the contemporary reader. My aim is to be both accurate and accessible. To fully appreciate Gogol's style in English is almost impossible in any translation, but I have done my best to capture his fantastic originality. The source of the Russian text for these stories is the *Sobranie sochinenii* (*Collected Works*) of N. V. Gogol, volumes 1 and 3, published by the Gosurdarstvennoe izdatel'stvo khudozhestvennoi literatury (The State Publisher of Artistic Literature), Moscow, 1952.

Gogol's influence on both Russian and Western literature is unmistakable. In the famous words (mistakenly) attributed to Dostoevsky, "We all came out from under Gogol's 'Overcoat.'" The relationship between Gogol and Dostoevsky is complex, involving both attraction and repulsion. The petty clerks, dreamers, and madmen of Dostoevsky's early writings come from the characters of Gogol's *Petersburg Tales*. In Dostoevsky's first literary work, *Poor Folk* (1845), a downtrodden civil servant reads and comments on Gogol's "The Overcoat." Appalled at the author's lack of empathy for his hero, he promises to write in a different manner altogether.

---

3. Christopher English in *The Encyclopedia of Literary Translation into English*, ed. Olive Classe, vol. 1 (Chicago: Fitzroy Dearborn, 2000), 547–8.

In the West, writers including Franz Kafka, Sholem Aleichem, and Vladimir Nabokov reveal the powerful influence of the themes and style of Gogol's prose and plays. His work features prominently in Jhumpa Lahiri's novel *The Namesake* in which the main character is even named Gogol. Truly, his legacy lives on.

And just who was the real Nikolai Gogol? Was he a humane critic of social conditions who hoped to arouse the reader's outrage and sympathy for the downtrodden, or was he a witty humorist and bitter satirist laughing both with us and at us for our foibles and our vanity? Can one reconcile these two disparate views of the author? This new translation of Gogol's most famous short stories aims to render the author's deep compassion and wicked humor in all their glory and to allow the reader to answer this question for him or herself.

Table of Ranks

The following is a list of Russian civil and army titles, in order of rank, introduced by Tsar Peter I and used from 1722 to 1917. These titles appear throughout Gogol's works.

Civil title	Army title
1. Chancellor	Field Marshal
2. Actual Privy Councilor	General
3. Privy Councilor	Lieutenant General
4. Actual State Councilor	Major General
5. State Councilor	Brigadier
6. Collegiate Councilor	Colonel
7. Court Councilor	Lieutenant Colonel
8. Collegiate Assessor	Major
9. Titular Councilor	Captain
10. Collegiate Secretary	Staff Captain
11. Senate Secretary	———
12. Provincial Secretary	Lieutenant
13. Senate Registrar	Second Lieutenant
14. Collegiate Registrar	Ensign

Nikolai Gogol

Selected Tales

Ivan Fyodorovich Shponka and His Auntie

There's a story connected to this story: it was told by Stepan Ivanovich Kurochka from Gadyach. You should know that my memory is incredibly bad: whatever you tell me goes in one ear and out the other. It's just like pouring water through a sieve. Knowing this about myself, I deliberately asked him to write it down in a notebook. Well, God grant him good health; he was always kind to me, so he picked up a notebook and wrote it down. I put it in the drawer of a small table; I think you know it well: it stands in the corner just where you come in the door. . . . But I forget you've never visited me there. My old woman, with whom I've lived for about thirty years, never learned to read—there's no reason to hide it. So one day I notice she's baking little meat pies and placing them on some sort of paper. She makes the most wonderful pies, dear readers; you won't find better ones anywhere. I happen to look at the underside of a pie and there I see some written words. I felt it in my heart at once; I went to the little table—half the notebook was missing! She had taken those pages for her pies. What could I do? There's no sense in quarreling at our age!

Last year I happened to pass through Gadyach. Before reaching town, I tied a knot in my handkerchief on purpose so as not to forget to ask Stepan Ivanovich about it. That wasn't all: I promised myself that as soon as I sneezed in town, I'd remember it. But it was all in vain. I drove through town, sneezed, blew my nose into my handkerchief, but still forgot all about it; I remembered only when I had gone about six miles past the town gate. What was to be done? I had to publish it without the ending. However, if someone absolutely wants to know what happened subsequently in this tale, all he should do is go to Gadyach and ask Stepan Ivanovich. He'll relate it with great pleasure, only he'll tell the whole story from beginning to end. He lives not far from the stone church. There's a small lane: as soon as you turn into it, his house will be at the second or third gate. Better still: when you see a large post in the yard with a quail sitting on top, and a heavyset old woman in a green skirt comes out to meet you (there's no harm in saying that he's a bachelor), it's his house. However, you can meet him at the market where he goes every morning before nine o'clock to select some fish and greens for his table and where he chats with Father Antip or the Jewish tax-farmer.° You'll recognize him immediately because nobody else wears trousers made from printed linen and a yellow cotton coat. Here's another indication: he always swings his arms when he walks. The late local assessor, Denis Petrovich, catching sight of him from a distance, always used to say: "Look, look, here comes the windmill!"

1

Ivan Fyodorovich Shponka

It's been four years since Ivan Fyodorovich Shponka retired and has been living on his small estate in Vytrebenki. When he was still known as Vanyusha, he was a student at the Gadyach district school, and it must be said that he was an extremely well-behaved and conscientious lad. The teacher of Russian grammar, Nikifor Timofeevich Deeprichastie,° used to say that if all his pupils were as diligent as Shponka, he wouldn't have to bring his maple-wood ruler into class, which, as he himself admitted, he used to smack the hands of lazy and mischievous boys. Shponka's notebook was always clean, with a ruled margin and no blotches anywhere. He always sat quietly, arms folded, his eyes fixed on the teacher; he didn't attach any papers to the back of the boy sitting in front of him, didn't carve anything into the school bench, and never fooled around by shoving anyone off the bench before the teacher came into the room. If anyone needed to sharpen his pen, he could turn immediately to Shponka, knowing that he always carried a little pocket knife; and Ivan, then still known simply as Vanyusha, took out his knife from a small leather pouch attached to a buttonhole in his gray jacket, and asked that the sharp side not be used to sharpen the pen, saying that the blunt side would better suit that purpose. Such good behavior soon attracted the attention even of the Latin teacher, whose cough in the hall alone would induce fear in the entire class even before his heavy wool overcoat and pock-marked face could be glimpsed at the classroom door. This terrifying teacher, who always had two bundles of birch twigs on his desk, and half of whose pupils were always down on their knees, made Shponka a monitor, even though there were many others in his class who had greater abilities.

Here we can't omit an incident that influenced Shponka's entire life. One of the boys entrusted to his charge, in order to induce the monitor to write *scit*° on his paper, even though he really didn't know his lesson, brought into class a pancake drenched in butter and wrapped in paper. Ivan Fyodorovich, although he usually behaved properly, on this occasion was very hungry and unable to resist temptation; he took the pancake, placed a book in front of him, and began eating. He was so engrossed that he didn't even notice when a deathly silence suddenly fell upon the class. He came to his senses with horror only when a terrible hand, extending from a heavy woolen overcoat, grabbed him by the ear and pulled him into the middle of the room. "Give me that pancake! Give it here, I say, you rascal!" said the severe teacher, seizing the buttery pancake with his fingers and tossing it out the window, sternly forbidding the boys in the schoolyard to pick it up. Right after this he landed some painful blows on Shponka's hands. And that was only fitting: his hands were to blame and not some other part of his body because they had taken the pancake. Be that as it may, from that time forward, Shponka's timidity, which had always been one of his attributes, increased all the more. Perhaps that very incident was the reason he never had the desire to enter government service, having

learned by experience that one is not always successful in conceal-
ing one's crimes.

He was almost fifteen years old when he was promoted to the
second class, where, moving on from the abridged version of the catechism and the four rules of arithmetic, he progressed to the extended
catechism and a book about the duties of man and about fractions.
But seeing that the further he went into the forest, the thicker the
woods became, and having received news that his father had passed
away, he stayed on in school another two years and then, with his
mother's consent, enlisted in an infantry regiment.

This regiment was not at all like any other; for the most part it
was stationed in villages, but was on the same footing as other regiments, even some cavalry regiments. A large number of the officers would drink heavily and drag Yids° around by their side curls
just as well as the hussars could. A few men could even dance the
mazurka; the corporal of the regiment never missed a chance to
mention this fact when he was talking in company. "In our regiment, sir," he used to say, patting himself on the belly after every
word, "a large number of us dance the mazurka, sir, a very large
number, sir, an extremely large number, sir." To demonstrate further the cultural level of this regiment, we'll add that two officers
were terrible gamblers and lost their uniforms, caps, overcoats,
sword knots, and even their underwear, which is more than you can
say about many other regiments.

Contact with such comrades, however, in no way diminished
Shponka's timidity. And since he didn't drink heavily, preferring a
glass of vodka before dinner and supper, and since he didn't dance
the mazurka or gamble at cards, then, naturally, he was always left
alone. Thus, while others were gallivanting around on hired horses
visiting small landowners, he remained in his quarters and engaged
in pursuits fitting his timid and kind character: he polished his buttons, read a fortune-telling book, or placed mousetraps in the corners of his room; then at last, removing his uniform, he would lie
down on his bed. On the other hand, there was no one in his regiment more meticulous than Shponka. He drilled his men so well
that the company commander always held him up as an example.
As a result, in a short time, only eleven years after becoming an
ensign, he was promoted to second lieutenant.

During this time he received the news that his mother had passed away; his aunt, his mother's sister, whom he knew only because in his childhood she would bring him or even send him dried pears and delicious homemade spice cakes (she had quarreled with his mother and therefore he didn't see her afterwards)—this aunt, being very kind-hearted, took over the management of his small estate, about which he learned from a letter in due course. Ivan Fyodorovich, being convinced of his aunt's good sense, continued to perform his duties as before. Another person in his place, having received such a promotion, would have been proud; but he knew no such thing as pride, and having become a second lieutenant, he remained the same Shponka as he was when he had the rank of ensign. Four years after this remarkable event, he was preparing to leave the province of Mogilyov and move to Russia proper when he received a letter with the following content:

"Dear nephew, Ivan Fyodorovich!

"I'm sending you some linen: five pairs of cotton socks and four shirts of fine material; and I would also like to speak with you about some business. Since you now hold a rank of some importance, I think you know that you have reached an age when it is time for you to manage your own estate; there's no reason for you to remain in military service any longer. I'm already old and can't oversee everything on your estate; besides, there is much that I would like to discuss with you personally. Come home, Vanyusha! In expectation of the genuine pleasure of seeing you, I remain your loving aunt,

"Vasilisa Tsupchevska

"P.S.: A splendid turnip has grown in our garden, more like a potato than a turnip."

A week after receiving this letter, Shponka wrote the following reply:

"Honored madam, Auntie Vasilisa Kashporovna!

"Many thanks for the package of linen. My socks especially are very old; my orderly has darned them four times and as a result they have become very tight. Concerning your opinion about my military service, I agree with you entirely and I resigned my position several days ago. As soon as I receive my discharge, I shall hire a driver. I could not carry out your previous commission concerning wheat seeds and Siberian grain: there isn't any to be had in all of Mogilyov province. Here for the most part pigs are fed brewers' mash mixed with a little flat beer.

"With sincere respect, dear madam Auntie, I remain your nephew,

"Ivan Shponka."

At last Shponka received his discharge with the rank of lieutenant, hired a Jew for forty rubles to take him from Mogilyov to Gadyach, and took his place in the carriage at the same time as the trees were scantily decked in young leaves, the whole earth was turning bright green with fresh growth, and it smelled of spring throughout the fields.

2

The Journey

Nothing too remarkable happened during the drive home. He traveled a little more than two weeks. Shponka might have arrived sooner, but the devout Jew would observe the Sabbath on Saturdays: after covering himself with the horse blanket, he prayed all day long. However, as I've had the chance to mention previously, Ivan Fyodorovich was the sort of person who didn't allow himself to get bored. During that time he would untie his suitcase, take out his linen, and examine it carefully: was it properly washed and folded? He carefully removed the fluff from his new uniform without epaulets, then folded it again in the best possible way. In general he was not fond of reading; if he sometimes glanced into a fortune-telling book, it was because he liked to find familiar passages that he'd read several times before. In the same way a resident of a town sets off to the club every day, not to learn anything new, but to meet those acquaintances, whom, from time immemorial, he's grown accustomed to seeing there. In the same way a civil servant reads his address book several times a day, not for any diplomatic reasons, but because he finds perusing the printed list of names extremely amusing. "Ah! There's Ivan Gavrilovich!" he repeats to himself. "Ah! And here I am again! Hmm!" And the next time, he rereads it with the very same exclamations.

After a two-week journey Shponka reached a little village located some eighty miles from Gadyach. It was on a Friday. The sun had already set a long time ago when the Jew drove his carriage up to an inn.

This inn wasn't distinguished in any way from others built in small villages. In them the traveler is usually treated to hay and oats, as if he were a post horse. But if he wants to have something to eat, as decent people usually do, he would have to save his appetite for some other opportunity. Knowing all this, Shponka had provided himself beforehand with two bundles of bagels and some sausage; after asking for a glass of vodka, of which there's never a shortage in any village inn, and having seated himself on a bench in front of an oak table firmly fixed on the clay floor, he began eating his supper.

Meanwhile, the sound of a carriage could be heard. The gates squeaked, but the carriage took a long time to enter the courtyard. A loud voice was abusing the woman who ran the inn. "I'll come in," heard Shponka, "but if even one bedbug bites me in your establishment, I swear I'll give you a beating, so help me God, I will, you old witch! And I won't pay for any hay!"

A moment later the door opened and a fat man in a green coat walked in, or rather, squeezed in. His head rested motionless on his short neck, which seemed even thicker on account of his double chin. He appeared to belong to that group of men who never trouble over trifles and whose lives pass effortlessly.

"I wish you good day, kind sir!" he said, catching sight of Shponka.

Ivan Fyodorovich bowed silently.

"Allow me to inquire, with whom do I have the honor of speaking?" continued the fat arrival.

At such an interrogation Shponka involuntarily rose from his place and stood at attention, which he used to do when the colonel of his former regiment would ask him a question.

"Retired Lieutenant Ivan Fyodorovich Shponka," he replied.

"And, may I ask, where are you traveling to?"

"To my own farm, sir, Vytrebenki."

"Vytrebenki!" cried the stern inquisitor. "Allow me, honored sir, allow me!" he said, approaching him and waving his arms, as if someone was restraining him or he was pushing his way through a crowd; having approached, he grabbed Ivan Fyodorovich in an embrace and kissed him first on the right cheek, then on the left, and then on the right cheek again. Shponka very much appreciated these kisses because his lips felt that the stranger's large cheeks were like soft pillows.

"Allow me, kind sir, to make your acquaintance!" continued the fat man. "I'm a landowner in the same Gadyach district and your neighbor. I live no more than four miles from your farm at Vytrebenki, in the village of Khortishche; my name is Grigory Grigorevich Storchenko. You must, absolutely must pay me a visit, dear sir, or else I'll have nothing more to do with you. Now I'm hurrying on business. . . . But what's this?" he said in a gentle voice to his servant, a lad wearing a Cossack jacket with tattered elbows, who was placing some bundles and boxes on the table with a bewildered look. "What's this? What?" Storchenko's voice became imperceptibly louder and louder. "Did I order you to put those here, my dear sir? Did I really tell you to put them here, you rascal? Didn't I tell you to heat up the chicken first, you scoundrel? Get out!" he cried, stamping his foot. "Wait a minute, you beast! Where's the basket with the bottles? Ivan Fyodorovich!" he said, pouring some liquor into a glass: "I beg you, have some of this medicinal cordial!"

"I can't, so help me God, sir. . . . I've already had some," said Shponka with a stutter.

"I won't hear of it, kind sir!" the landowner said, raising his voice. "I won't hear of it! I won't leave here until you try some. . . ."

Ivan Fyodorovich, seeing that it was impossible to refuse, drank some, not without enjoyment.

"This is a chicken, my dear sir," continued the obese Grigory Grigorevich, carving it with a knife in its wooden box. "I must tell you that my cook, Yavdokha, likes to tipple every so often; as a result, she sometimes overcooks my food. Hey, lad," he said, addressing the young man in the Cossack jacket, who had carried in a featherbed and pillows. "Make up my bed on the floor in the middle of the room! Be sure to put down some extra hay to raise the pillow! And grab a bit of hemp from the old woman's spindle so I can plug my ears! You should know, kind sir, that I have had the custom of plugging my ears at night since that awful time when a cockroach crawled into my left ear in one Russian inn. Those damned Russians, as I found out later, will even eat their cabbage soup with cockroaches in it. It's impossible to describe what was going on: it tickled my ear, it really did . . . it nearly drove me mad! A simple old woman in our district helped me. How do you think she did it? Simply by whispering some special words. What can you say, kind sir, about doctors? I think they simply confuse and deceive us. Some of these old women know twenty times more than those doctors."

"As a matter of fact, that's absolutely true, sir. These women know . . ." He paused here, as if unable to find the right word.

It wouldn't hurt to note here that in general Shponka wasn't lavish with his words. Perhaps that was a result of his timidity, or else of his desire to express himself more eloquently.

"Shake the hay well, very well!" Storchenko said to his servant. "The hay here is so nasty that you can suddenly find a twig in it. Allow me, kind sir, to wish you a good night! We won't see each other tomorrow: I'll leave before dawn. Your Jew will celebrate the Sabbath because tomorrow's Saturday, so there's no reason for you to get up early. Don't forget my request: if you don't come to visit me in Khortishche, I won't even want to know you."

Then his servant removed his jacket and boots, and helped him into a dressing gown. When Storchenko stretched out on the bed, it seemed as if one huge featherbed lay down on top of another.

"Hey, boy! Where have you gone to, you rascal? Come here and fix my blanket! Hey, boy, put some more hay under my head! Well, have the horses been watered? More hay! Here, under this side! Fix the blanket properly, you rascal! Like that, more! Ugh!"

Storchenko heaved a few more sighs and then emitted a terrible whistle from his nose that filled the whole room, snoring so loudly at times that the old woman, who was snoozing on the stove bench, woke up and suddenly looked around on all sides, but, seeing nothing, settled down again and fell asleep.

The next day, when Shponka woke up, the fat landowner was nowhere to be seen. That was the only remarkable occurrence that happened to him during his journey. Two days later, he drew near his own farmstead.

Here he felt his heart begin to pound as he saw a windmill waving its sails and, as the Jew began urging his nags up the hill, he caught sight of a row of willows below. The pond shone clearly and brightly between them, and it smelled very fresh. In this same pond Ivan Fyodorovich used to go wading up to his neck, angling for crayfish. The carriage climbed up the mound and he saw the same little old house thatched with reeds, the same apple trees and cherry trees in which he had secretly climbed. When he had just driven into the courtyard, dogs of various kinds came running from all sides: brown, black, gray, and spotted. Some of them rushed forward, barking under the legs of the horses; others ran behind, having noticed that the axle was smeared with lard; one of the dogs, standing next to the kitchen and covering a bone with his paw, began barking as loudly as he could; another barked from a distance and ran back and forth, wagging his tail and seeming to say, "Look at me, good Christian folk, and see what a fine young fellow I am!" Young boys in dirty shirts came running to stare. A sow, crossing the courtyard with her sixteen piglets, raised her snout with a curious glance and grunted louder than usual. On the ground in the courtyard lay a multitude of sheets with wheat, millet, and barley drying in the sun. There were also many different kinds of herbs drying on the roof: wild chicory, hawkweed, and others.

Shponka was so busy examining everything that he came to his senses only when the spotted dog bit the Jew on the calf as he was climbing down from the box. The servants came running: the cook, an old woman, and two young women in woolen undergarments. After their initial exclamations, "It's our young master!" they told him that his aunt was out planting wheat in the garden with the maid Palashka and the coachman Omelko, who often performed the roles of gardener and watchman. But his aunt, who had seen the covered cart from a distance, was already there. Ivan Fyodorovich was astonished when she almost picked him up in her arms, hardly able to believe that this was the same aunt who had written to him about her own infirmity and illness.

3

Auntie

At this time Aunt Vasilisa Kashporovna was about fifty years old. She had never been married and usually claimed that her single life was better than anything else in the world. However, as best I can recall, no one had ever courted her. That's because all men felt some hesitancy in her presence and never had the courage to propose to her. "Vasilisa has a great deal of character!" prospective suitors used to say, and they were absolutely correct, because there wasn't anyone alive she couldn't put in his place. Every day she would yank the totally useless drunken miller by his long braid with her own powerful hand, without any other means, and could turn him from a simple soul into pure gold. She was of almost gigantic height and both her breadth and strength were completely commensurate. It seemed that nature had made an unforgivable mistake in assigning her to wear a dark brown dress with small pleats on weekdays, and a red cashmere shawl on Sunday and her name-day, when a mustache and the high jackboots of a dragoon would have suited her much better. On the other hand, her activities corresponded completely to her appearance: she could row her own boat, handling the oars more skillfully than many a fisherman; she hunted game; she stood guard over the mowers; she knew exactly how many watermelons and other melons grew in her garden; she collected a toll of five kopecks from every cart that crossed her dam; she climbed up pear trees and shook down the fruit; she would beat lazy servants with her fearsome hand, and serve a glass of vodka to the deserving ones with the very same hand. Almost at one and the same time she could abuse the servants, dye the yarn, and run to the kitchen to make kvass and honey preserves; she was busy all day long, yet had time for everything everywhere. The result of all this was that Shponka's small estate, consisting of a mere eighteen serfs according to the last count, was flourishing in the full sense of the word. In addition, she loved her nephew fervently and carefully saved every kopeck for him.

Upon his arrival home, Ivan Fyodorovich's life decidedly changed and proceeded in a different direction. It seemed that nature had created him to run his eighteen-serf estate. His aunt thought that he would make a good landowner, but didn't allow him to interfere in the various aspects of estate management. "He's still a young lad," she used to say, in spite of the fact that Ivan Fyodorovich was almost forty years old. "How could he know everything?"

However, he was always out in the fields with the reapers and the mowers, and this afforded his gentle soul inexpressible enjoyment. The uniform sweep of a dozen or more shining scythes; the sound of the sheaves of grass falling in straight rows; the songs of the reapers pouring forth from time to time, now cheerful, as if greeting guests, then mournful, as if parting from them; and the peaceful, clear evening, and what an evening it was! The air was so fresh and pure! How full of life everything was then: the steppe was turning red and blue and was aflame with flowers; quails, bustards, gulls, grasshoppers, and thousands of insects, and from them, whistling, buzzing, droning, and crackling at once merged into a harmonious choir; nothing was silent, even for a moment. The sun was setting and going into hiding. Oh! How fresh and fine! In the fields, first here, then there, campfires were burning with cauldrons placed over them; reapers sporting mustaches sat around the fires, steam rising from the dumplings. Twilight was setting in. . . . It's difficult to relate what Ivan Fyodorovich was feeling at that time. He would forget everything and join the mowers to sample the dumplings, which he loved very much, and would stand still, following with his gaze a gull disappearing in the sky or counting the heaps of harvested grain lying in the field.

In a short time people began describing Ivan Fyodorovich as a wonderful landlord of his estate. His aunt couldn't have been more overjoyed with her nephew and never missed a chance to brag about him. One fine day—it was already toward the end of the harvest, that is, the end of July—Vasilisa Kashporovna took Ivan Fyodorovich by the hand with a mysterious look, and said that she wanted to talk to him about a matter that had been concerning her for some time.

"You know, my dear Ivan Fyodorovich," she began, "you have eighteen serfs on your estate; however, that is according to the census; it may be that since then the number has grown and there might now be as many as twenty-four. But that's not what I want to talk to you about. You know that grove, the one behind our wetland, and you probably also know the broad meadow behind that wood: it's at least forty acres; there's so much grass that you'd be able to sell the hay every year for more than one hundred rubles, especially if, as they say, a cavalry regiment is to be stationed in Gadyach."

"Of course, Auntie, I know it: the grass there is very fine."

"I know the grass is fine; but do you know that all that land is really yours? Why are you staring at me like that? Listen, Ivan Fyodorovich! Do you remember Stepan Kuzmich? What am I saying: how could you remember him? You were so little then that you couldn't even pronounce his name. Indeed! I recall that when I came here during Advent and took you in my arms, you almost spoiled my new dress; fortunately I managed to hand you off to your wet-nurse Matryona. You were such a nasty little child then! But that's not the point. All of the land beyond our farm, as well as the village of Khortishche, belonged to Stepan Kuzmich. I must tell you that, long before you were born, he had begun to visit your mother—true, it was only when your father wasn't home. I'm not saying this to reproach her—may God rest her soul!—although she was always unfair to me. But that's not the point. Be that as it may, Stepan Kuzmich gave you a deed of gift to the very piece of land I was telling you about. But your late mother, just between us, had a very strange character. Even the devil himself, God forgive me for mentioning his name, could never understand her. God only knows where she hid that deed. I think, simply, that it's in the hands of that old bachelor Grigory Grigorevich Storchenko. That tubby rascal inherited that estate. I'm willing to bet you God knows what that he's concealed that deed of gift."

"Forgive me, Auntie: isn't that the same Storchenko I met at the post station?"

Here Shponka recounted the story of his meeting.

"Who knows?" his aunt replied after thinking for a while. "Perhaps he's not such a scoundrel. True, it's only been half a year since he came here to live; you don't get to know a man in so short a time. The old woman, his mother, I hear, is a very smart woman, and they say she's excellent at pickling cucumbers. And her servant girls know how to make fine rugs. But if, as you say, he treated you well, go and pay him a visit! Perhaps the old sinner will listen to his conscience and give you back what doesn't belong to him. Perhaps you could drive over there in our carriage, only those damned kids pulled out all the nails from the back. I'll tell the coachman Omelko to attach the leather properly."

"What for, Auntie? I'll take the cart you use when you go out shooting game."

With this the conversation ended.

4

Dinner

Shponka drove into the village of Khortishche at dinnertime and began to feel timid as he approached the manor house. The house was long and its roof was wooden, not thatched like so many of the surrounding structures. Two barns in the courtyard also had wooden roofs; the gates were made of oak. Ivan Fyodorovich felt like a dandy who, having arrived at a ball, sees everyone else, no matter where he glances, dressed more elegantly than he is. Out of respect he stopped his cart near the barn and proceeded on foot to the porch.

"Ah! Ivan Fyodorovich!" cried the fat Storchenko, who was crossing the courtyard wearing a jacket, but without a tie, a vest, or suspenders. But even this attire seemed to burden his portly figure because he was sweating profusely. "Why did you say that as soon as you saw your aunt you'd come visit me, but you didn't come?" After these words Shponka's lips encountered those familiar soft pillows.

"For the most part I was busy on my estate. . . . I've come to see you for a minute, actually on business. . . ."

"For a minute? I won't allow it. Hey, boy!" shouted the fat landowner, and the same lad in a Cossack coat came running from the kitchen. "Tell Kasyan to bolt the gates at once, do you hear, lock them tight! And unharness this gentleman's horses this very minute! Please come in; it's so hot out here that my shirt's soaking wet."

Upon entering the room, Shponka decided not to waste any time; in spite of his timidity, he attacked resolutely.

"My aunt had the honor of . . . she told me that a deed of gift left by the late Stepan Kuzmich . . ."

It's difficult to depict the unpleasant expression that appeared on Storchenko's face as soon as these words were uttered.

"So help me God, I can't hear a thing! I must tell you that I had a cockroach in my left ear. Those damned Russians always have so many cockroaches in their cottages. It's impossible to describe in writing what a torture it is. It tickles and tickles. An old woman helped me once with a simple remedy. . . ."

"I wanted to say"—Shponka dared interrupt him, seeing that Storchenko intended to change the subject—"that the late Stepan Kuzmich's will mentions a deed of gift, so to speak . . . and that according to it, I should . . ."

"I know what nonsense your aunt has filled your head with. It's a lie, so help me God, a lie! Your uncle left no deed of gift. Although, it's true, there's a mention of it in his will, but where is it? No one's presented it. I'm telling you this 'cause I sincerely wish you well. So help me God, it's a lie!"

Shponka fell silent, thinking that perhaps his aunt had only imagined it.

"Here comes Mother with my sisters!" said Storchenko. "Therefore, dinner is served. Let's go!" Having said this, he dragged Shponka by the arm into the room in which the vodka and some snacks were already set out on the table.

At the same time a short, old woman, resembling a coffeepot wearing a cap, entered the room with two young ladies—one blond and the other with dark hair. Shponka, like a well-brought-up gentleman, went up first to kiss the old woman's hand, and then to kiss the hands of the two young ladies.

"This, Mother, is our neighbor, Ivan Fyodorovich Shponka!" said Storchenko.

The old woman stared at Shponka, or perhaps it only seemed that way to him. However, she was kindness itself. She seemed to want to ask him, "How many cucumbers have *you* pickled for the winter?"

"Did you have some vodka?" asked the old woman.

"Mother, you probably didn't get enough sleep," said Storchenko. "Who asks a guest if he's had some vodka? You merely offer it to him: it's our business whether we've already had some or not. Ivan Fyodorovich! Would you prefer centaury-flavored vodka or raw vodka? And you, Ivan Ivanovich, what are you doing over there?" Storchenko asked, turning around; Shponka noticed another man approaching the table with the vodka; he was wearing a long frock coat with a large high collar that covered the back of his neck entirely so that his head seemed to be sitting on the collar, as if in a carriage.

Ivan Ivanovich went over to the vodka, rubbed his hands, examined a goblet carefully, took some, raised it to the light, and poured it from the glass into his mouth, but didn't swallow; instead he rinsed it methodically around his mouth and only then did he swallow it; after eating a piece of bread and a pickled mushroom, he turned to Shponka.

"Don't I have the honor of addressing Ivan Fyodorovich Shponka?"

"Yes, indeed," replied Shponka.

"You've changed a great deal since I first met you. Why," Ivan Ivanovich continued, "I remember you from when you were only this tall." After saying that he lowered his hand to about two feet above the floor. "Your late father, may he rest in peace, was a rare breed. The watermelons and other melons he grew—you won't find the likes of those anywhere. Whereas here," he continued, taking him aside, "they serve you melons, but what sort are they? You don't even want to look at them! Believe me, kind sir, your father's watermelons," he uttered with a mysterious look, spreading his arms as if he wanted to encircle a large tree, "were this big, so help me God!"

"Come to the table!" said Storchenko, taking Shponka by the hand.

Everyone went into the dining room. Grigory Grigorevich sat in his usual place at the head of the table, fastened an enormous napkin around his neck, and in this guise resembled the heroic figures that barbers like to depict on their signboards. Shponka, blushing, sat down at the place indicated to him, opposite the two young ladies; Ivan Ivanovich didn't miss the chance to sit next to him, genuinely delighted that he could share his knowledge with him.

"You shouldn't take the tail, Ivan Fyodorovich! It's a turkey!" said the old woman, turning to Shponka, just as the village waiter wearing a gray frock coat with a black patch was offering him the platter. "Take the back instead!"

"Mother! No one's asking you to interfere!" Storchenko declared. "You can be sure that our guest knows what part to take! Ivan Fyodorovich, take a wing, the other one, with the gizzard! Why have you taken so little? Take a leg! What are you staring at? Ask him! Go down on your knees, you scoundrel! Say at once, 'Ivan Fyodorovich, take a leg!'"

"Ivan Fyodorovich, take a leg!" said the waiter, kneeling with the serving plate.

"Hmm, what sort of turkey is this?" said Ivan Ivanovich in a low voice with a look of disdain, turning to his neighbor. "Is this what turkey should look like? You should see my turkeys! I can assure you that there's more fat on one of my birds than on ten of these. Believe me, kind sir, it's even disgusting to look at them as they strut across my courtyard—they're so fat!"

"Ivan Ivanovich, you're lying!" uttered Storchenko after hearing his words.

"I tell you," Ivan Ivanovich continued speaking to his neighbor, as if he hadn't heard Storchenko's words. "Last year, when I sent them to Gadyach, they paid me fifty kopecks for each one. And I didn't want to take that little."

"Ivan Ivanovich, I tell you you're lying!" uttered Storchenko, emphasizing each syllable and speaking loudly for greater clarity.

But Ivan Ivanovich pretended that these words had nothing to do with him; he continued in the same way, only in a much softer voice.

"Yes, sir, good sir, I didn't want to take that little. Not one other landowner in Gadyach . . ."

"Ivan Ivanovich! You're simply stupid, and that's that," said Storchenko in a loud voice. "Why, Ivan Fyodorovich knows all this better than you do, and surely he won't believe you."

Now Ivan Ivanovich was completely offended; he fell silent and took to eating his turkey, in spite of the fact that it wasn't as fat as those it was so disgusting to look at.

For a while the sound of knives, spoons, and plates replaced conversation; but loudest of all was the noise made by Storchenko, as he sucked the marrow out of the lamb bones.

"Have you read," Ivan Ivanovich asked Ivan Shponka after some silence, sticking his head out of his carriage, "Korobeinik's *Journey to Holy Places*?° It's a genuine delight for the heart and soul! Such books don't get published nowadays. I'm very sorry that I didn't look to see what year it was issued."

Shponka, having heard that the conversation concerned a book, briskly began to serve himself some gravy.

"It's genuinely remarkable to think, good sir, that a simple merchant visited all those places. He traveled over two thousand miles, kind sir! More than two thousand miles! It must be that God Himself facilitated his trip to Palestine and Jerusalem."

"So you say," said Shponka, who had heard a great deal about Jerusalem from his servant in the regiment, "that he visited Jerusalem?"

"What are you talking about, Ivan Fyodorovich?" Storchenko asked from the head of the table.

"I, that is, had the occasion to remark that there are such distant places in the world!" said Shponka, being greatly content that he had managed to utter such a long and difficult sentence.

"Don't believe him, Ivan Fyodorovich!" said Storchenko, not listening very carefully. "It's all lies!"

Meanwhile, dinner was finished. Grigory Grigorevich headed into his own room, as was his custom, to take a little nap; the guests followed the old woman and the young ladies into the living room, where the same table on which the vodka had been served before dinner had been transformed and was now covered with saucers containing various preserves and dishes of watermelon, cherries, and other melons.

Storchenko's absence was noticeable in all regards. The hostess became more talkative and revealed many secrets, without anyone asking, concerning the making of pastilles and the drying of pears. Even the young ladies started talking: but the blond, who seemed six years younger than her sister and who appeared to be some twenty-five years old, was more reticent.

But Ivan Ivanovich talked more than anyone else. Being certain that no one would interrupt him or interfere, he spoke about cucumbers, planting potatoes, and how there used to be such clever people in the old days—as opposed to nowadays—and about how everything was getting smarter and leading to the invention of clever things. In a word, he was one of those people who, with the greatest enjoyment, love to talk and will do so about everything under the sun. If the conversation concerned important and spiritual subjects, Ivan Ivanovich would sigh after every word, nodding his head slightly; if it concerned domestic matters, then he would stick his head out of his carriage and make such faces that just by looking at them it seemed that one could tell how to make pear kvass, or how large his melons were, or how fat the geese were that ran around his yard.

At last with great difficulty, already toward evening, Shponka managed to say goodbye. And in spite of his tractability and the fact that they insisted vehemently that he stay the night, he stuck to his decision to leave and left.

5

Auntie's New Scheme

"Well, so? Did you wheedle the deed out of the old villain?" That was the question with which his aunt greeted Shponka; she had been waiting for him impatiently on the porch for several hours; finally, she was unable to resist running out of the gates.

"No, Auntie!" said Shponka, climbing out of the cart. "Grigory Grigorevich has no deed of gift."

"And you believed him! He's lying, damn him! One day I'll go to see him and give a beating with my own hands. I'll take care of some of his fat for him! However, we should talk to our lawyer first, to see if we can take him to court. . . . But that's neither here nor there. Well, how was dinner?"

"Very good . . . yes, extremely so, Auntie."

"Well, and tell me, what did they serve? I know the old woman is first-rate at looking after the food."

"There were cheese fritters with sour cream, Auntie. Stuffed pigeons with gravy . . ."

"And was there turkey with prunes?" asked the aunt, because she herself was a master at preparing that dish.

"There was turkey, too! And very pretty young ladies, Grigory Grigorevich's sisters, especially the blond."

"Ah!" said the aunt and stared intently at Shponka, who blushed and lowered his eyes to the floor. A new idea swiftly occurred to her. "Well, then," she asked with curiosity and sparkle, "what sort of eyebrows did she have?"

It needs to be said that the aunt always considered eyebrows an indication of a woman's beauty.

"Her eyebrows, Auntie, were very much like yours, such as you had when you were young. And she had little freckles all over her face."

"Ah!" said the aunt, satisfied with Shponka's remark, though it hadn't been intended as a compliment. "What sort of dress was she wearing? Although these days it's hard to find the sort of sturdy material such as I have, for example, in this dress. But that's not the point. Well, then, what did you talk about with her?"

"What do you mean? Me, Auntie? Perhaps you're already thinking that. . . ."

"So? What's so strange about that? It's as God wills it! Perhaps you're fated to live with her in wedlock."

"I don't know how you can say that, Auntie. It shows that you don't know me at all. . . ."

"Now, now, you've already taken offense!" said the aunt. "He's still only a child," she thought to herself.° "He doesn't know a thing! They must be brought together so they can get acquainted."

At this point the aunt went to look into the kitchen and left Shponka alone. But from that time on she thought only about how to see her nephew married off soon and about taking care of his little ones. Her head was chocked full of plans in preparation for the wedding, and it was evident that she was much busier around the house than before; however, everything she did now turned out worse. Often making some pie, which task in general she never delegated to the cook, the aunt, forgetting herself and imagining that a little child was standing next to her asking for some pie, would absentmindedly stretch out her hand holding a choice morsel; the courtyard watch-dog, taking advantage of this fact, would seize the tasty bit and, with its loud chomping, would end her reverie, for which the dog was always beaten with a poker. She even gave up her favorite pastimes and no longer went hunting, especially after she shot a crow instead of a partridge, something that had never happened to her before.

At last, about four days after this, everyone saw the carriage dragged from the barn into the courtyard. The coachman Omelko, who also served as gardener and watchman, wielded his hammer from early morning and attached a piece of leather to it, constantly shooing away the dogs, which were licking the wheels. I consider it my duty to inform readers that this was the very same carriage that Adam had used; therefore, if someone else should claim to have Adam's carriage, it's a baldfaced lie: that one is undoubtedly a fake. It's not known how the carriage managed to escape the great flood. One has to conclude that in Noah's ark there was a special space reserved for it. I'm very sorry that I can't describe its appearance to my readers. Suffice it to say that Vasilisa was very satisfied with its structure and always declared her regret that such old carriages had gone out of fashion. The shape of the carriage, a little lopsided, that is, with the right side much higher than the left, she found very convenient, because, as she used to say, a short person could climb in from one side, and a tall person from the other. However, there was enough space in the carriage for five short people or three of the aunt's girth.

Around noon Omelko, having finished work on the carriage, led out of the stable three horses, not much younger than the carriage itself, and began to harness them with a rope to the majestic conveyance. Shponka and his aunt, he from the left, she from the right, climbed into the carriage and set off. The peasants whom they met along the way, seeing such a fine carriage (the aunt rarely went out in it), paused respectfully, doffed their caps, and bowed from the waist. About two hours later the carriage stopped in front of the porch—I think it unnecessary to specify: it was Storchenko's house. Grigory Grigorevich was not at home. The old woman came out with the young ladies to greet the guests in the dining room. The aunt walked up to them with a majestic stride; placing one foot forward with great agility, she said loudly:

"I'm very glad, madam, that I have the honor of personally conveying my respects to you. Together with my respects, allow me to thank you for the hospitality shown to my nephew Ivan Fyodorovich, who praised your generosity. You have very fine buckwheat, madam! I saw it as we approached the village. Allow me to inquire how many sheaves you harvest from an acre."

After this there occurred a general exchange of kisses. When they had already seated themselves in the living room, the old woman began:

"As for the buckwheat, I can't tell you: that's Grigory Grigorevich's affair. I no longer have anything to do with it; nor can I: I'm already too old! In former times, I recall, our buckwheat used to reach up to our waist; now goodness knows how it grows. Although they say that everything's better now." Here the old woman sighed. Some observer might have heard in that sigh the sound of the long-gone eighteenth century.

"I've heard, madam, that your serf girls know how to make excellent rugs," said Vasilisa, and in so doing she touched the old lady's most sensitive nerve. Upon hearing these words, the old woman seemed to come to life and began talking a blue streak about how to dye yarn and prepare threads. From rugs the conversation quickly shifted to salting cucumbers and drying pears. In a word, before an hour was up the two ladies were talking as if they'd known each other for years. Vasilisa even began whispering to her in a low voice, such that Shponka couldn't hear a thing.

"Wouldn't you care to have a look?" the old woman asked, standing up.

The young ladies and Vasilisa stood up after her and they all started to make their way to the serf girls' workroom. But the aunt signaled to Shponka that he should stay behind and said something softly to the old woman.

"Mashenka!" said the old woman, turning to the blond. "Stay here with our guest and talk to him so he won't be bored."

The blond stayed behind and sat down on the sofa. Shponka sat on his chair as if on pins and needles; he blushed and lowered his eyes; but the young lady seemed not to notice and sat calmly on the sofa, carefully examining the windows and walls, or else following the cat with her eyes, as it timidly scurried under the chairs.

Shponka worked up some courage and was about to begin a conversation; but it seemed that he'd lost all of his words along the way. Not one idea occurred to him.

The silence lasted almost a quarter of an hour. The young lady just sat there.

At last Shponka summoned up his courage:

"There are many flies in the summer, madam," he uttered in a half-trembling voice.

"A great many!" replied the young lady. "My brother made a fly swatter out of Mama's old slipper, but there are still very many."

Here the conversation ended. Shponka couldn't find his tongue, no matter how hard he tried.

At last the hostess returned with his aunt and the dark-haired young lady. After talking a little longer, Vasilisa bade farewell to the old woman and the young ladies, in spite of an invitation to spend the night. The old woman and the young ladies escorted the guests out to the porch, and for a long time they waved to the aunt and her nephew, who peered out of the carriage.

"Well, Ivan Fyodorovich! What did you talk about when you were together with the young lady?" asked his aunt along the way home.

"Marya Grigorevna is a very modest and well-bred young lady!" said Shponka.

"Listen, Ivan Fyodorovich! I want to have a serious talk with you. You're thirty-eight years old, thank God. You already hold a good rank. It's time to think about having children! You must take a wife. . . ."

"What, Auntie?" cried Shponka, growing frightened. "What do you mean, a wife? No, Auntie, do me a favor. . . . You're making me feel quite ashamed. . . . I've never been married. . . . And I wouldn't know what to do with a wife!"

"You'll find out, Ivan Fyodorovich, you'll find out," his aunt uttered with a smile, and she thought to herself, "My goodness! He's still so young; he doesn't know a thing!" She continued aloud, "Yes, Ivan Fyodorovich! You won't find a better wife than Marya Grigorevna. And besides, you liked her very much. The old woman and I discussed this quite a bit: she would be very glad to have you as her son-in-law; it's still not clear, however, what that old sinner

Storchenko will say about it. But we won't pay him any attention; if he refuses to provide her with a dowry, we'll take him to court. . . ."

At this time the carriage drew up to the porch; the old nags grew lively, sensing the nearness of their stall.

"Listen, Omelko! Let the horses have a good rest; don't lead them to the water-trough right away after you've unharnessed them! They're too hot. Well, Ivan Fyodorovich," his aunt continued after climbing out of the carriage, "I advise you to think it over carefully. I have to run into the kitchen; I forgot to order supper from Solokha and that good-for-nothing won't ever think of it herself."

But Shponka stood there as if thunderstruck. True, Marya Grigorevna was not bad-looking; but to get married! That idea seemed so strange to him, so peculiar, that he couldn't think about it without fear. To live with a wife! It's incomprehensible! He wouldn't be alone in his own room, but there would always be two of them! Sweat broke out on his face the more he became absorbed in his thoughts.

He went to bed earlier than usual, but in spite of all his efforts, there was no way he could fall asleep. At last wished-for sleep, that universal soother, visited him; but what a sleep it was! He had never had such incoherent dreams. First he dreamed that everything was whirling noisily around him; he was running and running, as fast as his legs could carry him. He was at his last gasp. All of a sudden someone caught him by the ear. "Ouch! Who is it?" "It's me, your wife!" a voice resounded. And suddenly he woke up. Then he imagined that he was already married, that everything in their little house was so peculiar, so strange: a double bed stood in his room instead of single bed. His wife was sitting on a chair. He felt strange; he didn't know how to approach her, what to say; and then he noticed that his wife had the face of a goose. Inadvertently turning to one side, he saw another wife, also with the face of a goose. Turning to the other side, there was a third wife. Behind him, still another. He panicked and ran out into the garden, but out there it was very hot. He took off his hat and there was a wife sitting in it. Beads of sweat ran down his face. He put his hand in his pocket for a handkerchief, and there was a wife in there, too. He took a wad of cotton out of his ear, and there was a wife there, too. Then he suddenly began hopping on one leg and his Auntie, looking at him, said with a dignified air, "Yes, you must hop now, because you're a married man." He went toward her, but his aunt was no longer his aunt, but a belfry. And he felt that someone was dragging him by a rope up the belfry. "Who's dragging me?" he asked plaintively. "It's me, your wife. I'm dragging you because you are a bell." "No, I'm *not* a bell. I'm Ivan Fyodorovich!" he cried. "Yes, you *are* a bell," said the colonel of his infantry regiment, who just happened to be passing by. Then he suddenly dreamed that his wife was not a person at all, but some kind of woolen fabric; and that he went into a shop in Mogilyov. "What sort of material would you like?" asked the shopkeeper. "You had better take some wife, it's the latest thing. It wears very well. Everyone's having coats made from it nowadays." The shopkeeper measured and cut him off a wife. Shponka put her under his arm and went off to the Jewish tailor. "No," said the Jew, "this is poor fabric. No one has coats made from it anymore. . . ."

Shponka woke up terrified and beside himself. Cold sweat dripped from his face.

As soon as he got up that morning, he turned at once to his fortune-telling book, at the end of which the generous bookseller had placed an abridged dream manual. But there was absolutely nothing there even remotely resembling such an incoherent dream.

Meanwhile, an entirely new idea was developing in his aunt's head, about which you will learn in the next chapter.

Nevsky Prospect

There is nothing finer than Nevsky Prospect, at least not in Petersburg; it is the be-all and end-all. What splendor does that street lack—this beauty of our capital? I know for a fact that not one pale civil servant living there would trade Nevsky Prospect for all the happiness in the world. Not only someone who's twenty-five years old, sports a splendid mustache, and wears a handsomely tailored suit, but even someone with white hairs appearing on his chin and a head as smooth as a silver plate, even that person is ecstatic about Nevsky Prospect. And the ladies! Oh, Nevsky Prospect is even more appealing to the ladies. And indeed, to whom isn't it appealing? As soon as you arrive on Nevsky Prospect you are immersed in merriment. Even if you have some sort of important, necessary business, as soon as you set foot on it, you probably forget all about it. It's the only place where people come not out of necessity, driven by need and the mercantile interest that engulfs all of Petersburg. A person encountered on Nevsky Prospect seems less of an egoist than those on other streets, where avarice, greed, and necessity are manifested in those who walk or drive in carriages or carts. Nevsky Prospect is a universal means of communication in Petersburg. Here a resident of the Petersburg or Vyborg district who hasn't visited his acquaintance in the Peski district or near the Moscow Gate, can be certain he'll encounter him for sure. No list of addresses or information bureau can supply such accurate information as Nevsky Prospect. Omnipotent Nevsky Prospect! It is the sole source of amusement for a poor resident of Petersburg! How clean are its pavements and, my goodness, how many feet have left their marks on it! Both the clumsy, dirty boots of the retired soldier, under whose weight the very granite seems to crack; and the miniature little shoes, light as smoke, of a young lady, turning her head toward the lighted shop windows, like a sunflower to the sun; and the rattling saber of the hopeful lieutenant, which makes a sharp scratch along it—everything displays the extent of its strength or weakness. What a rapid phantasmagoria is enacted on it in the course of a single day! How many changes it endures in just twenty-four hours!

Let's begin with very early morning, when all Petersburg is filled with the smell of hot, freshly baked bread and with old women wearing tattered dresses and boots who are making their raids on churches and sympathetic passersby. Then Nevsky Prospect is deserted: the stout shopkeepers and their assistants are still asleep in their shirts of Dutch linen, or else they're soaping up their noble cheeks or drinking coffee; beggars gather at the doors of the confectioner's shop where a sleepy Ganymede,° who was buzzing around like a fly yesterday serving cups of chocolate, with a broom in his hands, without a necktie, tosses them stale pies and scraps. Working people move through the streets: sometimes Russian peasants cross over, hurrying to work, wearing boots, covered in lime, which even the waters of the Ekaterinsky Canal, known for its cleanness, are unable to wash off. At this time it is usually indecent for women to be out, since simple Russian folks like to express themselves in such sharp language that one doesn't even hear spoken in a theater. Sometimes a sleepy civil servant trudges along with a briefcase under his arm, if his path to the department takes him to Nevsky Prospect. It may be said definitively that at this time, that is, until twelve o'clock, Nevsky Prospect doesn't serve as a destination for anyone, but simply as a means: it gradually fills up with people who have their occupations, their cares, their disappointments, but who don't think about the street. The Russian peasant talks about ten kopecks or seven copper half-kopeck pieces; old men and women wave their arms or talk to themselves, sometimes with rather striking gestures, but no one listens or laughs at them, except perhaps for young lads wearing colorful shirts, carrying empty bottles or repaired boots in their hands, streaking like lightning down Nevsky Prospect. At this time no matter what you wear, even if you put a cap on your head instead of a hat, or your collar is sticking out too far from under your tie—no one will notice.

At twelve o'clock tutors from all nations make forays onto Nevsky Prospect with their pupils wearing cambric collars. English Joneses and French Cocos walk hand-in-hand with their charges entrusted to their parental care, and, with proper solidity, explain to them that signs hanging above the shops are put there so that one can tell what is for sale inside. Governesses, pale misses and rosy-cheeked Slavic girls, walk majestically behind their light and nimble young girls, ordering them to raise their shoulders a little and stand up straighter; to put it briefly, at this time Nevsky Prospect is pedagogical. But the closer it gets to two o'clock, the more the number of tutors, pedagogues, and children decreases: they are finally pushed out by their gentle fathers walking arm-in-arm with their colorfully dressed, high-strung wives. Gradually they're joined by all those who have completed rather important domestic chores, such as: conferring with their doctor about the weather and a small pimple that has just erupted on their nose; asking about the health of their horses and their children, who, by the way, have demonstrated great promise; who have read in the newspapers the announcement of and an important article about various arrivals and departures; and lastly who have consumed a cup of coffee or tea; and they are also joined by those whom enviable fate has blessed with the honored title of civil servant for special commissions. They're also joined by those who serve in the Department of Foreign Affairs and who are distinguished by the dignity of their profession as well as by their habits. My goodness, what splendid positions and employment! How they ennoble and enhance the soul. But, alas! I'm not in the service and am deprived of the pleasure of seeing the refined conduct of my superiors. Everyone that you encounter on Nevsky Prospect is replete with decorum: men in long jackets with their hands in their pockets, ladies in pink, white, and pale blue satin riding coats and hats. Here you meet remarkable side-whiskers, tucked behind neckties with extraordinary and astonishing art-istry; velvety side-whiskers, satiny, black as sable or coal, but, alas, belonging only to the members of the Department of Foreign Affairs. Providence has denied black side-whiskers to those work-ing in other departments; they have to sport reddish whiskers, to their extreme displeasure. Here you'll encounter magnificent mus-taches, ones that can't be described by any writer's pen or any art-ist's brush; mustaches to which the better half of life has been devoted—the object of prolonged attention by day and night; mustaches that are drenched in enchanting perfumes and scents, and anointed with all sorts of expensive and uncommon pomades; mustaches wrapped up at night in the most expensive vellum paper; mustaches toward which the owners manifest the most ten-der affection, and which are envied by passersby.

Thousands of different kinds of hats, dresses, and kerchiefs—light and colorful, toward which their owners sometimes feel an attachment over the course of two whole days—dazzle everyone on Nevsky Prospect. It seems as though a whole sea of butterflies has risen from flower stalks and is hovering in a brilliant cloud above black male beetles. Here you'll encounter waists such as you've never even dreamt of: slim, narrow waists, no thicker than a bot-tleneck; meeting them, you respectfully step aside, so that you don't poke them carelessly with your impolite elbow; your heart is over-powered by timidity and fear, that somehow, even as a result of your incautious breathing, this most splendid creation of nature and art might break.

And here you'll meet all sorts of ladies' sleeves! Ah, what a delight! They can resemble two balloons, so that the lady might soon float up into the air if her male companion wasn't keeping hold of her, because it would be as easy and as pleasant for a woman to float up into the air as it is to raise a glass of champagne to one's lips. Nowhere do people bow so graciously and naturally as they do to each other on Nevsky Prospect. Here you can meet a singular smile, a smile that is the height of art, sometimes a smile that makes you melt with pleasure, sometimes one that makes you suddenly bow your head and feel humble, and sometimes one that makes you lift up your head and feel higher than the spire of the Admiralty build-ing. Here you'll meet people conversing about a concert or about the weather with unusual graciousness and a feeling of their own self-worth. Here you'll meet a thousand inscrutable characters and phenomena. Oh, Creator! What strange characters can be encountered on Nevsky Prospect! There's a large number of such people, who, after meeting you, immediately stare at your boots and, when they have passed you by, turn back to have a look at your coattails. I still don't understand why this happens. At first I thought that they were shoemakers; however, that was not the case: for the most part they serve in various departments, many of them are superb at referring a matter from one official department to another; or they are people who take walks or who read the newspapers in pastry shops—in a word, most of them are decent folk.

At this blessed time, from two to three o'clock in the afternoon, Nevsky Prospect becomes a capital in perpetual motion: there takes place the main display of all the best works of mankind. One person wears a fashionable overcoat trimmed with expensive beaver fur; another has a splendid Grecian nose; the third sports superb side-whiskers; the fourth—a pair of lovely little eyes and a striking hat; the fifth—a signet ring on his little finger; the sixth—her little foot in a charming shoe; the seventh—an astonishing necktie; the eighth—a mustache that elicits amazement. But when the clock strikes three and the display ends, the crowd thins out. . . .

At three o'clock—there comes a new change. It's suddenly springtime on Nevsky Prospect: it is filled entirely by civil servants wearing green uniforms. Hungry titular councilors, court councilors, and others try with all their strength to speed up their movements. Young collegiate registrars, provincial and collegiate secretaries hasten to make use of the time and stroll along Nevsky Prospect with a look as if they hadn't spent the last six hours sitting in an office. But the older collegiate secretaries, titular and court councilors walk along swiftly, their heads lowered: they're not interested in observing passersby; they haven't quite torn themselves away from their worries; their thoughts are in confusion, and full of a whole bunch of started, but unfinished affairs; instead of signboards they still see in front of them a box of documents or the full face of their office head.

From four o'clock Nevsky Prospect is empty, and it is unlikely you will meet even one civil servant on it. Some seamstress coming out of a shop carrying a box runs across Nevsky Prospect. Some pitiful victim of a benevolent attorney, wandering about in his heavy woolen overcoat; some eccentric visitor who considers all hours equal; some tall, skinny Englishwoman who has a handbag and a book in her hands; some porter, a Russian wearing a high sturdy cotton jacket, with a narrow beard, living his whole life in constant haste, in whom everything is in motion: his back, hands, feet, and head as he deferentially makes his way along the sidewalk; and sometimes a lowly tradesman: you won't meet anyone else on Nevsky Prospect.

But, as soon as twilight descends on houses and streets, and a policeman, covered in burlap, scrambles up the ladder to light a streetlamp, and engravings, which dare not show themselves by day, peek out of the small, low windows of a shop, then Nevsky Prospect comes to life again and everything starts moving. That's when the mysterious time begins, when the lamps cover everything with a wonderful, enchanting light. You meet a large number of young people, mostly bachelors, in warm frock coats and overcoats. At this time you feel there's a goal, or better to say, something like a goal, something exceptionally inexplicable; everyone's steps speed up and, in general, become very uneven. Long shadows flit across the walls and pavement, and their heads almost reach the Police Bridge. Young collegiate registrars, provincial and collegiate secretaries stroll for a very long time; but older collegiate registrars, titular and court councilors stay at home for the most part, either because they're married, or because the German cooks who live in their homes are preparing good meals. Here you'll meet venerable old men, who with such dignity and astonishing decorum were strolling along Nevsky Prospect at two o'clock. You'll see them running just like the young collegiate registrars, in order to glance under the hat of a lady first glimpsed at a distance, whose thick lips and cheeks are covered in rouge, are well liked by so many people, most of all by shopkeepers, tradesmen, and merchants who always wear German frock coats and stroll in crowds, usually arm-in-arm.

"Stop!" cried Lieutenant Pirogov at that moment, yanking the sleeve of the young man walking alongside him wearing a tailcoat and cloak. "Did you see her?"

"I did; she's lovely; a regular Bianca painted by Perugino."°

"Who are you taking about?"

"About her, the one with the dark hair. And what eyes! My God, what eyes! Her entire bearing, her lines, and the cast of her face—marvelous!"

"I'm talking about the blond, who was walking behind her in the other direction. Why don't you follow the brunette, if you liked her so much?"

"Oh, how could you!" exclaimed the young man in the tailcoat, blushing. "As if she were one of those women who stroll along Nevsky Prospect at night. She must be a very distinguished lady," he continued, sighing: "her cloak alone must cost some eighty rubles!"

"You simpleton!" cried Pirogov, forcefully pushing him in the direction where her bright cloak was fluttering. "Go on, you ninny, you'll lose her! I'll go after the blond."

The two friends parted.

"We know what you're like," thought Pirogov to himself with a self-satisfied and self-assured smile, certain that no beautiful woman could resist him.

The young man in the tailcoat and the cloak proceeded with a timid and anxious step in the direction where the bright cloak was flickering in the distance, first shining brightly as it drew closer to the streetlamp, then momentarily fading in the darkness as it got further away from him. His heart was pounding, and he unintentionally quickened his pace. He dared not even think about obtaining some right to any attention from the lovely woman running ahead of him, let alone admit to such a dark thought as that hinted to him by Lieutenant Pirogov; he merely wanted to see her house, to observe where this splendid creature resided, she who seemed to have descended from heaven right onto Nevsky Prospect, and probably would rush off to somewhere unknown. He dashed along so quickly that he kept bumping into stolid gentlemen with gray sidewhiskers and forcing them from the pavement.

This young man belonged to that class of people who make up a rather strange phenomenon and belong to the citizens of Petersburg as a person who appears to us in a dream belongs to the real world. This exclusive class is very unusual in a city where everyone else is either a civil servant or a merchant, or a German tradesman.

He was an artist. Isn't that a strange phenomenon? A Petersburg artist! An artist in a land of snowfalls, an artist in a country of Finns, where everything is wet, slippery, uniform, pale, gray, and misty. These artists in no way resemble Italian artists, proud and passionate like Italy and its skies; on the contrary, they are for the most part kind gentle people, bashful, carefree, quietly loving their art, sipping tea with their two friends in their small rooms, modestly discussing their favorite subject, and in general ignoring anything unnecessary. He is constantly inviting to his room some poor old woman and forcing her to sit there for some six hours straight in order to convey her pitiful, unfeeling countenance onto his canvas. He depicts the perspective of his room in which all sorts of artistic rubbish appears: plaster-of-Paris arms and legs that have become coffee-colored from the passage of time and a coating of dust, broken painting easels, and an overturned palette, a friend strumming on a guitar, walls splattered with paint, and an open window through which one can catch a glimpse of the pale Neva and some poor fishermen wearing red shirts. In all their work you almost always see the same gray, drab colors—the indelible imprint of the north. In spite of it all, they slave over their work with genuine enjoyment. They often nourish true talent in themselves, and if the fresh air of Italy merely wafted on them, this talent would probably develop just as freely, broadly, and brightly as a plant carried at last from indoors into the fresh air. In general, they're very timid: military stars and thick epaulets occasion such confusion that they inadvertently lower the price of their works. Sometimes they like to dress fashionably, but this tendency always seems too sharp and somewhat resembles a patch. At times you can meet them wearing a fine tailcoat and a splattered cloak, an expensive velvet vest, and a frock coat covered in paint. In the same way as on one of their unfinished landscapes, you sometimes see drawn the upside-down head of a nymph, for which he could find no other place, sketched onto the soiled background of an earlier work once painted with pleasure. He never looks you directly in the eye; if he does look at you, his glance will be vague and uncertain; he doesn't fix on you the hawk-like glare of an observer or the falcon-like stare of a cavalry officer. That's because at the same time as he sees your features, he also sees the features of some plaster-of-Paris Hercules standing in his room, or imagines his own picture that he's planning to paint. As a result he sometimes replies incoherently, sometimes irrelevantly, and the objects all mixed up together in his head further increase his timidity.

The young man we've just described belongs to such a class of people, the artist Piskarev, bashful, timid, but bearing in his soul the sparks of feeling ready to burst into flame at the right time. With secret trepidation he hastened after the young woman who had made such a strong impression on him, and he seemed to be surprised by his own audacity. The unknown creature on which his eyes, thoughts, and feelings were engaged suddenly turned her head and looked at him. Oh, God, what divine features! Her most magnificent forehead of blinding whiteness was framed by hair that was as beautiful as agate. They curled, these marvelous locks, and some of them, escaping from her hat, brushed her cheeks, which were flushed by a delicate fresh color, chilled by the evening cold. Her lips were closed on a whole swarm of the most splendid visions. Everything that remains of our childhood memories, everything that occasions dreaming and quiet inspiration by the light of an icon-lamp—all of this seemed to be gathered up, joined together, and reflected on her sweet lips. She glanced at Piskarev and his heart began to flutter as a result; she glared severely, a feeling of indignation appeared on her face as a result of his bold pursuit; but on this splendid face, even rage was enchanting. Overcome by shame and timidity, he stopped, lowering his eyes; but could he risk losing this divine creature and not get to see the sanctuary in which she lived? Such thoughts occurred to the young dreamer and he decided to pursue her. But so as to remain unobserved, he followed her at a distance, looked casually from side to side, and examined the signboards, meanwhile not letting even one of the steps of the unknown woman out of his sight. The number of passersby began to diminish and the street became quieter; the beauty glanced back at him and it seemed to him that a slight smile flitted across her lips. He was trembling from head to toe and could scarcely believe his eyes. No, the deceptive light of this streetlamp revealed something like a smile on her face; no, it's his own dreams laughing at him. He held his breath and trembled all over; all his feelings were aflame and everything before him was covered over by some sort of fog. The sidewalk seemed to be sliding under his feet, the carriages with their galloping horses seemed to be standing still, the bridge stretched out and seemed to be breaking in the middle, the house stood upside down on its roof, the policeman's booth seemed to be rushing toward him, and the policeman's halberd, together with the gold letters and scissors of the signboards, seemed to be shining on his very eyelashes. And all of this was caused by her one glance, one turn of her pretty little head. Without hearing, seeing, or understanding anything, he flew after the light traces of these magnificent little feet, trying his best to moderate his pace, which was racing with the beat of his heart. At times he was overcome with doubt—was the expression on her face really so favorable?—and then he would pause for a minute; but the beating of his heart, and the indefinable power and apprehension of all his emotions, impelled him forward. He didn't even notice how there suddenly loomed ahead of him a four-story building; all four levels of windows, brightly illuminated, stared at him at once and the iron railings of the entrance administered a sudden shock. He saw how the unknown woman flew up the staircase, turned to glance back, placed her finger on her lips, and signaled him to follow. His knees trembled; his thoughts and feelings burned; a pang of joy pierced his heart with unbearable swiftness. No, this was no dream! Lord, how much happiness is contained in one moment! Such wonderful life in two minutes!

But isn't it all taking place in a dream? Was it really true that she, for whose single heavenly glance he was ready to give his entire life, to approach the domicile that he already considered inexplicably holy, was it really true that she was just now so well disposed and attentive to him? He flew up the stairs. He was experiencing no earthly thoughts; he was not warmed by the flame of earthly passion; no, at this moment he was pure and innocent, like a young virgin, still inhaling the vague spiritual craving for love. And that which would have aroused impertinent thoughts in a debauched man, that same emotion, on the contrary, merely sanctified them even more. This trust, which the splendid, weak creature showed him, this trust imposed on him a sacred duty of chivalrous severity, the duty to fulfill all her orders slavishly. He merely wished that her orders were as difficult and wearisome as possible, so that he could rush to carry them out with greater effort. He didn't doubt that some sort of secret and, at the same time, important event had forced the unknown woman to trust him; and that most likely significant service would be required of him, and that he already felt the internal strength and resoluteness to perform.

The staircase wound around, and with it, his swift dreams did, too. "Be careful!" rang out a voice like a harp, filling all his fiber with new excitement. In the darkness on the fourth floor the strange young woman knocked at the door—it opened and they entered together. A rather nice-looking woman met them with a candle in her hand, but she regarded Piskarev in such an unusually bold manner that he involuntarily lowered his eyes. They entered the room. There he could see three women's figures in different corners. One was laying out a deck of cards; another was sitting at a piano, picking out some pitiful version of an old polonaise with two fingers; the third was sitting in front of a mirror combing her long hair and was in no way disposed to forsake her toilette at the arrival of this stranger in their midst. Some sort of unpleasant disorder, which one encounters only in the neglected room of a bachelor, prevailed in everything. The rather fine furniture was covered with dust; a spider was spinning its web on the molded cornice; through the open door of another room shone a pair of boots with spurs and the braid of a uniform; a loud man's voice and a woman's laughter resounded without any restraint.

My God! Where had he come? At first he didn't want to believe it and began examining the objects filling the room more closely; but the bare walls and windows without curtains showed no indication of the presence of a caring mistress; the exhausted appearance of these pitiful creatures, one of whom sat down almost right in front of him and scrutinized him as serenely as a stain on someone's dress—all of this convinced him that he had entered a revolting haunt where pitiful vice resides, born out of the tawdry education and the vast overpopulation of the capital. It was that haunt where man sacrilegiously tramples and mocks all that is pure and sacred, all that beautifies life; where a woman, this beauty of the world, this crown of creation, has turned into some sort of strange, ambiguous creature; where, together with her purity of soul, she is deprived of all that is feminine, and disgustingly acquires the manner and arrogance of a man; she ceases to be that weak, splendid creature, so different from us. Piskarev surveyed her from head to toe with his astonished eyes, as if still not wishing to believe that it was she who had so enchanted and enticed him to follow her along on Nevsky Prospect. But she stood before him just as pretty; her hair was just as beautiful; her eyes seemed even more divine. She was young and fresh, only seventeen; it was apparent that she had only recently entered on the path of horrible vice; it hadn't yet affected her cheeks; they were still fresh and lightly flushed with color—she was magnificent.

He stood motionless before her and was ready to sink into a reverie, as he had before. But the young beauty was bored by such a long silence and smiled knowingly, looking right into his eyes. But this smile was filled with some sort of pitiful insolence; it was so strange and so incompatible with her face, just as an expression of piousness would suit the face of a bribe-taker, or an accounting book would suit a poet. He shuddered. She opened her pretty little mouth and began to say something, but it was all so stupid, so vulgar. It was as if together with her innocence a person's intelligence also disappears. He didn't want to hear anything. He felt extremely foolish and naïve, like a child. Instead of taking advantage of such good graces, instead of rejoicing at such an opportunity, which would have pleased another in his place, he scampered away as fast he could, like a wild goat, and ran out to the street.

Hanging his head and lowering his arms, he sat in his own room like a poor fellow who'd found a valuable pearl and immediately dropped it into the sea. "Such a beauty, such divine features— but where is she? In what sort of place?" That was all that he could utter.

As a matter of fact, grief never overcomes us so powerfully as it does at the sight of beauty, touched by the putrid breath of depravity. If only ugliness went along with it; but beauty, tender beauty . . . it combines only with innocence and purity in your thoughts. The beautiful woman, who had so entranced poor Piskarev, was a genuinely amazing, extraordinary creature. Her presence in this despicable setting seemed even more extraordinary. All her features were so purely formed, the expression of her beautiful face was marked by such graciousness, that there was no way to think that depravity had gotten its claws into her. She should have been a priceless pearl, the whole world, all of paradise, the fortune of a passionate husband; she should have been a beautiful, quiet star in some inconspicuous family circle, and should have been issuing sweet orders by the single movement of her lovely lips. She should have been the goddess in a crowded ballroom, on a sparkling parquet floor, under candlelight, and met by the silent adoration of the crowd of astounded admirers prostrated at her feet—but alas, she'd been cast into the abyss with a loud laugh by the horrible will of some infernal spirit hoping to destroy the harmony of life.

Exhausted by heartbreaking pity, he sat before a spluttering candle. Midnight had long since passed, the bell tower chimed half past twelve, and he sat motionless, neither sleeping nor fully awake. Drowsiness, taking advantage of his stillness, was already beginning to overtake him gently, the room had begun to disappear, and only the flame of the candle shone through the dreams that were starting to overpower him, when suddenly a knock at the door caused him to shudder and come to his senses. The door opened and a footman in rich livery entered. Such livery had never before appeared in his lonely room, let alone at such an unusual hour. . . . He was perplexed and regarded the footman with impatient curiosity.

"That lady," the footman said with a courteous bow, "whom you visited a few hours ago, asks to see you; she has sent her carriage to fetch you."

Piskarev stood in silent amazement: "Carriage? A footman in livery? No, there must be some mistake.

"My dear sir," he continued timidly, "you must have come to the wrong place. No doubt the lady sent you to fetch someone else, not me."

"No, sir, I've made no mistake. Didn't you accompany a lady on foot to her house on Liteiny Prospect, to a room on the fourth floor?"

"Yes, I did."

"Well, then, please come quickly; the lady definitely wishes to see you and asks that you come straight to her house."

Piskarev ran down the stairs. There really was a carriage standing in the courtyard. He took a seat in it, the doors slammed shut, the cobblestones rumbled noisily under the wheels and the horses' hooves—and soon a lighted panorama of houses with bright signs passed by the carriage windows. Piskarev pondered all along the way, but he was unable to explain the adventure. Her own house, a carriage, and a footman in rich livery—he was unable to reconcile all of this with a room on the fourth floor, dusty windows, and an out-of-tune piano.

The carriage stopped in front of a brightly lit entrance, and at once he was struck by a row of carriages, the chatter of coachmen, the brightly lit windows, and the sound of music. The footman in rich livery helped him out of the carriage and politely escorted him into a hall with marble columns, a doorman decked out in gold, cloaks and fur coats scattered around, and with a bright lamp. An ethereal staircase with dazzling railings, fragrant with perfumes, led upstairs. He was already on it, already entering the first room, frightened and drawing away at first from the enormous crowd. The extraordinary diversity of faces completely bewildered him; it seemed as if some demon had cut the whole world into a multitude of different pieces and then mixed all these pieces together without any sense or order. The gleaming shoulders of women, the black tailcoats, chandeliers, lamps, airy floating gauzes, ethereal ribbons, and the fat double-bass looking out from behind the railings of the magnificent gallery—everything seemed so overwhelming to him. He saw at one time so many respectable older and middle-aged men wearing stars on their frock coats; ladies so elegantly, proudly, and gracefully stepping onto the parquet floors or sitting nearby; he heard so many French and English words; besides, the young people in black frock coats were filled with such nobility, were speaking and keeping silent with such dignity, knowing how not to say too much; they joked so splendidly, smiled so respectfully, sporting such superb side-whiskers, displaying their fine hands so skillfully as they straightened their ties; and the ladies were so ethereal, so steeped in self-satisfaction and rapture, and they lowered their eyes so charmingly, that . . . but just Piskarev's humble appearance, as he leaned against a column, showed that he was completely overwhelmed. At that moment the crowd surrounded a group of dancers. They whirled around, dressed in the transparent creations of Paris, in dresses woven out of the very air; their lovely little feet tenderly touched the parquet floor, and they were more ethereal than if they hadn't touched the floor at all.

But one lady stood out among all the rest, dressed more elegantly and dazzlingly than the others. An inexpressible, most subtle taste was expressed in her entire apparel, and yet it seemed as if she had taken no trouble at all over it, as if it came naturally, of its own accord. She looked and then refrained from looking at the surrounding crowd of spectators; she lowered her lovely, long eyelashes indifferently, and the dazzling whiteness of her face became even more blinding when a light shadow fell across her ravishing brow as she bent her head.

Piskarev exerted all his strength to make his way through the crowd and get a closer look at her; but, to his great annoyance, some enormous head with dark curly hair kept getting in his way; moreover, the crowd pressed against him so hard that he dared not move forward or backward, fearing that he might somehow shove some privy councilor. But then he finally made his way forward and glanced down at his attire, wanting to be sure that everything was in order. Heavenly Father, what's this? He was wearing a coat spotted with paint: in his hasty departure he had forgotten to change into appropriate clothing. He blushed to the roots of his hair, lowered his head, wanted to escape, but there was nowhere to flee: court chamberlains in bright suits formed an impenetrable wall behind him. He wished that he were as far away as possible from the beautiful lady with the lovely eyebrows and long lashes. He raised his eyes, fearing to see if she were looking at him. Oh, God, she was standing right in front of him. . . . But what's this? What's this? "It's she!" he exclaimed almost at the top of his voice. Indeed, it was she, the very one whom he'd met on Nevsky Prospect and followed home.

Meanwhile, she raised her eyelashes and looked at everyone with her bright eyes. "Oh, my goodness, how lovely she is," was all he could utter with bated breath. Her eyes roamed around the room; all the men were vying with each other for her attention; but with weariness and boredom, she soon turned away from them and then her eyes met Piskarev's. Oh, good heavens! What paradise! Lord, give me strength to endure this! His life could not encompass such joy; it threatened to overwhelm his soul. She made a sign. Not with her hand, nor with a nod of her head—no: this sign was expressed by her striking eyes in such a subtle, imperceptible manner that no one could see it; but he saw it and understood it. The dancing lasted a long time; the languid music seemed to fade and die away, and then it burst forth again, shrieked and thundered; finally—it was over. She sat down, her breast heaving under a light cloud of gauze; her hand (oh, Lord, what a wonderful hand!) dropped into her lap, crushed the ethereal dress beneath it, and the dress seemed to breathe with the music; its light lilac color made the brilliant whiteness of her lovely hand even more obvious. He only wanted to touch it—nothing more! No other desires—they would be impertinent. . . . He stood near her behind her chair, not daring to speak, not daring to breathe.

"Were you feeling bored?" she asked. "I was also bored. I suspect you hate me," she added, lowering her long lashes.

"Hate you! Me? I . . ." Piskarev, completely taken aback, was just about to say, and probably would have said, a lot of very confused things, but at that moment a court chamberlain approached with a beautifully curled tuft of hair, and began spouting witty and pleasant observations. He rather charmingly displayed a row of fine teeth and every witty remark he made drove a sharp nail into Piskarev's heart. Fortunately, a stranger finally turned to the court chamberlain with a question.

"How unbearable this is!" she said, raising her heavenly eyes to him. "I will sit down at the other end of the room; meet me there!"

She slipped through the crowd and disappeared. Like a madman, he shoved the crowd aside and was there at once.

So it was she; she was sitting like an empress, better than all the others, lovelier than all the others, and her eyes were looking for him.

"You're here," she said quietly. "I'll be frank with you: the circumstances of our meeting must have seemed strange. Did you really imagine that I could belong to that despised class of creatures among whom you first encountered me? My actions may seem strange to you, but I'll tell you a secret. Will you be in a position," she asked, looking him straight in the eye, "never to betray it?"

"Oh, yes, I will, I will, I will."

But just at that moment a rather elderly man approached, began conversing with her in a language that Piskarev didn't understand,

and offered her his arm. She looked at Piskarev with an imploring glance and gave him a sign—to wait there for her return; but in a burst of impatience he was unable to obey any commands, even those she uttered. He set out after her, but the crowds separated them. He could no longer see the lilac dress; he passed from room to room in agitation, shoving everyone away unmercifully; but in all the rooms sat important people plunged in deep silence, playing games of whist. In one corner several elderly people were arguing about the superiority of military over civil service. In another, people in magnificent tailcoats were casting aspersions on the voluminous labors of a hard-working poet. Piskarev realized that one elderly gentleman with a distinguished look had buttonholed him and was presenting for his opinion one of his very judicious observations, but he rudely pushed him away, not even noticing that he was wearing a rather important order around his neck. He ran into another room—she wasn't there either. Into a third—not there. "Where is she? Give her to me! Oh, I can't go on living without another look at her! I must hear what she wanted to tell me." But all his searching was in vain. Agitated, exhausted, he remained in his corner and looked at the crowd; but then his straining eyes began to see everything in unclear form. At last the walls of his own room began to appear clearly. He opened his eyes; the candlestick stood before him flickering, almost extinguished; the whole candle had burned down; there was wax spilled all over his table.

So he'd been asleep! Good Lord, what a dream! And why did I wake up? Why didn't I wait a moment longer: surely she would have appeared again! The annoying light peeked in through his windows with its dull illumination. The room was in such gray, dreary disarray. . . . Oh, reality is so loathsome! What was it compared to dreams? He got undressed quickly and climbed into bed, wrapped himself up in a blanket, hoping to summon the fleeting dream back for a moment. Sleep, as a matter of fact, didn't delay in overtaking him, but he dreamt something very different from what he'd hoped to see: first Lieutenant Pirogov appeared, smoking his pipe, then he saw the porter from the Academy, then an actual civil councilor, then the head of a Finnish woman, whose portrait he had once painted, and other similar things.

He lay in bed until midday, wishing to fall asleep; but he couldn't even doze. If only she'd shown her lovely features for a minute, if only he could have heard her light step swishing, if only her pretty bare hand, shining bright as fresh snow, would have flashed before him.

Forsaking everything, forgetting everything, he sat with a defeated, hopeless look, full of nothing but his dream. He never thought of touching anything; his eyes, lacking all feeling and sparkle, stared at the window looking out on the courtyard, where the muddy water-carrier was pouring water that froze in midair, and the bleating voice of a peddler cried, "Old clothes for sale." Everyday actual life struck his ears strangely. Thus he sat until late in the evening and greedily threw himself into bed. For a long time he struggled with insomnia, but then finally overpowered it. Once again he had some sort of vulgar, disgusting dream. "God, have mercy on me: even for a minute, show her to me at least for a minute!" Once again he waited for the evening, once more he fell asleep, once again it was some civil servant, who was both a civil servant and a bassoon at the same time; oh, how unbearable! At last she appeared! Her little head and her curls . . . she looks . . . Oh, but how briefly! Once again, the fog, and again some sort of stupid dream.

Finally dreams became his whole life and from that time forth his life took a strange turn: one could say that he slept while awake and came to life in his sleep. If someone saw him sitting still in front of his empty table or even walking along the street, probably he would take him for a madman or someone deranged by heavy drinking; his eyes had a vacant look, and his natural absentmindedness had worsened and powerfully banished all feelings from his face, all movement. He would come to life only with the approach of nightfall.

Such a state depleted his strength, and the most terrible torment for him was that sleep had begun to forsake him altogether. Wanting to preserve this one resource he possessed, he employed all possible means to restore it. He heard that there was a way to bring back sleep—to do so one must only take some opium. But where could he procure it? He remembered a certain Persian, who owned a shop where shawls were sold, who almost always asked

Piskarev, whenever they met, to paint him a picture of a beautiful woman. He decided to go see him; he supposed that he would undoubtedly have some opium. The Persian received him sitting on his divan, his legs folded under him.

"What do you need opium for?" he asked him.

Piskarev told him about his insomnia.

"Fine, I'll give you some, but you must paint me a picture—of a very beautiful woman! With black eyebrows and eyes large as olives; and so that I myself was lying next to her and smoking a pipe! You hear? She should be very pretty! A beauty!"

Piskarev promised to do everything as requested. The Persian left for a minute and returned with a small bottle filled with a dark liquid, carefully poured some into another small bottle, and gave it to Piskarev with instructions to use no more than seven drops in a glass of water. He greedily grabbed hold of the valuable bottle, which he would not have sold even for a pot of gold, and ran home as fast as he could.

Upon arrival home, he measured a few drops into a glass of water and, after swallowing it, fell fast asleep.

Oh, God! What joy! It was she! Once again it was she! But in a completely different guise. Oh, she was lovely, sitting near the window of a bright little country cottage. Her attire was simplicity itself—such as that in which only the thought of a poet clothes itself. And her coiffure . . . oh, Lord, how simple it was and how it suited her! A small kerchief was thrown lightly around her graceful neck; everything about her was modest; everything revealed a secret, inexplicable sense of taste. How sweet her graceful walk! How musical the sound of her footsteps and how elegant her plain dress! How lovely her arm, encircled by a ringlet of hair. With tears in her eyes, she says, "Do not despise me; I am not the sort of woman you take me for. Look at me, look closely and ask: can I really be capable of doing what you think?" "Oh, no, no! Let anyone who thinks so, let anyone . . ."

But he woke up, moved, disturbed, with tears in his eyes.

"It would be better if you didn't exist at all—didn't live in the real world—and if you were the creation of an inspired artist! I would never move away from the canvas, I'd stare at you all the time and kiss you. I would live and breathe for you, like a magnificent dream, and then I would be happy. I would ask for nothing more. I would summon you, like a guardian angel, before sleep and waking, I would wait for you, whenever I happened to paint the sacred and divine. But as for now . . . what a terrible life! What good is it that she's alive? Can a madman's life be pleasant to his friends and relatives who once loved him? Good Lord, what is our life? An eternal struggle between dreams and reality!"

Thoughts almost like these occupied him constantly. He couldn't think about anything else; he ate almost nothing; with the impatience of a lover he waited for the evening and the desired vision. The incessant striving of his thoughts toward one and the same thing at last took such control over his entire existence and his imagination that the desired image would appear to him almost every day, always in a situation that was contrary to reality, because his thoughts were absolutely innocent, like the thoughts of a child. Through these dreams the object itself became somehow more innocent and was completely transformed.

The taking of opium further enflamed his thoughts, and if there ever was a man in love to the last degree of madness, impetuously, terribly, destructively, and rebelliously, then he was that unfortunate fellow.

Of all these dreams, one was more joyful to him than all the rest: he dreamt of his studio. He was so happy; with such enjoyment he sat with palette in hand! And she was there, too! She was already his wife. She sat alongside him, resting her lovely elbows on the back of his chair and looking at his work. Her languid, tired eyes expressed the burden of blissfulness; everything in the room breathed of paradise; it was so right, so neat. Oh, Lord, she leaned her lovely little head against his chest. . . .

He had never had a better dream than this. He woke up after it feeling fresher and less distracted than before. Strange thoughts were conceived in his head: "Perhaps," he thought, "she was drawn into vice by some terrible, involuntary misfortune; perhaps her soul is ready to repent; perhaps she herself wishes to escape from her own awful predicament. Is it really possible to be indifferent and allow her to ruin herself, when in fact all one has to do is extend a hand to her and save her from drowning?" His thoughts stretched ever further. "Nobody knows me," he said to himself, "and no one

cares what I do and I don't care at all what they do. If she declares
pure repentance and alters her life, then I will marry her. I really
ought to marry her, and surely I will do much better than many
people who marry their housekeepers or even the most despicable
characters. But my feat will be fair-minded and perhaps even great.
I shall return this most magnificent ornament to the world."

After having devised such a frivolous plan, he felt a blush covering his face; he went to the mirror and was frightened by his
sunken cheeks and the pallor of his own face. He began to dress
with care; he washed thoroughly, combed his hair, put on a new
frock coat, a stylish vest, threw on a cloak, and went into the street.
He breathed in the fresh air and felt the freshness in his heart, like
a recovering patient who's decided to go outside for the first time
after a prolonged illness. His heart was pounding as he approached
the street, where he hadn't set foot since that fateful meeting.

He searched for the house a long time; his memory seemed to
betray him. He walked up and down the street twice and didn't
know which house it was. Finally one seemed to be the right one.
He quickly ran up the steps and knocked at the door: it opened and
who should come out to meet him? It was his ideal, this mysterious image, the original of his dream picture, she for whom he lived,
so terribly, ardently, blissfully. She herself stood before him. He
began trembling; he could scarcely stand from weakness, overcome
by a burst of joy. She stood before him just as lovely, though her eyes
were sleepy, though pallor had covered her face and she was no longer fresh, but still she was beautiful.

"Ah!" she cried upon seeing Piskarev, and rubbing her eyes (it
was already two o'clock). "Why did you run away from us then?"

In exhaustion he sat down on a chair and stared at her.

"I just woke up; they brought me home at seven o'clock. I was
completely drunk," she added with a smile.

Oh, better if you were deaf and dumb, deprived of the ability
to speak, than to utter such words! She suddenly revealed to him,
as in a panorama, her entire life. However, in spite of this, taking
heart, he resolved to see if his admonitions would have any impact
on her actions. Gathering his strength, he began in a trembling, but
at the same time heated, voice to present her awful predicament to
her. She listened to him with an attentive expression and with the

same feeling of astonishment that we manifest in the face of something strange and unexpected. She glanced with a slight smile at her friend sitting in the corner, who, ceasing to clean her comb, also listened with attention to this new preacher.

"It's true, I'm poor," Piskarev said at last, after a long and instructive admonition, "but we'll work; we'll try, striving with one another, side by side, to improve our life. There is nothing more pleasant than to be obligated to oneself for everything. I'll sit and paint pictures, and you'll sit next to me and inspire my work, you'll sew or pursue other tasks, and we won't be lacking for anything."

"What?" she interrupted his speech with an expression of some indignation. "I'm not a washerwoman or a seamstress who has to work."

Oh, God! Those words expressed the entire base, despised life—a life filled with desolation and idleness, genuine consequences of vice.

"Marry *me* instead!" inserted a friend impertinently, who until then had been sitting quietly in the corner. "If I become your wife, I will sit just like this!"

Having said that, she assumed a foolish expression on her pitiful face, which greatly amused the young beauty.

Oh, this was more than he could bear! He lacked the strength to tolerate it. He rushed out, having lost both feeling and thoughts. His mind was clouded: unthinkingly, without a goal, not seeing anything, not hearing, not feeling, he wandered around the city all that day. No one could know whether he spent the night somewhere or not; it was only the next day that by some stupid instinct he made his way back to his own apartment, pale, looking awful, with disheveled hair, with signs of madness on his face. He locked himself in his room, wouldn't let anyone in, and asked for nothing. Four days passed, but the door to his room never opened once; finally a week passed and his room was still locked. They knocked at the door, began calling him, but there was no reply; finally they broke down the door and found his lifeless corpse with his throat slit. His bloody razor sprawled on the floor next to him. But his convulsive and outstretched arms and his horribly distorted appearance led to the conclusion that his hand was unsteady and that he suffered for a long time before his sinful soul parted from his body.

Thus perished the victim of insane passion, poor Piskarev, quiet, timid, modest, child-like, simple-hearted man, carrying within himself the spark of talent, which might with time have burst into bright, brilliant flame. No one wept for him; no one attended his lifeless corpse, besides the ordinary figure of the police inspector and the indifferent face of the town doctor. His coffin was carried quietly, even without any religious ritual, to the cemetery at Okhta; only one soldier walking behind it wept, and that was because he had drunk an extra bottle of vodka. Even Lieutenant Pirogov didn't come to view the body of the poor, unfortunate man to whom he had offered his noble patronage during his life. He had no time for that: he was busy with an extraordinary adventure. But we will soon turn to him.

I don't like corpses or dead bodies, and I always find it unpleasant when a long funeral procession crosses my path with some invalid soldier, dressed like a Capuchin monk, inhaling snuff with his left hand because his right hand is holding a torch. I always feel annoyed at the sight of a sumptuous hearse with a velvet-lined coffin; but my annoyance is mixed with sadness when I see a carter dragging the red, uncovered coffin of some poor fellow, and only one beggar woman, who met it at the crossroads, follows behind because she has nothing else to do.

It seems that we left Lieutenant Pirogov after he bade farewell to poor Piskarev and was following the blond. This woman was a lively, rather pretty little creature. She would pause in front of every shop to look at the items on display—sashes, kerchiefs, earrings, gloves, and other trifles; she twisted and turned continually, peered in all directions, and looked behind her. "You little doe, you," said Pirogov with self-confidence, continuing his pursuit, and wrapping his face up in the collar of his overcoat, so that he wouldn't meet any of his acquaintances. But it wouldn't hurt to tell the reader what sort of fellow this Lieutenant Pirogov really was.

But before we tell you about him, it wouldn't hurt to tell you something about the society to which Lieutenant Pirogov belonged. There are officers comprising a sort of middle class in Petersburg society. In the evening, you'll always find them at dinner at some state councilor's or active civil councilor's, who earned this promotion after some forty years of service. Their daughters are a bit pale, completely colorless, just like Petersburg, some of whom have already passed their prime; a tea table, a piano, dances—everything inseparable from the councilor's bright epaulets, which sparkle in the lamplight between the well-behaved blond and the black frock coat of her brother or a domestic acquaintance. It's very difficult to amuse these cold-blooded young ladies or to make them laugh; great skill is needed for this, or, better to say, no skill at all. One must speak in a way that's not too clever, not too funny, so that one talks about the trivialities that women adore. For this, one must render justice to those gentlemen we are discussing. They have a special talent for making these colorless beauties listen and laugh. Exclamations, smothered in laughter: "Oh, do stop! Aren't you ashamed to be so funny?" are often their highest form of reward. They wind up in upper-class settings very rarely, better to say, never. They are completely supplanted from this society by so-called aristocrats; however, they are considered learned and well brought up. They love to talk about literature; they praise Bulgarin, Pushkin, and Grech, and speak with contemptuous and witty remarks about A. A. Orlov.° They don't miss even a single public lecture, even if it's about accounting or forestry. No matter what the play, you will always find one of them in the theater, unless it's a vaudeville like *Filatka*,° which is sure to offend their refined taste. In the theater they are priceless and constitute the most valuable people for the directors. They especially like fine verse in the plays, and also like to call out loudly for the actors to appear; many of them, teaching in government institutions or preparing students to study in such institutions, acquire a cabriolet and a pair of horses. Then their circle becomes wider; they finally end up marrying some merchant's daughter who can play the piano, and who has a hundred thousand rubles or almost that, plus a host of bearded relatives. However, they can't attain that honor until they have at least achieved the rank of colonel. This is because bearded Russians, in spite of the fact that they still reek of cooked cabbage, don't want to see their daughters marrying anyone lower than a general, or at least a colonel. Such are the main characteristics of this kind of young people.

But Lieutenant Pirogov had many talents belonging to him alone. He could recite verse splendidly from *Dmitry Donskoi* and *Woe from Wit*,° and he had a special knack for blowing smoke rings from his pipe, able to produce a dozen of them, one after another. He could very pleasantly relate the anecdote about the fact that an ordinary cannon is one thing, while a unicorn cannon is another. However, it's somewhat difficult to enumerate all the talents with which fate had endowed Pirogov. He loved to talk about actresses and dancers, but less harshly than young ensigns discourse on this subject. He was very satisfied with his rank, to which he had been promoted not long ago; and although at times, reclining on his divan, he would say, "Oh, oh! Vanity, all is vanity! What difference does it make if I'm a lieutenant?" he was secretly very much flattered by this new distinction. In conversation he frequently tried to allude to it offhandedly, and once, when he encountered some sort of scribe on the street who treated him rudely, he immediately stopped him and in a few harsh words, let him know that he was standing in front of a lieutenant, and not some other officer. Moreover, he tried to express this more eloquently, for just then two extremely attractive women happened to pass by. In general Pirogov manifested a passion for elegance and he encouraged the artist Piskarev; however, this may have been because he very much wanted to see his own manly face portrayed on a canvas. But that's enough about the qualities of Pirogov. Humankind are such miraculous creatures that it's impossible ever to enumerate all their distinctions at once, and the closer you look, the more new traits emerge: a description of them would be endless.

And so, Pirogov kept on pursuing the unknown young woman, from time to time addressing questions to her to which she replied abruptly, sharply, and with some indistinct sounds. They entered Meshchanskaya Street through the heavy Kazan Gates, a street of tobacconists and other small shops, German craftsmen, and Finnish nymphs. The blond ran faster and darted into the gates of a rather soiled house. Pirogov followed her. She ran up a narrow, dark staircase and entered a door, which Pirogov also boldly forced his way through. He found himself in a large room with black walls and a sooty ceiling. A pile of iron screws, a metalworker's tools, shiny coffeepots and candlesticks stood on the table; the floor was strewn with copper and iron filings. Pirogov immediately grasped that this was a workman's apartment. The unknown woman darted into a side door. He hesitated, but, following the Russian rule, he decided to forge ahead. He entered the room, which in no way resembled the first room; it was very neatly arranged, indicating that the owner was a German. He was struck by an unusual, strange sight.

Before him sat Schiller, not the Schiller who wrote *William Tell* and *The History of the Thirty Years' War*,° but the well-known Schiller, the metalworker of Meshchanskaya Street. Next to him stood Hoffmann, not the writer Hoffmann,° but the rather skilled cobbler of Ofitsersky Street, Schiller's good friend. Schiller was drunk and sitting on a chair, stamping his foot and speaking with enthusiasm. All this would not have struck Pirogov, but what astonished him was the extremely strange position of the two men. Schiller was seated, his head raised, his rather large nose protruding; while Hoffmann held this nose in his two fingers and was twisting the blade of his cobbler's knife over its surface. Both men were speaking German, and therefore Lieutenant Pirogov, who only knew how to say "*Guten Morgen,*" couldn't understand a word of this whole scene. However, the meaning of Schiller's words was as follows:

"I don't want a nose; I don't need one!" he said, waving his arms. "My own nose consumes three pounds of snuff every month. And I buy it in a filthy Russian shop, because the German store doesn't stock Russian snuff, and I pay forty kopecks for every pound in that shop; that comes to one ruble and twenty kopecks; twelve times one ruble and twenty kopecks equals fourteen rubles and forty kopecks. You hear that, my friend Hoffmann? Fourteen rubles and forty kopecks for one nose. And on holidays I take some rapé,° because I don't want to take that filthy Russian snuff on holidays. In a year I take several pounds of rapé—so that's twenty rubles and forty kopecks for tobacco alone. That's robbery! I ask you, my friend Hoffmann, isn't it true?"

Hoffmann, who was drunk himself, replied affirmatively. "Twenty rubles and forty kopecks! I'm a Swabian German;° I have a king in Germany. I don't want a nose! Cut off my nose! Here's my nose!"

And if it hadn't been for the sudden appearance of Lieutenant Pirogov, then, without any doubt, Hoffmann would have cut off Schiller's nose for no good reason at all, because he had already brought his knife into position, as if he were going to cut out a sole for a shoe.

Schiller seemed very annoyed that suddenly an unfamiliar, uninvited person had interrupted him so inopportunely. In spite of the fact that he was in an intoxicated haze of beer and wine, he felt that it was somewhat indecent to be found in such a state and engaged in such action in the presence of a witness. Meanwhile, Pirogov bowed slightly and with his usual pleasant manner said:

"Excuse me. . . ."

"Get out!" Schiller drawled.

This reply puzzled Lieutenant Pirogov. Such a mode of address was entirely new to him. The slight smile, which had appeared on his face, suddenly vanished. With a feeling of wounded dignity, he said:

"I find it strange, dear sir . . . surely you didn't notice that . . . I am an officer. . . ."

"What's officer? I am Swabian German. Me, too" (here Schiller banged his fist on the table) "vill be officer: one and haff year cadet, two year lieutenant, and tomorrow I vill be officer. But I don't vant to serve. Mit officer I make this: Phoo!" And with this Schiller raised his palm and snorted into it.

Lieutenant Pirogov realized that there was nothing left for him to do but beat a hasty retreat; however, he considered such behavior, completely unbefitting his rank, very unpleasant. He paused on the staircase several times, as if trying to pull himself together and to think how he might let Schiller know of his audacity. At last he determined that he could excuse Schiller because his head was filled with beer; besides, he had a vision of the attractive blond, so he decided to consign this episode to oblivion. The next day Lieutenant Pirogov appeared early in the morning in the workshop of the ironworker. The pretty blond met him in the entrance hall and in a rather stern voice, which was very becoming to her little face, she asked:

"What do you want?"

"Ah, greetings, my dear! Don't you recognize me? You little imp, you, what lovely little eyes!" Saying this, Lieutenant Pirogov wanted to lift up her chin with his fingers.

But the blond emitted a frightened cry and repeated with the same severity:

"What do you want?"

"To see you; I don't want anything more than that," said Lieutenant Pirogov, smiling rather nicely and moving closer to her; but noticing that the frightened young woman wanted to slip out the door, he added: "I need to order some spurs, my dear. Can you make me some spurs? Although to love you, I don't need any spurs; a bridle will do. What sweet little hands!"

Lieutenant Pirogov was always very affectionate in declarations of a similar manner.

"I will call my husband at once," cried the German woman and went out; in a few minutes Pirogov caught sight of Schiller, emerging with sleepy eyes, barely recovered from yesterday's binge. After he saw the officer, he recalled, as in a vague dream, yesterday's events. He didn't remember anything very clearly, but he felt that he had done something foolish, and therefore he received the officer with a very stern look.

"I can't accept less than fifteen rubles for a pair of spurs," he said, wishing to get rid of Pirogov because, as an honest German, he found it embarrassing to meet anyone who had seen him in an indecent situation. Schiller loved to drink without any witnesses, with two or three friends, and he would lock himself away during these times even from his own workers.

"Why so expensive?" Pirogov asked warmly.

"German workmanship," Schiller replied coolly, stroking his chin. "A Russian would do it for two rubles."

"Well, to prove that I like you and would like to make your acquaintance, I will pay the fifteen rubles."

For a minute Schiller paused to consider: as an honest German, he was feeling somewhat guilty. Wishing to talk him out of his order, he declared that he couldn't fulfill it in less than two weeks. But Pirogov, without any contradiction, stated his complete agreement with the terms.

The German sank into thought and began to ponder how he could complete the work so that it was really worth the price of fifteen rubles. At that moment the blond walked into the workshop and began to search for something on the table that was covered with the coffee pots. The lieutenant took advantage of Schiller's moment of reflection and stepped up to her and squeezed her arm, which was bare up to her shoulder. Schiller didn't like that one bit.

"*Mein Frau!*" he cried.

"*Was wollen Sie doch?*" replied the blond.

"*Gehen Sie* to the kitchen!"°

The blond obeyed.

"So, ready in two weeks?" said Pirogov.

"Yes, in two weeks," replied Schiller in deep thought. "I have a great deal of work at the moment."

"Goodbye! I'll drop in on you."

"Goodbye," replied Schiller, locking the door after him.

Lieutenant Pirogov resolved not to cease his pursuit, in spite of the fact that the young German woman had rebuffed him so directly. He couldn't understand how anyone could refuse him, all the more so since his courtesy and brilliant rank gave him the full right to attention. However, one must state that in spite of her good looks, Schiller's wife was also very stupid. And, stupidity constitutes a special attraction in a pretty wife. At least I have known many husbands who are in ecstasy over their stupid wives and see in them all the traits of child-like innocence. Beauty creates absolute miracles. All spiritual deficiencies in a beautiful woman, rather than induce disgust, become somehow extraordinarily attractive; vice itself adds to their attraction; but, if it vanishes, then a woman must be twenty times cleverer than a man to inspire if not love, then at least respect. However, Schiller's wife, for all her stupidity, was always faithful to her vows, and therefore Pirogov found it rather difficult to succeed in his bold undertaking; but there is always pleasure in overcoming obstacles, and the blond became more and more interesting to him day after day. He began to inquire rather frequently about his spurs, so that Schiller finally grew fed up with it. He used all of his efforts to finish the spurs more quickly; finally the spurs were ready.

"Ah, what excellent work!" cried Lieutenant Pirogov when he saw the spurs. "Good Lord, they are so well made! Our generals don't have spurs as nice as these."

A feeling of self-satisfaction filled Schiller's soul. His eyes began to look rather merry, and he made it up completely with Pirogov. "The Russian officer is a smart man," he thought to himself.

"So, are you able to make a sheath for a dagger and other items?"

"Of course, I am," said Schiller with a smile.

"So make me a sheath for a dagger. I'll bring it to you; I have a very fine Turkish dagger, but I'd like to have a new sheath for it."

This hit Schiller like a bomb. He suddenly knitted his brows. "How do you like that?" he thought to himself, cursing himself silently for bringing it on himself for his own work. He thought it dishonorable to refuse; besides the Russian officer had praised his work. Shaking his head slightly, he agreed to do it; but the kiss that Pirogov planted so boldly on the lips of the pretty blond as he was leaving left him in a state of utter confusion.

I consider it appropriate to acquaint the reader more closely with Schiller. He was a true German, in the full sense of that word. When he was only twenty years old, that happy time when a Russian lives without a care in the world, Schiller had already measured out his own life and made absolutely no exceptions. He rose regularly at seven o'clock, dined at two, was prompt in all things, and got drunk every Sunday. He resolved to accumulate a capital of some fifty thousand rubles in the course of ten years, and this was already assured and unalterable as fate, because a civil servant would sooner forget to glance into the porter's lodge of his superior than a German would decide to break his word. Under no circumstances would he increase his expenditures, and if the price of potatoes rose higher than normal, he wouldn't add one kopeck, but would reduce the amount he bought; although he would sometimes be left a little hungry, still, he grew accustomed to it. His precision extended so far that he made it a practice to kiss his own wife no more than twice a day, and in order not to kiss her an extra time, he never put more than one spoonful of pepper into his soup; however, on Sunday, this rule was not so strictly enforced, because then Schiller drank two bottles of beer and one bottle of herb-flavored vodka, which, however, he always insulted. He drank not at all like an Englishman, who right after supper bolts the door and gets drunk all alone. On the contrary, as a German, he drank enthusiastically, either with the cobbler Hoffmann, or with the cabinet-maker Kuntz, who was also a German and a known drunk. Such was the character of the worthy Schiller, who, at last, was placed in an extremely difficult situation. Although he was a phlegmatic sort and a German, still Pirogov's advances aroused something in him akin to jealousy. He wracked his brain and was still unable to conceive of a way to get rid of this Russian officer. Meanwhile, Pirogov, smoking his pipe in a circle of his comrades—because that was how providence had arranged it so that where there are officers, they are smoking pipes—so, smoking his pipe in a circle of his comrades, he hinted meaningfully and with a pleasant smile about his little intrigue with the pretty German woman, with whom, in his own words, he was already on intimate terms, although as a matter of fact he had lost all hope of winning her over to his side.

One day he was strolling along Meshchanskaya Street, gazing at the house above which hung the sign of Schiller displaying coffeepots and samovars; to his great delight, he saw the head of the little blond, hanging out of the window and surveying the passersby. He stopped, blew her a kiss, and said: "*Guten Morgen!*" The blond nodded to him as if he were an acquaintance.

"Is your husband at home?"

"He is," replied the blond.

"When does he go out?"

"On Sundays he's not here," said the foolish blond.

"That's not bad," thought Pirogov to himself. "I must use that opportunity."

The next Sunday, like a bolt from the blue, he appeared before the blond. In fact, Schiller wasn't home. His pretty wife was frightened; but this time Pirogov behaved rather cautiously, treated her very respectfully, and, after greeting her, displayed all the beauty of his slender, attractive build. He made very pleasant and polite jokes, but the foolish German woman replied only in monosyllables. Finally, having approached her from all sides and seeing that nothing would entertain her, he proposed to dance with her. She agreed at once, because German women always love to dance. Pirogov placed great hopes in this approach; in the first place, it provided her with enjoyment; in the second place, it would demonstrate his dexterity and grace; in the third place, during a dance he could get closer to her and put his arm around the pretty woman, and establish the basis of everything else; in a word, he counted on his complete success from this dancing. He began with some gavotte, knowing that the German needed a gradual approach. The pretty woman went to the middle of the room and raised her lovely little foot. This position so enchanted Pirogov that he rushed forward to kiss her. The German started to scream, and this greatly enhanced her attractiveness in Pirogov's eyes; he showered her with kisses. All of a sudden the door opened and in came Schiller and Hoffmann and the cabinetmaker Kuntz. All three of these crafts-men were drunk as cobblers.

But I leave it to the reader to imagine Schiller's rage and indignation.

"You boor!" he cried in great indignation. "How dare you kiss my wife? You're a scoundrel, not a Russian officer. To hell with you! I'm a German, not a Russian swine! Isn't that right, my friend Hoffmann?"

Hoffmann replied in the affirmative.

"Oh, I don't want to be a cuckold. Grab him, Hoffmann, my friend, by the collar; I won't have it," he continued, waving his arms vigorously, while his face turned the color of his red vest. "I've been living in Petersburg for eight years; my mother lives in Swabia and my uncle in Nuremberg. I'm a German and not a horned ox! Away with him, my friend Hoffmann! Hold his arms and legs, my com-rade Kuntz!"

And the Germans grabbed hold of Pirogov's arms and legs.

He struggled in vain to free himself; these three tradesmen were the most sturdy men of all Petersburg Germans, and they treated him so rudely and curtly that, I confess, I can hardly find the right words to describe this unfortunate incident.

I'm certain that the next day Schiller suffered from a high fever, that he trembled like a leaf, waiting minute by minute for the arrival of the police, that he would have given God knows what so that everything that had happened the day before was all a dream. But what's transpired can never be altered. Nothing could be compared with Pirogov's fury and indignation. One thought of such a terri-ble insult drove him into a rage. He considered that Siberia and the lash would be a minimum punishment for Schiller. He rushed home so that, after having changed his clothes, he could go straight to the general and describe for him the German tradesmen's unruly con-duct in the most expressive terms. At the same time he wanted to file a written complaint with the general staff. If the designated punishment turned out to be unsatisfactory, then he would take the matter higher and higher.

But all this ended in a rather strange manner: along the way he dropped into a confectioner's shop, ate two cream puffs, read something out of the *Northern Bee*,° and left the shop in a less indignant frame of mind. Besides, the rather pleasant, cool evening made him take a little stroll along Nevsky Prospect; by nine o'clock he had calmed down and decided that it was unwise to disturb a general on Sunday; besides, he was undoubtedly off visiting someone, and therefore he went to spend the evening with one of the directors of the College of Inspectors,° where there was a very nice gathering of civil servants and officers. He spent a pleasant evening and so distinguished himself in dancing the mazurka that not only the women, but even their partners were filled with admiration.

"What an astonishing world we live in!" I thought as I strolled along Nevsky Prospect several days ago and pondered these two incidents. "How strangely, how incomprehensibly fate toys with us! Do we ever get what we wish for? Do we ever attain that for which our strengths seem marshaled? Everything happens in the opposite way. One person to whom fate grants the most splendid horses gallops on them with indifference, not noticing their beauty—while another person, whose heart is consumed by a passion for horses, goes on foot, and has to be content with clicking his tongue when trotters pass him by. One person has a fine cook, but, unfortunately, has such a small mouth that he can't take in more than two bites of food; another has a mouth as big as the arch at the General Staff, but, alas, has to content himself with some sort of German meal consisting of potatoes. Fate toys with us in such a strange way!

But the strangest things of all take place on Nevsky Prospect. Oh, don't trust that Nevsky Prospect! I always wrap myself up tighter in my coat when I'm walking along it, and in general I try not to look at things I meet along the way. It's all deception, it's all a dream: everything is not what it seems to be. You think that this fellow walking along in a splendidly made frock coat is very rich? Nothing of the sort: that frock coat is all he owns. You think that those two corpulent men standing in front of that church that is still being built are talking about its architecture? Not at all: they're talking how strange it is that two crows are sitting there, facing one another. You think that that enthusiastic fellow who is waving his arms about is talking about how his wife tossed a little ball out of a window at a completely unknown officer? Not in the least; he is talking about Lafayette.° You think that these ladies . . . but least of all you should trust ladies. Don't glance into shop windows: the trifles exhibited there are magnificent, but they smell of a lot of money. And God preserve you from looking under ladies' hats! However the coat of a beautiful woman may flutter in the distance, I would never follow her to get a better look. Keep away, for God's sake, keep away from streetlamps! And go past them, as quickly as you can pass them by. It's fortunate if you can escape with nothing more than a few drops of their smelly oil on your dashing frock coat. But besides the streetlamp, everything breathes deception. It lies at all times, this Nevsky Prospect, but most of all it lies when night falls in thick masses of shadows and you can see only the white and pale yellow walls of houses, and when the entire town is transformed into noise and brilliance; when myriads of carriages roll off bridges, postilions shout and jump up on their horses, and the devil himself lights the streetlamps so as to show everything in an unreal aspect.

Notes of a Madman

October 3

An extraordinary adventure happened today. I woke up this morning rather late, and when Mavra brought my cleaned boots, I asked her what time it was. After hearing it was long past ten o'clock, I hastened to dress more quickly. I confess I wouldn't have gone to the Department at all, knowing in advance what sort of sour face our Section Head would make. He'd been saying for some time: "Why is it, brother, that your thoughts are always so confused? Sometimes you go rushing around like a madman, and you jumble things so badly that even Satan can't figure it out; you write headings with small letters instead of capitals and you leave out the day and month." That damned frog-pecker! No doubt he envies me because I get to sit in the Director's office and sharpen His Excellency's quills. In a word, I wouldn't go to the Department if I didn't have the hope of seeing the treasurer and asking that Yid if I could receive some of my salary in advance. What a creature he is! For him to issue my salary a month in advance—good Lord, the Last Judgment will occur sooner than that. Ask until you burst, even in great need—he won't pay it, that old devil. And in his own apartment, his cook slaps him across the face. The whole world knows that. I don't understand the advantage of working in the Department. There are no opportunities at all. In the provincial government, or in the civil and state offices, it's another matter entirely: there, you may see someone squeezed into a little corner and copying. His frock coat is wretched and his face is such that you feel like spitting, but just look at the dacha he rents every summer! It's no use offering him a gilded porcelain cup: "That," he says, "is a present for a doctor." Give him a pair of trotters, or a carriage, or a beaver-fur coat worth some three hundred rubles. His appearance is so timid and he speaks so politely: "Lend me your little penknife so that I can sharpen my little quill." But then he robs you so that all you have left is the shirt on your back. On the other hand, it's true that our office is very well mannered; cleanliness prevails, such as you've never seen in government offices: the tables are made of fine wood, and all the supervisors use the formal form to address us. Yes, I confess if it weren't for the prestige of the service, I would have left the Department long ago.

I put on my old overcoat and took an umbrella, because it was pouring rain. There was no one out on the streets; I met only some old women, covering their heads with their skirts, some Russian merchants carrying umbrellas, and some couriers. Of the better class of folk, I encountered only a fellow clerk. I met him at a crossroads. As soon as I saw him, I said to myself immediately: "Oho! No, my dear fellow, you're not heading to the Department; you're hurrying after that woman who's running ahead of you, and you're looking at her little feet." What a beast that clerk is! So help me God, he's just as bad as any officer: if some woman goes by wearing a hat, he'll definitely latch onto her. While I was thinking about this, I caught sight of a carriage approaching a shop that I was walking past. I recognized it at once: it was our Director's carriage. He had no reason to go into that shop, and I thought: "It's probably his daughter." I pressed myself up against the wall. The footman opened the carriage doors and she darted out like a little bird. How she glanced from right to left, how she fluttered her eyes and brows. . . . Oh, good Lord! I'm lost, completely lost! Why did she go out in such rainy weather? Don't try to tell me that women don't have a passion for new clothes. She didn't recognize me, and I tried to wrap myself up more because I was wearing a very dirty, old-fashioned overcoat. Nowadays people wear coats with long collars, while mine had short collars, one over another; and the material wasn't waterproof. Her little dog, which hadn't managed to scurry through the shop door, remained outside on the street. I know that dog. She's called Midgie. I hadn't been there longer than a minute when suddenly I heard a thin little voice: "Hello, Midgie!" How do you like that? Who said that? I looked around and saw two ladies walking along under their umbrellas: an old woman and a younger one; but they'd already gone past when next to me I heard, "Shame on you, Midgie!" What the devil! I saw that Midgie was sniffing around the little dog following the two ladies. "Aha!" I said to myself: "that will do. Am I drunk? But that, it seems, rarely happens to me." "No, Fidèle, you were wrong." I myself saw that Midgie spoke: "I was bow-wow, bow-wow, I was bow-wow, bow-wow, bow-wow, very ill!" Oh, so it's you, you little dog! I confess that I was very surprised to hear her speak like a person. But afterwards, when I thought hard about all this, I was no longer so surprised. As a matter of fact, many similar examples have already occurred in this world. They say that in England a fish surfaced and spoke several words in such a strange language that scholars have been trying to decipher it for the last three years and have yet to understand it. I also read in the newspaper about two cows that walked into a shop and ordered a pound of tea. But I confess that I was much more surprised when Midgie said, "I wrote to you, Fidèle; probably Polkan failed to deliver my letter!" I'd stake my salary on it! Never in my life did I ever hear that a dog could write. Only a member of the gentry can write correctly. Of course, it's true that some shopkeepers and even some serfs can sometimes write a bit; but their writing is for the most part mechanical: no commas, no periods, no style.

This surprised me. I confess I've recently begun to see and hear such things that no one else has ever seen and heard. "I'll follow this little dog," I said to myself, "and find out who she is and what she's thinking."

I unfurled my umbrella and set off after the two ladies. We crossed into Gorokhovaya Street, turned into Meshchanskaya, from there to Stolyarnaya, finally to Kokushkin Bridge, and then stopped in front of a large house. "I know this house," I said to myself. "It's

Zverkov's house." What a place! So many different people live there: so many cooks, so many guests! And our fellow clerks—they crowd in like dogs, one after another. I also have one friend there who plays the trumpet very well. The ladies went up to the fifth floor. "Fine," I thought. "I won't go in now; I'll merely note the place and won't miss the first opportunity to take advantage of it."

October 4

Today is Wednesday and that's why I was in the Director's office. I came in early on purpose and, after getting seated, sharpened all his quills. Our Director must be a very clever man. His whole study is filled with bookcases. I read the titles of a few of the books: they're all so very learned and beyond anyone like me. They're all either in French or German. And when you look into his face: phew, what importance shines in his eyes! I've never heard him utter a point-less word. It's only when you hand him some documents, he'll ask: "What's it like outside?" "It's damp, Your Excellency!" He's no match for us! A real statesman. I notice, however, that he likes me a great deal. If only his daughter would, too. . . . Hey, what knav-ery! . . . Never mind, never mind, silence! I read the *Bee*. What stu-pid people those Frenchmen are! Well, what do they want? I'd take them all, so help me God, and thrash them with birch rods! It was there I read a very pleasant description of a fancy ball written by a merchant from Kursk. Those merchants are good writers. After that I noticed that it was already half past twelve, and our Director still hadn't come out of his bedroom. But around half past one there took place an event that no pen could describe. The door opened and I thought it was the Director, so I jumped up from my chair with the documents; but it was she, she herself! Holy Fathers, how she was dressed! She was wearing a dress as white as snow: phew, how luxurious! And how she glanced around: like the sun, so help me God, just like the sun! She bowed and said, "Papá hasn't been here yet?" Ai, ai, ai, what a voice! Like a canary, a little canary! "Your Excellency," I was about to say, "don't have me punished, but if you want to punish me, then do it with your own *magnificent* little hand." But, devil take it, my tongue wouldn't budge, and I said merely, "No, ma'am." She looked at me, at the books, and dropped her handkerchief. I moved as fast as I could, slipped on the damned parquet floor, and almost fell flat on my face; but I recovered and managed to pick up her handkerchief. Oh, saints alive, what a handkerchief! The most delicate fabric, light muslin—amber, pure amber! The fragrance of nobility. She thanked me and almost smiled, so that her sweet little lips barely moved, and then she left. I sat there another hour and then all of a sudden the footman arrived and said, "Go home, Aksenty Ivanovich, the master has already left the house." I can't stand footmen and the like: they're always loitering in the hall and don't even take the trouble to nod to me. And that's not all: once one of these creatures offered me his snuffbox, without even standing up. Don't you know, you stupid lackey, that I'm a civil servant and a member of the gentry? However, I took my hat and put on my overcoat myself, because these people never help me, and I left. At home I lay on my bed for the most part. Then I copied out some very fine verses:

> I didn't see my love for one whole hour,
> It seemed to me more like a year;
> I grew to hate my own life,
> I said, "How can I possibly go on living?"

It must be something Pushkin wrote.° Toward evening, wrapped up in my overcoat, I went to the entrance to Her Excellency's house and waited for a long time to see if she would come out and get into her carriage, so that I could get another look at her—but no, she didn't appear.

November 6

The section head made me furious today. When I arrived, he summoned me and began speaking like this: "Well, tell me, please, what are you up to?" "What do you mean? I'm not up to anything," I replied. "Well, think about this carefully! You're already over forty—it's time to get some sense into your head. What on earth do you imagine? You think I don't know your tricks? You're running after the Director's daughter! Just look at yourself and think, what are you? Why, you're nothing, nothing at all. You haven't a kopeck to your name. Take a look at your face in the mirror: how can you even think about that?" The devil take him: just because his face looks a bit like an apothecary bottle and he has a tuft of hair twisted into a topknot on his head, which he holds erect, and he uses pomade to make it look like a rosette, he thinks that he can do anything he likes. I understand, I understand why he's so angry with me. He's envious; perhaps he's noticed the indications of preference shown to me. But I spit on him! As if a court councilor was so important! He hangs his watch on a gold chain and orders boots worth thirty rubles—may the devil take him! Does he think I'm descended from some commoners, tailors, or noncommissioned officers? I'm a member of the gentry. I, too, can rise in the ranks. I'm still only forty-two years old—I'm at a time when my service is just beginning. Just you wait, my friend! I'll become a lieutenant, and perhaps, if God's willing, even something higher. I'll establish a reputation even better than yours. How did you get it into your head that besides you, there are no decent men? Just give me a fashionable frock coat, and let me put on a necktie like yours—and you won't be able to hold a candle to me. It's just that I lack the means, that's all.

November 8

I was in the theater. They were presenting the Russian fool Filatka.° I laughed a great deal. There was also a vaudeville with amusing lines about lawyers, especially about one collegiate registrar, written without restraint, such that I was surprised that the censor had allowed it to pass; it also said plainly that merchants cheat people and that their sons are debauched and imitate the gentry. There was also a very funny couplet about journalists: they like to abuse everything and the author was requesting that the public defend him. Our writers compose very amusing plays these days. I love going to the theater. As soon as a few kopecks turn up in my pocket—I can't wait to go. Among our fellow clerks there are such pigs: they simply won't go the theater, the peasants; even if you give them free tickets. One actress sang very well. I thought about you know who. . . . Ah, what knavery! Never mind, never mind. . . . Silence.

November 9

I set off for the Department at eight o'clock. The section head pretended that he didn't notice my arrival. I also behaved as if there hadn't been anything between us. I kept looking through and checking some papers. I left at four o'clock. I walked past the Director's apartment, but didn't see anyone there. After dinner I lay on my bed for the most part.

November 11

Today I sat in our Director's office; I sharpened twenty-three quills for him and for her, ai, ai . . . for Her Excellency, four quills. He very much likes there to be lots of quills. Oh! He must be very smart! He always sits in silence, but I think he's mulling things over in his head. I'd like to know what he thinks about most of all; what's really going on in that head? I'd like to get a closer look at the life of these people, all the subtleties and court doings—how they are, what they do in their own circle—that's what I'd really like to find out! Several times I thought about initiating a conversation with His Excellency, but, devil take it, my tongue just wouldn't behave: you say only whether it's warm or cold outside, and you can't say anything more than that. I'd like to take a look into his living room, where you sometimes see an open door, and after that into one other room. Hey, what luxurious furniture! What mirrors and china! I'd like to look into that part of the house where Her Excellency lives— that's what I would like to do! Into her boudoir: where there are all sorts of little jars, bottles, and flowers, such that one is afraid even to breathe on them; to see her dress lying there, more like thin air, than a dress. I'd like to glance into her bedroom . . . there, I think, must be wonders, there, I think, must be paradise, such as doesn't even exist in the heavens. To have a look at the little bench on which she places her little foot as she gets out of bed; how she puts on a stocking, white as snow, on her little foot . . . ai, ai, ai. . . . Never mind, never mind. . . . Silence.

Today, however, a light dawned on me; I remembered the conversation between the two dogs, which I overheard on Nevsky Prospect. "Fine," I thought, "now I'll find out everything. I have to seize the correspondence that these two nasty dogs have been conducting. There I'm sure I'll find out something." I confess that once I called Midgie over and said to her, "Listen, Midgie, now we're alone; if you like, I'll lock the door so that no one will see us. Tell me everything you know about the young lady; what's she like? I swear to you that I won't tell anyone." But the sly dog put her tail between her legs, cringed, and went out of the room quietly, as if she hadn't heard a thing. For a long time I've suspected that dogs are much smarter than people; I was even certain that she could speak, but that she was simply being very stubborn. She's very diplomatic: she notices everything, all of a person's footsteps. Tomorrow I'll set off for the Zverkovs' house, question Fidèle, and if I succeed, I'll confiscate all the letters that Midgie has written to her.

November 12

At two o'clock in the afternoon I set off determined to see Fidèle and to question her. I can't stand the smell of cabbage, which wafts from all the little shops along Meshchanskaya Street; besides, such a hellish stench comes from the gates of every house that I held my nose and raced along at full speed. And the nasty draftsmen produce such soot and smoke from their workshops that it's absolutely impossible for a respectable person to take a stroll there. When I had made it up to the sixth floor and rung the bell, a young girl emerged, not too bad-looking, with little freckles. I recognized her. She was the same one who had been walking together with the old woman. She blushed a little, and I guessed right away: you, my dear, are looking for a husband. "What do you want?" she said. "I need to speak with your little dog." The girl was stupid! I knew it at once! At that moment the little dog came running in, barking; I wanted to grab her, but the nasty creature kept trying to snap at my nose. However, I spied her basket in the corner. Hey, that's just what I needed. I went up to it, fished around in the straw in the wooden box, and, to my indescribable delight, pulled out a little packet of small notes. The horrid pooch, seeing this, at first sank her teeth into my calf, and then, after sensing that I had taken the letters, began to whine and fawn on me, but I said, "No, my dear, goodbye!" and started to run. I think the girl took me for a madman, because she grew very frightened. After I got home I wanted to set to work immediately and decipher these notes, because I have some trouble seeing in candlelight. But Mavra had decided to wash the floor. These stupid Finnish women always decide to clean at the wrong time. Therefore I went for a stroll to ponder this whole incident. Now, at last, I will find out all the activities, thoughts, and sources, and finally understand the whole thing. These letters will reveal everything to me. Dogs are a clever lot, they know all the political relationships, and therefore the letters will contain everything: a picture and an account of this man. And there will be something about the young woman, who . . . Never mind. Silence! I returned home toward evening. For the most part I lay on my bed.

November 13

Well, now. Let's see: the letter's written rather clearly. However, there seems to be something canine about the handwriting. Let's read it:

"Dear Fidèle! I still can't get used to your vulgar name. Couldn't they manage to give you a better name? Fidèle, Rosa—what bad taste! But all that's beside the point. I'm very glad we decided to write to each other."

The letter was written in very correct Russian. The punctuation and even the spelling were all accurate. Even our section head can't write that well, though he claims that he studied in some university. Let's read on:

"It seems to me that to share one's thoughts, feelings, and impressions with another is one of the greatest blessings on earth."

Hmm. That idea is borrowed from some work translated from German. I don't remember its title.

"I say this from experience, although I haven't seen the world beyond the gates of our house. Don't I spend my life in great comfort? My young lady, whom Papá calls Sophie, is crazy about me."

Ai, ai! . . . Never mind, never mind. Silence!

"Papá also pets me very often. I drink tea and coffee with cream. Ah, *ma chère*, I must say that I find nothing attractive in the large chomped bones that our Polkan gnaws in the kitchen. Tasty bones come only from wild game, and only when no one has sucked out the marrow. It's very nice to mix several sauces, but only without capers and greens; but I don't know of anything worse than feeding dogs little balls of bread. Some gentleman sitting at the table, who has had all sorts of filthy things in his hands, begins to squeeze balls of bread with those very same hands, calls you over, and thrusts one of them into your mouth. It's somehow rude to refuse, so you eat it; with disgust, but you eat it. . . ."

The devil knows what this is! What nonsense! As if there wasn't a better subject to write about. Let's look at another page. We'll see if there's something more sensible.

"With great pleasure I'm ready to tell you about all the events that have occurred here. I've already told you something about the principal gentleman, whom Sophie calls Papá. He's a very strange man."

Ah! At last! Yes, I knew it: they have political views about everything. Let's see what they write about Papá:

". . . a very strange man. He maintains silence for the most part. He rarely speaks; but a week ago he was constantly talking to himself: 'Will I get it or not?' He takes a piece of paper in one hand, makes a fist with the other hand, and says: 'Will I get it or not?' Once he turned to me with the question: 'What do you think, Midgie? Will I get it or not?' I couldn't understand a thing; I sniffed his boot and walked away. Then, *ma chère*, a week later Papá arrived home in great joy. All morning men in uniforms came to offer him their congratulations. He was so cheerful at the table, such as I've never seen before; he told anecdotes and after dinner lifted me up to his neck and said: 'Have a look, Midgie, what's this? I saw some sort of little ribbon. I sniffed it, but it didn't have any odor whatsoever; finally I gave it a quiet little lick: it was a bit salty.'"

Hmm! This mutt, it seems to me, is already too much . . . she ought to be beaten! Ah! And he's so ambitious! That must be taken into consideration.

"Farewell, *ma chère*, I have to run and so on . . . and so forth. . . . I'll finish my letter tomorrow.

"Well, hello! I'm with you again. Today my young lady Sophie . . ."

Ah! Well, let's see about Sophie. Hey, what knavery! Never mind, never mind. . . . Let's go on.

". . . my young lady Sophie was in a terrible tizzy. She was planning to attend a ball, and I was glad that in her absence I could write to you. My Sophie is always extremely pleased to go to a ball, although she almost always gets angry as she's getting dressed. I don't understand at all, *ma chère*, the pleasure of going to a ball. Sophie comes home at six o'clock in the morning, and I can almost always guess from her pale and exhausted expression that she, poor thing, was not given anything to eat there. I confess that I couldn't live that way. If they didn't give me some grouse with sauce or a wing of roast chicken, then . . . I don't know what would become of me. I also like kasha with gravy. But I never like carrots, or turnips, or artichokes. . . ."

What an extremely uneven style. It's immediately apparent that it couldn't have been written by a man. It begins appropriately, but ends in doggy fashion. Let's look at one more little letter. Something longer. Hmm! There's no date on this one.

"Ah, my dear! How one can feel the approach of spring. My heart beats faster, as if it were expecting something. I hear a constant noise in my ears, so that I frequently stand there, front paw raised for several moments, listening at the doors. I'll reveal to you that I have a great number of suitors. Often I sit at the window and scrutinize them. Ah, if you only knew what monstrosities there are among them. One of them is a very clumsy mongrel, terribly stupid; stupidity is written all across his mug; he walks along the street grandly, and imagines that he's an important creature; he thinks that everyone will be staring at him. By no means. I didn't even pay him any attention, as if I didn't see him at all. And what a terrifying Great Dane pauses in front of my window! If he stood up on his hind legs, which the lout probably doesn't know how to do, he would be half a head taller than my Sophie's Papá, who's also rather tall and fat. This oaf must be horribly ill mannered. I growled at him a bit but he didn't care at all. He didn't even frown! He stuck out his tongue, hung his huge ears, and looked in the window— what a bumpkin! But do you really think, *ma chère*, my heart is indifferent to all these overtures? Ah, no. . . . If you could only see one of my cavaliers, Trezor by name, clambering over the fence of the next house. Ah, *ma chère*, what a fine snout he has!"

Phew! Devil take it! What nonsense! How can one fill letters with such stupidities? Give me a person! I want to see a person; I demand food—that which would nourish and soothe my soul, and not these inanities. . . . Let's turn the page and see if it gets any better.

".... Sophie was sitting at a table and sewing something. I was looking out the window because I love to scrutinize people passing by. Suddenly the footman came to announce: 'Teplov!'—'Ask him in,' Sophie cried and rushed to embrace me. 'Ah, Midgie, Midgie! If you only knew who this is: a dark-haired man, a chamberlain, who has such eyes! Black and flashing, like fire.' Sophie ran into her own room. A minute later the young chamberlain with dark side-whiskers came in, went up to the mirror, smoothed his hair, and looked around the room. I growled and sat down in my place. Sophie soon came out and bowed cheerily to his shuffling; I behaved as if I hadn't noticed anything and kept staring out the window; however, I leaned my head a bit to one side and tried to listen to what they were saying. Ah, *ma chère*, what nonsense they talked! They spoke about how a certain lady executed one dance figure instead of another; also how one fellow named Bobov who wore a ruffle on his shirt looked very much like a stork and nearly took a tumble; and how someone named Lidina imagines that she has blue eyes, but they're really green; and so on and so forth. 'My goodness,' I thought to myself, 'if one were to compare that chamberlain with Trezor!' Heavens! What a difference! In the first place, the chamberlain has a completely smooth, broad face, with whiskers around the sides, as if he had wrapped his head up in a black kerchief; while Trezor has a delicate little snout, and a white patch on his forehead. You can't even compare Trezor's figure with the chamberlain's. And the eyes, his movements, and his manners are not the same at all. What a difference! I don't know, *ma chère*, what she sees in her Teplov. Why is she in such rapture about him?"

Something seems to be wrong here. It can't be that the chamberlain has so charmed her. Let's read further:

"It seems to me that if she likes this chamberlain, she'll soon also be attracted by that civil servant who sits in Papá's office. Ah, *ma chère*, if you only knew how ugly he is. He looks like a turtle in a sack. . . ."

Who could this civil servant be?

"He has a very strange surname. He's always sitting there and sharpening quills. The hair on his head is very much like hay. Papá always sends him out on errands instead of a servant. . . ."

It seems to me that this nasty little mutt is alluding to me. Since when is my hair like hay?

"Sophie can hardly refrain from laughing when she sees him."

You're lying, you damned mutt! What a nasty tongue! As if I didn't know that this is a result of envy. As if I didn't know whose tricks these were. These all come from the section head. That fellow's sworn to implacable hatred—and now he's harming me, again and again, at every step he's harming me. However, let's read one more letter. Perhaps the matter will be cleared up by itself.

"*Ma chère* Fidèle, forgive me for not writing to you in so long. I was in absolute ecstasy. Some writer accurately maintains that love is a second life. Besides, we're now experiencing big changes at home. The chamberlain visits us almost every day now. Sophie is head over heels in love with him. Papá is very cheerful. I've even heard from our Gregory, who sweeps the floor and almost always talks to himself, that soon there'll be a wedding; because Papá wants to see Sophie married either to a general, a court chamberlain, or an army colonel. . . ."

Damn it all! I can't read any more. . . . It's all about the chamberlain or the general. All that's best in the world always goes to chamberlains or generals. You find yourself some poor treasure, you think you'll be able to keep it—and some chamberlain or general snatches it away from you. Devil take it! I myself would like to be a general: not just to marry her and all the rest of it; no, I would like to be a general simply because I want to see how they would hang around me and play all those various courtly tricks and intricacies, and then I would tell them that I spit on both of you. Damn it all. How annoying! I tore that stupid mutt's letters to shreds.

December 3

It can't be. It's nonsense! There won't be a wedding! So what if he's a court chamberlain? It's nothing more than a high rank; it's not something tangible that you can pick up in your hands. Just because he's a chamberlain doesn't mean he has a third eye in the middle of his forehead. His nose isn't made of gold; it's just like mine and like everybody else's; it can sniff, but not eat; it can sneeze, but not cough. Several times I wanted to try to understand where all these distinctions come from. Why am I a titular councilor? On what grounds am I a titular councilor? Perhaps I'm some sort of count or general, and I only seem to be a titular councilor? Perhaps I myself don't know who I am? After all, there are so many examples in history: some simple, humble tradesman or peasant, not even a member of the gentry, and all of a sudden it turns out that he's some grandee, or sometimes even a sovereign. If a peasant can sometimes turn into somebody else, then what can happen to a member of the gentry? For example, I could suddenly come in wearing a general's uniform: I'd have an epaulet on my right shoulder and one on my left, and a blue ribbon across my chest—well, won't my lovely girl sing a different tune then? And what will Papá himself say, our Director? Oh, he's an extremely ambitious man! He's a Mason, absolutely a Mason, although he pretends to be this and that, but I noticed immediately that he was a Mason: if he shakes someone's hand, he sticks out only two fingers. Might I not be appointed this very minute a governor-general or a quartermaster, or something like that? I'd like to know why I'm a titular councilor. Why precisely a titular councilor?

December 5

Today I read the newspapers all morning. Strange events are occurring in Spain. I couldn't even understand it very well. They write that the throne is vacant and that officials are in a difficult position concerning the selection of an heir and as a result there are uprisings. It seems to me that is very strange. How can the throne be vacant? They say that some *donna*° should ascend to the throne. A *donna* cannot ascend to the throne. No way can she. There has to be a king on the throne. But, they say there's no king. It can't happen that there's no king. There can't be a kingdom without a king. There is a king, but he's somewhere in hiding. He may be in hiding, but some kind of family reasons, or threats from a neighboring state, like France or another country, are forcing him to hide, or else there must be some other reasons.

December 8

I was prepared to go into the Department today, but various reasons and reflections detained me. I couldn't get the events in Spain out of my mind. How can it be that a *donna* would become queen? They won't allow it. And in the first place, England won't permit it. Besides, there's the politics of all Europe: the Austrian emperor and the Russian tsar. . . . I confess, these events have so affected and shaken me that I couldn't do anything the whole day. Mavra remarked that I seemed extremely distracted at the table. As a matter of fact, I was so absentminded that I threw two plates on the floor, and they shattered at once. After dinner I went for a walk down the mountains. But I couldn't learn anything edifying. For the most part I lay on my bed and thought about the events in Spain.

April 43, 2000

Today is a day of the greatest rejoicing! There's a King of Spain. He's been found. I am that King. It was only today that I found this out. I confess it dawned on me like a flash of lightning. I don't understand how I could think and imagine that I was just a titular councilor. How could that ridiculous idea ever have entered my head? It's a good thing that no one thought of putting me into a madhouse. Now everything has been revealed to me. Now I see everything clearly, as if it was in the palm of my hand. Previously, I didn't understand; previously, everything appeared to me as if in some sort of fog. And that all happened, I think, because people imagined that the human brain was located in the head; but that's not the case: it comes with the wind from the Caspian Sea. First I told Mavra who I was. When she heard that the King of Spain was standing in front of her, she threw up her hands and almost died of fright. Foolish woman that she is, Mavra still has never seen the King of Spain. However, I tried to calm her down and in courteous words persuade her of my benevolence; I said that I was not angry in the least that she sometimes didn't clean my boots properly. But she's one of the common people. It's no use talking to them about lofty matters. She was frightened because she was of the opinion that all the kings of Spain resembled Phillip II.° But I explained to her that there was no similarity between Phillip and me, and that I had not even one Capuchin monk. . . . I didn't go to the Department today. . . . To hell with it! No, my friends, you won't lure me there; I won't copy your filthy documents!

Martober 86. Between day and night.

Our Department administrator came today to tell me to report to the Department, and to observe that I hadn't been there for more than three weeks. As a joke I went to the Department. The head of our section thought that I would bow to him and apologize, but I regarded him with indifference, not too angrily or too favorably, and I sat down in my place as if I hadn't noticed a thing. I looked at all the scum in the office and thought: "If they only knew who's sitting among them. . . . My goodness! Wouldn't there be such a commotion, and the section head himself would begin bowing, the way he bows to the Director now." They put some documents in front of me, so that I would write a summary of them. But I didn't move a finger. A few minutes later everything was in an uproar. They said the Director was coming. Many civil servants dashed forward to show themselves off to him. But I didn't budge from my place. When he passed through our section, everyone buttoned up their frock coats; but I did absolutely nothing! What do I care about the Director? Why should I stand up to greet him? Never! What's a director? He's a cork, not a director. An ordinary cork, a simple cork, nothing more. The sort you can stop up a bottle with. The most amusing thing to me was when they brought me a paper to sign. They thought that I would write at the very bottom of the page: "such and such head clerk." Not a chance! Instead, on the most important line, where the Director signs his name, I wrote "Ferdinand VIII." You should have seen the reverential silence that ensued; but I merely waved my hand and said: "There's no need for signs of allegiance!" and I walked out. From there I went directly to the Director's apartment. He was not at home. The footman didn't want to admit me, but I said some things to him that caused him to drop his hands. I walked straight into her dressing room. She was sitting in front of a mirror; she jumped up and backed away from me. However, I didn't tell her that I was the King of Spain, I merely told her that happiness awaited her such as she couldn't even imagine, and that in spite of our enemies' intrigues, we would be together. I didn't want to say anything else and left. Oh, woman is a treacherous creature! Only now have I come to understand what a woman is. Up to this point no one knew whom she loved. I'm the first one to discover the secret. Woman is in love with the devil. Yes, no joke. Physicists write nonsense, that she is this or that—but she loves only the devil. Look over there, you'll see her in the first tier of a theater adjusting her lorgnette. You think she's staring at that fat man with the star on his chest? Not at all: she's looking at the devil standing behind his back. Now he's hiding in the fat man's star. Now he's motioning to her with his finger. She'll marry him. She will. And all these people, with their high-ranking fathers, all of them, who ingratiate themselves as best they can, who scramble at court, and who say they're patriots, as well as one thing and another: profit, profit is what these patriots want. They would sell their mother, their father, their God for money, those ambitious creatures, those Christ-sellers! It's all ambition, and this ambition is because under their tongue there's a small pimple and in it lives a small worm no bigger than the head of a pin, and it's all the doing of a barber who lives on Gorokhovaya Street. I don't remember his name, but it's well known that, together with a certain midwife, he's trying to spread Mohammedanism throughout the world, and that's why, they say, the majority of the people in France believe in the Mohammedan faith.

No date. The day had no date.

I walked along Nevsky Prospect incognito. His Majesty the Tsar rode past. The whole town doffed their hats, and so did I; However, I didn't give any indication that I was the King of Spain. I considered it inappropriate to reveal myself in front of everyone, because first I needed to present myself at court. The only thing that stopped me was that I still didn't have the proper royal attire. If I could at least acquire some sort of mantle. I was about to order one from a tailor, but they are complete asses, and besides, they neglect their work totally, engage in speculation, and for the most part wind up laying pavement stones. I decided to make a mantle from my new uniform, which I had worn on only two occasions. But so that these scoundrels wouldn't ruin it, I decided to sew it myself; I locked the door so that no one would see me. I cut the whole thing out with a pair of scissors, because the style of the mantle had to be completely different.

I don't recall the date. There was no month either. The devil knows what to make of it.

The mantle is completely sewn and ready. Mavra screamed when I put it on. However, I still haven't decided to present myself at court. Up to now there hasn't been any delegation to me from Spain. It wouldn't be proper to go without my delegation. It wouldn't convey my authority. I await them any time now.

The 1ˢᵗ

I'm extremely surprised by the slow speed of the delegation. What reasons could be detaining them? Could it be France? Yes, it's the most malevolent of countries. I went to the post office to inquire whether the Spanish delegation had arrived. But the postman was extremely stupid and didn't know anything: "No," he said, "there are no Spanish delegates here, and if you want to write a letter, we will send it according to the rules and regulations." Devil take him! What's a letter? A letter's rubbish. Even pharmacists can write letters. . . .

Madrid, February 30

And so, I'm in Spain, and it happened so quickly that I could hardly come to my senses. This morning the Spanish delegation came to see me, and I got into a carriage with them. The unusual speed of our journey seemed strange to me. We traveled so fast that we reached the Spanish border in half an hour. However, there are now railroads throughout Europe, and ships move very rapidly. Spain is a strange country: when we entered the first room, I saw many men with shaved heads. I surmised, however, that they must have been either grandees or soldiers, because they shave their heads.

The behavior of the State Chancellor seemed extremely strange; he led me by the hand, thrust me into a little room, and said, "Stay here: if you call yourself King Ferdinand, I'll knock that idea right out of you." But knowing that this was none other than a temptation, I replied in the negative—for which the chancellor hit me with a stick on the back so hard that I almost cried out. But I restrained myself, recalling that this was a chivalric custom upon admission to a high honor, because in Spain such chivalric customs persist even today. When I was left alone, I decided to occupy myself with state matters. I discovered that China and Spain were one and the same, and that it's only as a result of ignorance that they're considered two separate countries. I advise everyone to try to write the word "Spain" on a piece of paper: it will always turn out to be "China." But I'm most distressed by an incident that will happen tomorrow. Tomorrow at seven o'clock a strange event will occur: the earth will sit on the moon. Even the renowned English chemist Wellington has written about it. I confess that I experienced sincere discomfort when I imagined the extreme tenderness and brittleness of the moon. The moon's usually made in Hamburg, and it's very poorly made. I'm surprised that England pays no attention to this fact. It's made by a lame cooper, who's clearly a fool with no conception of the moon. He put in some tarred rope and wood-oil; that's why there's such a stench everywhere and why you have to plug up your nose. And that's why the moon itself is such a tender globe that people can't live on it; only noses live there now. And that's why we can't see our own noses, because they're all located on the moon. And when I imagined that the earth is a heavy object, and can grind our noses into powder, I was overcome by such distress that I put on my shoes and stockings and hurried to the hall of the State Council, intending to order the police to prevent the earth from sitting on the moon. The large number of shaved grandees, whom I met in the hall of the state council, were very clever people, and when I said: "Gentlemen, let's save the moon because the earth wants to sit on it," everyone rushed to carry out my sovereign wish, and many of them climbed up the walls to try to reach the moon; but just then the State Chancellor came in. Seeing him, everyone dispersed. As King, I remained there alone. But the Chancellor, to my astonishment, hit me with his stick and drove me back to my room. Such is the power of popular traditions in Spain.

January of the same year, occurring after February.

Up to now I still haven't been able to understand what sort of country Spain is. The popular traditions and customs of the court are completely unusual. I don't understand, I don't, I really don't understand a thing. Today they shaved my head, in spite of the fact that I shouted at the top of my voice that I didn't want to become a monk. But I can't even remember what happened when they started pouring cold water on my head. I've never experienced such hell before. I was almost so frenzied that they could scarcely hold me down. I don't understand at all the meaning of this strange custom. It's stupid, senseless! I can't fathom the reason other kings haven't abolished the custom before. Judging from all appearances, I wonder: have I fallen into the hands of the Inquisition, and is the man that I took for the State Chancellor, is he really the Grand Inquisitor? Only I still don't understand how the King can be subject to the Inquisition. It can only be the influence of France, and in particular, of Polignac.° Oh, that beast Polignac! He's sworn to hound me to death. He pursues me and persecutes me; but I know, my friend, that you're being led on by the English. The English are great schemers. They wriggle their way into everything. It's already well known to the whole world that when England takes a pinch of snuff, France sneezes.

The 25th

Today the Grand Inquisitor came to my room, but hearing his footsteps from a distance, I hid under a chair. Seeing that I wasn't there, he began to call me. At first he cried: "Poprishchin!" I said not a word. Then he called, "Aksenty Ivanovich! Titular Councilor! Member of the gentry!" I kept silent. "Ferdinand VIII, King of Spain!" I was about to stick my head out, but then I reconsidered: "No, my friend, you won't fool me! We know your tricks: you're going to pour cold water on my head again." However, he saw me and used his stick to drive me out from under the chair. That stick inflicts extremely painful blows. However, I was rewarded today with my discovery: I learned that every rooster has its Spain, and that it is located under its feathers. The Grand Inquisitor, however, went away furious and is threatening me with some sort of punishment. But I ignored his impotent malice, knowing that he's acting like a machine, like a tool of England.

The 34th. 349 *ʎɹɐnɹqǝℲ*

No, I don't have the strength to tolerate any more. My God! What are they doing to me? They're pouring cold water on my head! They don't hear me, don't see me, don't listen to me. What have I done to them? Why are they tormenting me? What do they want from a poor creature like me? What can I give them? I have nothing. I have no strength; I can't endure all their torments; my head's burning, and everything's spinning around me. Save me! Take me away! Give me a troika of horses, swift as a whirlwind! Take your seat, my driver, ring out, my bells, soar upwards, my steeds, and carry me away from this world! Further, further, so that nothing can be seen, nothing. The sky whirls in front of me; a little star twinkles in the distance; the forest rushes by with dark trees and the moon; a gray mist stretches out beneath my feet; a string sounds in the fog; there's sea on one side and Italy on the other; there are some Russian huts. Is that my house standing there in the distance? Is that my mother sitting by the window? Mama, save your poor son! Shed a tear on his suffering head! See how they torment him! Clutch your poor orphan to your bosom! There's no place for him in this world! They're persecuting him! Mother! Take pity on your poor, sick child! Do you know that the Dey of Algiers has a boil right under his nose?

The Nose

1

On March 25 an extremely strange event occurred in Petersburg. The barber Ivan Yakovlevich, who lived on Voznesensky Prospect (his surname has been lost; even on his sign—where a man is depicted with soaped-up cheeks and the inscription: "Also lets blood"—nothing else was written), the barber Ivan Yakovlevich awoke rather early and smelled the fragrance of warm bread. Raising himself up in bed, he saw that his wife, a rather respectable lady who loved to drink coffee, was taking some freshly baked loaves from the oven.

"Today, Praskovya Osipovna, I won't have any coffee," said Ivan Yakovlevich. "Instead I feel like eating some warm bread with onions."

(That is, Ivan Yakovlevich would have liked both, but he knew that it was absolutely impossible to request two things at the same time: Praskovya Osipovna really didn't like such caprices.) "Let the fool eat some bread; it's better for me," his wife thought to herself: "that will leave an extra portion of coffee." And she tossed one loaf of bread on the table.

For propriety's sake Ivan Yakovlevich put a frock coat over his shirt, sat down at the table, sprinkled some salt, peeled two onions, picked up his knife, and, making a serious face, set about slicing the bread. After cutting the loaf in half, he looked into the middle of it, and, to his surprise, noticed something white. Ivan Yakovlevich twisted his knife carefully and felt it with his finger. "It's thick!" he said to himself. "What on earth could it be?"

He thrust his fingers in and pulled out—a nose! Ivan Yakovlevich dropped his hands; he started to rub his eyes and to prod it: a nose, precisely, a nose! And it even seemed to be a familiar nose. The expression on his face was one of horror. But this expression was nothing compared with the indignation that overtook his wife.

"How did you manage, you beast, to cut off someone's nose?" she cried in a rage. "You scoundrel! You drunkard! I'll inform the police about you myself. What a villain! I've already heard from three people that while you're shaving them, you yank their noses so hard that they barely stay in place."

But Ivan Yakovlevich himself was feeling neither dead nor alive. He recognized that the nose was none other than that of the Collegiate Assessor Kovalyov, whose face he shaved every Wednesday and Sunday.

"Wait, Praskovya Osipovna! I'll take it, wrap it up in a cloth, and put it in the corner. Let it sit there for a little while; I'll take it away later."

"I don't want to hear a thing about it! I won't allow a sawn-off nose in my house. . . . You're a dried-up old biscuit! All you know how to do is sharpen a razor on a leather strap, but soon you won't be fit to carry out your conjugal duties at all, you swine, you ingrate! What on earth will I tell the police? Oh, you idiot, you dolt! Take it away! Out of here! Take it wherever you like! I never want to see it again!"

Ivan Yakovlevich stood there like someone thunderstruck. He thought and thought, but didn't know what to think.

"The devil only knows how this happened," he said finally, scratching behind his ear. "Was I drunk yesterday when I came home? I can't even say for certain. By all indications it must have been an extraordinary occurrence: for bread is the product of baking, but a nose is something entirely different. I can't make heads or tails of it!"

Ivan Yakovlevich fell silent. The idea that the police might search for the nose and blame him reduced him to a complete frenzy. Already he imagined the policeman's red collar, beautifully adorned with silver, the sword . . . he trembled all over. At last he found his underclothes and boots, put on all these items, and, accompanied by Praskovya Osipovna's harsh reproaches, wrapped the nose in a cloth and went outside.

He wanted to stash it somewhere: either under a curbstone by the gate or else drop it casually and then turn off into a side street. Unfortunately, he kept meeting acquaintances who immediately started asking, "Where are you going?" or else "Whom do you plan to shave so early?" The result was that Ivan Yakovlevich couldn't find the right moment. Another time he had just managed to drop the nose, but a policeman called him, pointing with his halberd, and said, "Pick it up! You dropped something!" And Ivan Yakovlevich had to pick up the nose and hide it in his pocket. He was overcome with despair, all the more so because more and more people were appearing on the street, especially since the stores and shops were beginning to open.

He decided to go to the Isakievsky Bridge: could he manage somehow to toss the nose into the Neva? But I'm somewhat at fault: up to now I haven't said anything about Ivan Yakovlevich, a reputable man in many respects.

Ivan Yakovlevich, like every decent Russian workman, was a terrible drunkard. And although he shaved other people's chins every day, his own chin was always unshaven. His tailcoat (Ivan Yakovlevich almost never wore a frock coat) was skewbald; that is, it was black with brownish-yellow and gray patches; the collar was shiny, and instead of three buttons, there was only one left hanging by a thread. Ivan Yakovlevich was a great cynic; when Collegiate Assessor Kovalyov would observe during a shave: "Ivan Yakovlevich, your hands always reek!" Ivan Yakovlevich answered this with a question: "Why would they reek?" The Collegiate Assessor would say, "I don't know, friend, but they do." And Ivan Yakovlevich, as a result, taking a pinch of snuff, lathered his cheek, under his nose, behind his ears and under his beard—in a word, wherever he felt like it.

This respectable gentleman was already standing on Isakievsky Bridge. First of all, he glanced around; then he leaned over the railing, as if to look under the bridge to see if there were many fish in the water; then he quietly tossed in the cloth with the nose. He felt as if at that moment a great weight had been lifted from his shoulders; Ivan Yakovlevich even smiled. Instead of going home to shave some civil servant's chin, he headed for an establishment with the sign "Tea and Refreshments," to drink a glass of punch, when suddenly he noticed at the end of the bridge a police inspector of respectable appearance, with broad side-whiskers, wearing a three-cornered hat, and carrying a sword. He froze: meanwhile, the policeman signaled to him and said:

"Step over here, my good man!"

Ivan Yakovlevich, knowing what to do, took off his cap while still at a distance; stepping up quickly, he said:

"I wish you good day, your honor!"

"No, no, my friend, I'm not your honor; tell me, what were you doing over there on the bridge?"

"I swear to God, sir, I am going to shave someone, and I was only having a look to see if the river was flowing swiftly."

"You're lying, you are! You won't get away with that. Please answer me!"

"I'm willing to shave your honor two or even three times a week without complaint," replied Ivan Yakovlevich.

"No, my friend, that's nonsense! Three barbers shave me already, and they think it's a great honor to do so. Now tell me what you were doing there."

Ivan Yakovlevich turned pale. . . . But from here on this incident is completely veiled in mist, and what happened next is simply unknown.

2

Collegiate Assessor Kovalyov awoke rather early and made the sound "brrr" with his lips, which he always did when he woke up, although he himself couldn't explain why. Kovalyov stretched and asked to be given a small mirror that stood on the table. He wanted to look at a pimple that had erupted on his nose yesterday evening; but, to his greatest astonishment, he saw that instead of a nose there was a completely smooth place. Growing frightened, Kovalyov asked for a glass of water and wiped his eyes with a towel: indeed, he had no nose! He began to feel with his hand to determine whether he was still asleep. It seemed he was wide awake. Collegiate Assessor Kovalyov jumped out of bed and became alarmed: he had no nose! He asked to get dressed immediately and rushed right to see the chief of police.

Meanwhile, it is essential to say something about Kovalyov so that the reader can see what sort of person this Collegiate Assessor was. Collegiate assessors in Petersburg, who receive this designation with the help of learned testimonials, can in no way be compared to those who are appointed in the Caucasus. They belong to two very different species. Learned collegiate assessors. . . . But Russia's such a strange place that if you talk about one collegiate assessor, then all collegiate assessors from Riga to Kamchatka, absolutely take it to heart. It's exactly the same with all grades and ranks. Kovalyov was a Caucasian collegiate assessor. He had assumed this rank only two years ago, and therefore was unable to forget it even for a moment; so, as to give himself more nobility and importance, he never referred to himself as a Collegiate Assessor, but always called himself Major.° "Listen, my good woman," he would say upon meeting someone in the street selling shirtfronts: "come to me at home; my apartment is on Sadovaya Street; merely ask if this is where Major Kovalyov lives. Anyone can show it to you." If he met some pretty young thing, he would also provide some secret directive, adding, "Ask, my dear, for the apartment of Major Kovalyov." Therefore, in the future we will refer to this Collegiate Assessor as Major.

Major Kovalyov had the habit of strolling along Nevsky Prospect every day. The collar of his shirtfront was always extremely clean and starched. His side-whiskers were such as you can see on provincial and district surveyors, architects, and regiment doctors, also on those engaged in various police obligations, and in general on those men who have full, ruddy cheeks and who play a game of boston very well:° these side-whiskers grow from the middle of the cheek and stretch right up to the nose itself. Major Kovalyov wore many cornelian seals, some with crests, others with an inscription: Wednesday, Thursday, Monday, and so forth. Major Kovalyov came to Petersburg out of necessity: namely, to search for a position that was appropriate to his rank: if he succeeded, he would become a vice-governor, and if not that, then an executive clerk in some important department. Major Kovalyov was also not opposed to getting married, but only in the case that his bride would contribute a capital of some two hundred thousand rubles. Therefore, the reader can judge for himself what sort of position this major was in when he saw that instead of a rather nice-looking, moderate-sized nose, there was now a stupid, empty, smooth place.

As luck would have it, not one cab appeared on the street, and he had to go on foot, wrapped up in his cloak, hiding his face with a handkerchief, as if he had a bloody nose. "Perhaps it was only my imagination: it couldn't be that my nose just up and vanished stupidly," he thought, and intentionally dropped into the confectioner's to glance at his face in a mirror. Fortunately, no one was in the shop; boys were sweeping the floors and arranging the chairs; several people with sleepy eyes were carrying hot pastries on trays; yesterday's newspapers covered with coffee stains were lying around on tables and chairs. "Well, thank heavens, no one's here," he said, "now I can take a look." He timidly approached the mirror and glanced at it. "Devil take it, what nonsense!" he said, spitting in disgust. "If only there was something there instead of a nose, but there's nothing!"

He bit his lip in annoyance, left the confectioner's shop, and decided, contrary to his usual practice, neither to look at anyone, nor to smile at anyone. All of a sudden he stood rooted at the door of a certain house; there, before his very eyes, appeared an indescribable phenomenon: in front of the entrance stood a carriage; the doors opened; a gentleman wearing a uniform jumped down, bending forward, and ran up the stairs. Imagine Kovalyov's horror and astonishment when he realized that it was none other than his own nose! At this extraordinary sight, it seemed to him that everything started reeling before his eyes; he felt that he could scarcely stand; but he resolved no matter what to await the return of the nose to the carriage; he stood there trembling all over as if feverish. A few moments later the nose really did emerge. It was dressed in a uniform, trimmed with gold braid, with a large standing collar; it was wearing buckskin trousers; there was a sword hanging at his side.° By his hat with fancy plumage one could conclude that he held the rank of a state councilor. From all appearances, he was going somewhere on an official visit. He looked to both sides, then shouted to the driver, "Let's go!" He climbed into the carriage and set off.

Poor Kovalyov nearly lost his mind. He didn't know what to think about such a strange occurrence. How was it really possible that a nose, which yesterday was still on his face, could walk and ride in a carriage—and be wearing a uniform? He ran after the carriage, which, fortunately, went only a short distance and stopped in front of the Kazan Cathedral.

He hastened into the cathedral, making his way through rows of old women begging for alms, their faces wrapped, with two slits for their eyes, at whom he used to laugh before, and entered the church. There were only a few people inside praying; they were all standing near the entrance. Kovalyov felt so upset that he couldn't possibly pray; his eyes searched for that gentleman in all corners of the church. He finally saw him standing to one side. The nose was hiding his face completely behind his high collar; he was praying with an expression of the greatest piety.

"How shall I approach him?" wondered Kovalyov. "By all appearances, his uniform and his hat, it's obvious that he's a state councilor. The devil only knows how to do this!"

He began coughing next to him; but the nose didn't forsake its pious position even for a moment and kept genuflecting.

"Kind sir . . . ," said Kovalyov, forcing himself inwardly to take heart. "Kind sir . . ."

"What do you want?" asked the nose, turning to look at him.

"It's strange, kind sir . . . it seems to me . . . you should know your place. And suddenly I find you where? In church. You'll agree that . . ."

"Excuse me, I don't understand a thing you're saying. . . . Explain yourself."

"How can I explain it to him?" wondered Kovalyov. Taking heart, he began:

"Of course, I . . . however, I'm a major. You'll agree that it's not appropriate for me to go around without a nose. Some trader who sells peeled oranges on Voskresensky Bridge can sit there without a nose; but, having in mind the possibility of a promotion . . . besides, visiting many houses and being acquainted with ladies: Chekhtareva, the wife of a state councilor, and others. . . . You can judge for yourself . . . I don't know, kind sir. . . ." (Saying this, Major Kovalyov shrugged his shoulders.) . . . "Excuse me . . . but if you regard this matter in accordance with the rules of duty and honor . . . then you yourself can understand . . ."

"I don't understand a thing," replied the nose. "Explain yourself in a more satisfactory manner."

"Kind sir . . . ," said Kovalyov, with a feeling of his own self-worth. "I don't know how to take your words. . . . It seems to me that the whole affair is perfectly obvious. . . . Either you wish to . . . After all, you're my own nose!"

The nose looked at the major and frowned slightly.

"You're making a mistake, kind sir. I'm a person in my own right. Besides, there can't be any close relations between us. Judging from the buttons of your uniform, you must serve in a different department."

After saying this, the nose turned away and continued praying.

Kovalyov was completely bewildered, not knowing what to do or even what to think. Just then he heard the pleasant rustling of a woman's dress. An elderly woman approached, dressed all in lace, accompanied by a slim young girl wearing a white dress, which looked very nice on her slender figure, and a pale yellow hat, light as a cream puff. A tall footman with large side-whiskers and at least a dozen collars stood behind them and opened his snuffbox.

Kovalyov moved closer to them, lifted the cotton collar from his shirtfront, adjusted his seals hanging on a gold chain, and, smiling to both sides, turned his attention to the slim young girl, who, like a spring blossom, bowed slightly and raised her white hand with her semitransparent fingers up to her forehead. Kovalyov's smile broadened even further when he glimpsed her round chin and a part of her cheek, white as could be, lightly colored like the first rose of spring. But all of a sudden he pulled back as if he'd been scalded. He remembered that instead of a nose, he had nothing there at all, and his eyes filled with tears. He turned around, intending to say directly to the gentleman in the uniform that he was a liar and a scoundrel, and that he really was nothing more than Kovalyov's own nose. . . . But the nose was no longer there: it had managed to dash away, probably to pay someone else a visit.

This drove Kovalyov to despair. He went back and paused for a moment under the colonnade, cautiously checking in all directions to see if the nose would turn up. He clearly recalled that it was wearing a hat with plumage and a uniform with gold braid; but he noticed neither its overcoat, nor the color of his carriage, nor his horses, nor even whether there was a footman wearing some sort of livery on the back of it. Besides, there were so many carriages going back and forth with such speed that it was hard to figure it all out; but even if he'd noticed any one of them, he lacked the means of stopping it. The day was splendid and sunny. There was a large crowd of people on Nevsky Prospect; ladies were scattered like an entire flowery waterfall all along the sidewalk, from Politseisky Bridge to the Anichkov Bridge. There he saw an acquaintance of his, a court councilor, whom he called lieutenant colonel, especially if he met him in the presence of others. There was Yaryzhkin, the head of a desk in the Senate, a good friend, who always got into trouble when he played an eight in boston. And there was another major, who had received the rank of collegiate assessor in the Caucasus, waving his arm, signaling to him. . . .

"Devil take it!" said Kovalyov. "Hey, driver, take me directly to the police superintendent!"

Kovalyov got into the carriage and shouted to the cabdriver, "Get going!"

"Is the police superintendent in?" he cried upon entering the hall.

"Not at all," replied the porter. "He just left."

"How do you like that!"

"Yes," added the porter, "it wasn't that long ago, but he left. If you'd come a minute earlier, then you might have found him here."

Kovalyov, without removing the handkerchief from his face, sat in the cab and cried in a frantic voice:

"Let's go!"

"Where to?" asked the cabdriver.

"Straight ahead!"

"How can I? There's a fork here: to the right or to the left?"

This question forced Kovalyov to stop and think again. In his situation, it was most appropriate for him to turn toward the Board of Public Order; not because it had any direct connection to the police, but rather because it might result in action much sooner than if he appealed to any other place; to seek satisfaction from the supervisor of the department where the nose claimed to be employed would have been unreasonable, because from the nose's own replies to the questions, it was clear that to this creature nothing was sacred, and it could be lying in this case as it was lying when it said that it had never seen him before. And so, Kovalyov was about to tell the cabdriver to drive to the Board of Public Order when once again the thought occurred to him that this liar and scoundrel, who at their first meeting had behaved in such an unscrupulous manner, could easily take advantage of the opportunity to slip out of town once again—and then all searches would be in vain, or they could go on, God forbid, for a whole month. At last it seemed that heaven itself gave him instruction. He decided to proceed right to the newspaper office and to publish in good time a detailed description of all the characteristics of the nose, so that anyone meeting it could bring it to him at once, or at least could inform him as to its whereabouts. And so, having resolved on this course of action, he ordered the cabdriver to drive to the newspaper office; all along the way he never ceased pummeling his back with his fist, adding, "Faster, you rascal! Faster, you scoundrel!" To which the cabdriver replied, "Hey, sir!" shaking his head and flicking the reins of his horse, whose coat was as long as a lapdog's. At last the cab stopped, and Kovalyov, gasping for air, ran up into the small reception room, where a gray-haired civil servant in an old frock coat and glasses sat behind a desk, a pen clenched in his mouth, counting some copper coins in front of him.

"Who here takes advertisements?" cried Kovalyov. "Ah, greetings!"

"Good day," said the gray-haired official, raising his eyes for a moment and then lowering them once again to the piles of coins.

"I wish to place an ad. . . ."

"By all means. I ask you to wait a bit," said the official, placing a number on the paper with one hand and moving a few beads on the abacus with the fingers of his other hand.

A footman with the braids and the appearance of someone whose behavior suggested that he served in an aristocratic household, stood next to the table with a note in hand, and considered it appropriate to display his social skills:

"Believe me, sir, that little dog isn't worth eight ten-kopeck pieces, that is, I wouldn't even pay eight half-kopeck pieces for it; but the countess loves it, so help me God, she does; she's offering a reward of one hundred rubles to the person who finds it! To put it politely, just as we do now, people's tastes differ: for example, a hunter's willing to pay five hundred rubles or even a thousand for a pointer or a poodle, as long as it's a good dog."

The worthy official listened to this with a meaningful expression, and at the same time continued counting the number of letters in the prospective advertisement. Many old ladies stood around, as well as shopkeepers and porters, all with ads to place. In one it said that a coachman of sober habits was looking for a position; another offered for sale a second-hand carriage brought from Paris in 1814; still another sought a position for a nineteen-year-old serf girl, a skilled laundress, capable of doing other tasks; a sturdy carriage, missing one spring; a spirited young horse with gray markings, only seventeen years old; new seeds, just received from London, to grow turnips and radishes; a dacha with all conveniences: two stalls for horses and land on which it was possible to plant splendid birches or fir trees; there was also an announcement for anyone who was looking to buy old boot soles, with an invitation to an auction every day from 8 a.m. to 3 p.m. The room in which all of these folks were gathered was small and the air was extremely dense, but Collegiate Assessor Kovalyov was unaware of the smell because he kept his handkerchief over his face, and because his own nose was God knows where.

"Kind sir, allow me to implore you. . . . I very much need . . . ," he said at last impatiently.

"One moment, one moment! Two rubles and forty-three kopecks! Immediately! One ruble and sixty-four kopecks!" said the gray-haired gentleman, tossing notes in the faces of the old women and the porters. "What do you want?" he said at last, turning to Kovalyov.

"I would like to ask . . . ," said Kovalyov. "A robbery or a swindle has occurred; up to now I don't know which it was. I would merely like to announce that whoever can identify the person who did it will receive a significant reward."

"Allow me to ask what your surname is."

"No, why do you need my surname? I can't tell you. I have a great deal of acquaintances: Chekhtareva, the wife of a state councilor; Palageya Grigorievna Podtochina, the wife of a staff officer. . . . All of a sudden, they'll find out, God forbid! You should only write down: a collegiate assessor, or, even better, a gentleman who holds the rank of major."

"Was the man who got away one of your serfs?"

"What do you mean? That wouldn't have been such a bad swindle! It's . . . my nose that has run away. . . ."

"Hmm. What a strange surname! And did this Mr. Nosov get away with a large sum of money?"

"No, my nose . . . you don't understand! My nose, my own nose has disappeared and I don't know where it is. The devil wanted to play a trick on me."

"How did it disappear? I still don't understand very much."

"I can't tell you how it happened; but the main thing is, my nose is going around town now, calling itself a state councilor. Therefore, I'm asking you to announce that whoever finds it should bring it back to me immediately, as quickly as possible. You can judge for yourself, as a matter of fact, what it's like to be without such a conspicuous part of one's body. It's not like losing your little toe, which can be hidden in your boot and no one will know whether it's there or not. On Thursdays I visit the state councilor's wife, Chekhtareva; Palageya Grigorievna Podtochina, the wife of a staff officer, and her very pretty daughter are good friends of mine; you can judge for yourself, how can I see them now? I can't possibly visit them now."

The official fell to musing, which was obvious from how he pursed his lips.

"No, I can't publish such an announcement in our newspaper," he said at last, after a long silence.

"What? Why not?"

"Just so. The newspaper might lose its reputation. If everyone started to write that his nose ran away, then . . . As it is, people say that we print a lot of nonsense and false rumors."

"In what way is this matter absurd? There's nothing of the sort here."

"Well, it seems like that to you. Why just last week there was a similar occurrence. A civil servant came in the same way, just as you did, and bought an advertisement; it came to two rubles and seventy-three kopecks, and the whole thing said that his poodle with black fur had disappeared. It seemed to be in order, right? But it turned out to be libel: that poodle was some cashier, I don't recall in which department."

"But I'm not placing an ad with you about some poodle, but about my own nose: it's just as if it concerned myself."

"No, there's no way I can place such an advertisement."

"Even though I really have lost my nose!"

"If it's gone, that's a medical matter. They say that there are some people who can attach any sort of nose you'd like. However, I note that you must be a man of a very cheerful manner, and you love to make jokes in society."

"I swear to you, as God is holy! Well, if it's come to that, I'll just have to show you."

"Why trouble yourself?" continued the official, taking some snuff. "However, if it isn't too much trouble," he added, spurred by his curiosity, "I wouldn't mind having a look."

The Collegiate Assessor removed the handkerchief from his face.

"As a matter of fact, that is extremely strange!" said the official. "The place is absolutely level, as if it were a freshly made pancake. Yes, it's incredibly smooth."

"Well, are you going to argue with me now? You can see that it's essential to print the ad. I'd be very grateful to you; I'm very glad that this circumstance has afforded me the pleasure of making your acquaintance. . . ."

The major, as is apparent from all this, had resolved to resort to flattery on this occasion.

"Of course, it isn't a very big deal to print it," said the official, "but I don't foresee any advantage in your doing so. If you like, give the story to someone who has a clever pen and who can describe it as a rare occurrence of nature and can publish an article in the *Northern Bee*"—here he took some more snuff—to benefit young people"—here he wiped his own nose—"or for general curiosity."

The Collegiate Assessor felt completely deprived of all hope. He dropped his eyes to the bottom of the newspaper; there were announcements of theatrical events; his face was just about to smile, noticing the name of a very pretty actress, and he was about to reach into his pocket to see if he had a blue five-ruble note there, because staff officers, in Kovalyov's opinion, should occupy seats in the stalls—but the thought of his nose spoiled everything!

The official himself seemed to be touched by Kovalyov's difficult predicament. Wanting to relieve his distress somewhat, he considered it fitting to express his concern in a few words:

"I'm very sorry that such an incident has happened. Would you like a pinch of snuff? It drives away headaches and gloomy moods; it even helps cure hemorrhoids."

Having said this, the official offered Kovalyov his snuffbox, rather skillfully raising the lid with a portrait of some lady wearing a hat.

This thoughtless action exhausted Kovalyov's patience.

"I don't understand how you can make light of it," he said with considerable feeling. "Can't you see that I am lacking that which is required for taking snuff? May the devil take your tobacco! Right now I can't even look at it, not merely at your horrid Berezinsky snuff, but even if you were to offer me some fine rapé."

After saying this, he left the newspaper office greatly saddened by his experience and headed for the office of the police commissioner, who happened to have a remarkable sweet tooth. His entire entrance hall, which also served as his dining room, was stacked with sugar loaves, which had been presented to him by merchants as tokens of friendship. Just at this moment the cook was engaged in removing the commissioner's jackboots; his sword and other military hardware were unobtrusively stashed in various corners of the room, and his three-year-old son was already fingering his imposing three-cornered hat; after a hard day of battles, he was preparing to enjoy the pleasures of some peace and quiet.

Kovalyov entered just as he was stretching, grunting, and saying: "Hey, I'll nap for a few hours!" Therefore one could tell in advance that the Collegiate Assessor's arrival wasn't coming at a good time at all; I don't know, even if he had brought him a few pounds of tea or a bolt of cloth, whether he would have been received more cheerfully. The commissioner was a fan of the arts and manufacturing, but he preferred receiving banknotes most of all. "There is," he usually said, "nothing better than that: they don't have to be fed, they take up very little space, they always fit nicely into one's pocket, and if you drop them—they don't break."

The commissioner received Kovalyov rather drily and said that after dinner was not the time to initiate an investigation, that nature itself had decreed that once having eaten, one should have a little rest (as a result of this the Collegiate Assessor could see that the police commissioner was familiar with the pronouncements of our ancient wise men), that a respectable man doesn't lose his nose, and that there are a great many majors in the world who lack even decent underwear and who frequent all sorts of disreputable places.

That added insult to injury. It must be said that Kovalyov was extremely quick to take offense. He could forgive whatever was said about him, but in no way could he excuse any insults to his rank or profession. He even supposed that in theatrical presentations one could tolerate anything related to officers of higher ranks, but no one had the right to attack those of lower rank. The commissioner's reception upset him so much that he shook his head and replied with a feeling of dignity, spreading his arms somewhat: "I confess, after such insulting remarks on your part, there's nothing I can add. . . ." And out he walked.

He went home, scarcely able to feel the ground under his feet. It was already growing dark. His apartment seemed sad or extremely repulsive after all these unsuccessful attempts. Entering his own hall, he saw his footman Ivan on his stained leather sofa; lying on his back, he was spitting at the ceiling and managing to hit the same spot rather successfully. The man's indifference infuriated him; Kovalyov smacked his forehead with his hat and said: "You, swine, you're always doing such stupid tricks!"

Ivan suddenly jumped up from where he was and rushed with all speed to take Kovalyov's cloak.

Upon entering his own room, the major, tired and gloomy, threw himself into his armchair and at last, after several deep sighs, said:

"My God! My God! Why am I punished with such terrible misfortune? If I had lost an arm or a leg—it would have been better; if I had lost my ears—it would be awful, but still more bearable; but without a nose—a man is devil knows what: neither fish nor fowl, neither man nor beast—simply grab hold of him and toss him out the window! And if only it had been cut off in a battle or a duel, or I myself was the cause of the loss; but it vanished all on its own, for no good reason, none at all! No, it couldn't be," he added, after a little thought. "It's unlikely that it just vanished; it couldn't have happened. It must be either a dream or hallucination; perhaps by some accident I drank some vodka instead of the water I use to wash my face after my shave. That fool, Ivan, didn't take it away, and I probably took it."

To convince himself that he wasn't drunk, the major pinched himself so hard that he cried out. That pain utterly convinced him that he was wide awake. He went up to the mirror slowly and at first squinted with the idea that perhaps his nose would appear in its rightful place; but just at that moment he sprang back, saying:

"What a ridiculous sight!"

It really was incomprehensible. If he had lost a button, a silver spoon, a watch, or something like that—but to lose a nose, and to lose it where? In his own apartment! Major Kovalyov, considering all the circumstances, came to the conclusion that what might lie closest to the truth was that no one other than the wife of Staff Officer Podtochin was responsible for it, since she wanted him to marry her daughter. He himself loved to flirt with her, but he avoided a definitive commitment. When Madame Podtochina directly declared her desire to have him wed her daughter, he put her off with his compliments, saying that he was still young, that he had to serve for five years so as to reach the age of forty-two. Therefore, Madame Podtochina, no doubt to exact her revenge, resolved to disfigure him, and hired for that purpose some peasant witches, since there was no way to suppose that his nose had been cut off: no one had entered his room; the barber Ivan Yakovlevich had shaved him last Wednesday, and all that day, as well as

Thursday, his nose had been intact—this he remembered and knew very well; besides, he would have felt the pain, and the wound couldn't have healed that quickly and now be flat as a pancake. He concocted plans in his head: he should summon Madame Podtochina formally to court, or appear before her and accuse her of the crime. His reflections were interrupted by light shining through the cracks in the door, which told him that Ivan had lit a candle in the hallway. Soon Ivan himself appeared, carrying a candle, lighting up the entire room. Kovalyov's first impulse was to seize his handkerchief and cover the place that, as recently as yesterday, his nose had occupied, so that the stupid fellow wouldn't gape seeing his master's strange predicament.

Before Ivan had withdrawn into his haunt, an unfamiliar voice rang out in the entrance hall:

"Is this the residence of Collegiate Assessor Kovalyov?"

"Come in, Major Kovalyov is here," said Kovalyov, jumping up quickly and opening the door.

A police officer came in: he was handsome, with side-whiskers not too light or too dark, with rather full cheeks, the same fellow who at the beginning of our story was standing at one end of the Isakievsky Bridge.

"Did you happen to lose your nose?"

"Yes, sir."

"It has been found."

"What are you saying?" shouted Major Kovalyov. Joy rendered him speechless. He stared directly at the police officer standing there, at his full lips and cheeks lit by the flickering light of the candle. "How was it found?"

"By pure chance: it was seized almost on the road. It was already seated in a coach, wanting to travel to Riga. It had a passport registered in the name of a civil servant. The strange thing was that at first I took him for a gentleman. But fortunately, I had my glasses with me, and saw at once that it was a nose. I'm nearsighted, and if you stand directly in front of me, I can only see that you have a face, but I can't see your nose, or your beard, or anything else. My mother-in-law, that is my wife's mother, also sees nothing."

Kovalyov was beside himself with joy.

"Where is it? Where? I'll go there at once."

"Don't trouble yourself. Knowing that you need it, I brought it with me. It's strange that the main culprit in this affair is the scoundrel of a barber on Voznesensky Street, who's now in custody. I've suspected him for some time of drunkenness and thievery; several days ago he carried off a dozen buttons from a shop. Your nose is exactly the same as it was."

Having said this, the policeman reached into his pocket and took out a nose wrapped in paper.

"That's it!" cried Kovalyov. "Precisely! Come have some tea with me this evening."

"I'd consider it a great honor, but I couldn't possibly accept: from here I have to visit the prison. . . . The price of all provisions is rising significantly. . . . At home I have my mother-in-law living with us, that is, my wife's mother, and my children; my eldest is very promising: he's a very clever lad, but we lack the means to pay for his education. . . ."

Kovalyov guessed accurately, and grabbing the red banknotes from the table, he thrust them into the policeman's hands; after bowing and scraping, he made his way to the door, and shortly thereafter Kovalyov heard his voice on the street, where he was upbraiding some foolish peasant for driving his cart up on the boulevard.

For several minutes after the policeman's departure the Collegiate Assessor remained in some sort of nebulous condition, and for several minutes was unable to see or feel anything: this unexpected joy drove him to such a state of stupefaction. He carefully picked up his recovered nose in his two hands and once again examined it attentively.

"Yes, that's it, precisely!" said Major Kovalyov. "There's the pimple on the left side that erupted yesterday."

The major almost laughed from delight.

But nothing on earth lasts a long time, and therefore his joy by the next moment was less; by the third moment, it lessened even further; and finally, it merged with the usual condition of the soul, just as a circle on the water, formed by tossing in a stone, finally merges with the smooth surface. Kovalyov began to ponder and realized that this business wasn't yet finished: the nose was found, but it had to be attached, restored to its rightful place.

"What if it won't stick?"

After posing such a question to himself, the major turned pale.

With a feeling of indescribable terror, he rushed to the table and took up the mirror so that he wouldn't attach the nose in crooked fashion. His hands trembled. Carefully and deliberately he placed the nose in its previous place. Oh, horror! The nose wouldn't stick! He raised it to his mouth, warmed it slightly with his breath, and once more placed it into the smooth place between his two cheeks; but the nose wouldn't stay on, no matter what.

"Come on! Come on! Stay there, you fool!" he said to the nose. But the nose was like a piece of wood and dropped onto the table with such a strange sound, as if it were a cork. The major's face was contorted feverishly. "Will it really not stick on?" he kept saying in a great fright. But no matter how many times he raised it to its rightful place, his attempts were as unsuccessful as before.

He called Ivan and sent him for the doctor who lived in the nicest apartment on the first floor of the same building. The doctor was a handsome man; he had splendid black side-whiskers, a lively, healthy wife, ate fresh apples every day, and kept his mouth extremely clean, rinsing it out every morning for almost three-quarters of an hour, and brushing his teeth with five different kinds of brushes. The doctor came immediately. After asking how long ago the unfortunate incident had occurred, he raised Major Kovalyov's chin and flicked his thumb onto the very same place where his nose had been; as a result the major had to jerk his head back with such force that he hit the back of his head against the wall. The doctor said that it was nothing and advised him to move slightly away from the wall, and told him to bend his head first to the right; feeling the place where the nose had been, he said, "Hmm!" Then he told him to bend his head to the left and said, "Hmm!" And in conclusion he once again flicked his thumb; as a result the major reared his head like a horse whose teeth are being examined. After completing this experiment, the doctor shook his head and said:

"No, it's impossible. It's better to leave it like that, or else you might make it even worse. Of course, it could be attached; I could attach it for you; but I assure you that it would be worse for you if I did."

"Fine for you to say! How can I remain without a nose?" asked Kovalyov. "It can't be any worse than now. It's simply the devil knows what! How can I show myself anywhere with this excuse for a face? I have some close acquaintances; why, today I've been invited to spend the evening in two different houses. I have many friends: the wife of State Councilor Chekhtarev, the wife of Staff Officer Podtochin . . . although after today's action, I'll have nothing more to do with her, except through the police. Do me a favor," said Kovalyov in an imploring voice, "is there no means? Attach it somehow; even if it's not quite right, as long as it holds; I can even support it with my hand in dangerous situations. Besides, I don't dance, so as to harm it by some inadvertent movement. Everything pertaining to showing my gratitude for the visit, you may be assured, I will do to the utmost of my means. . . ."

"Believe me," said the doctor in a voice neither too loud nor too soft, but extremely convincing and magnetic, "I never treat people for personal gain. It goes against my rules and my art. It's true I charge for my services, but that's only because I don't want to offend people by refusing. Of course, I could attach your nose; but I assure you on my honor, if you don't believe what I'm saying, that it will be much worse for you. Better to allow nature to take its own course. Wash it frequently in cold water, and I can assure you that even without a nose, you will be just as healthy as if you had one. And I advise you to put your nose in a jar with spirits, or even better, to pour in two tablespoons of strong vodka and warm vinegar—then you'll be able to get some real money for it. I might even take it myself, if you don't charge too much."

"No, no! I won't sell it for anything!" cried the desperate Major Kovalyov. "It would be better if it croaked!"

"Excuse me!" said the doctor, starting to take his leave. "I wanted to be of service to you. . . . What's to be done? At least you've seen my efforts."

After saying this, the doctor left the room with a majestic bow. Kovalyov didn't even notice his face, and, almost insensible, he saw only the cuffs of his clean shirt, white as snow, peeking out from the sleeves of his black frock coat.

The next day he resolved, before filing a complaint, to write to the wife of the staff officer, to see if she would agree to return to him without a struggle that which she had taken from him:

"Dear Madame, Aleksandra Grigorievna!

"I fail to understand the strange behavior on your part. You may be sure that such actions will achieve nothing and will not force me to marry your daughter. Believe me, I am fully aware of the tale being told about my nose, as well as the fact that you, and no one else, are the primary instigator. The sudden disappearance of my nose from its rightful place, its flight and disguise, first in the guise of a civil servant, and then finally in its own form, is nothing other than the result of sorcery, performed by you or by those who practice such refined pursuits. On my own part, I consider it my obligation to warn you: if the above-mentioned nose is not restored to its rightful place today, then I shall be compelled to resort to the assistance and protection of the law.

"Nevertheless, it is with complete respect that I have the honor of being

"Your obedient servant,

"Platon Kovalyov."

"My dear sir, Platon Kuzmich!

"Your letter astonished me greatly. I must frankly confess that I did not expect it, all the more so with your unjustified accusations. I can assure you that I never received the civil servant you mentioned at home, either in disguised form or in his own right. It is true that Filipp Ivanovich Potanchikov visited me. And he did in fact seek the hand of my daughter; he is a fine, sober man of great erudition, but I never gave him any hope at all. You also mention your nose. If you mean that I am leaving you out in the cold, that is, giving you a formal refusal, then I am surprised that you yourself are bringing that up, since, as you know, I hold the completely opposite opinion; if you are now going to court my daughter in a legitimate fashion, I am prepared to satisfy you at once, because this always constituted the object of my most earnest desire, in the hope of which I remain at your service,

"Aleksandra Podtochina."

"No," said Kovalyov after reading the letter, "she is not to blame. It can't be! The letter is written in such a way that a person guilty of a crime couldn't possibly write it." The Collegiate Assessor was knowledgeable about this because he had been sent several times to conduct investigations in the Caucasus. "How did it happen? How on earth could it happen? Only the devil can sort it out!" he said at last, dropping his hands.

Meanwhile, rumors about this extraordinary occurrence had circulated throughout the capital, and, as it happens, not without special embellishments. At that time all minds were particularly receptive to the fantastic: experiments in the field of magnetism had recently been attracting public attention. Besides, the story of the dancing chairs on Konyushennaya Street was so current, and therefore there was nothing to be surprised at when soon it was rumored that Collegiate Assessor Kovalyov's nose had been seen strolling along Nevsky Prospect at precisely three o'clock. Hordes of curious people gathered there every day. Someone said that the nose was in Yunker's shop—and next to the shop such a large crowd and press of people had gathered that even the police had to intervene. One speculator of respectable appearance, with side-whiskers, who used to sell various dry baked pies at the entrance to the theater, purposely constructed fine, solid wooden benches, on which he invited curious onlookers to stand for a fee of eighty kopecks from each visitor. One worthy colonel left home early on purpose and with great difficulty managed to fight his way through the crowd; but, to his great indignation, he saw in the window of the shop, not the nose, but an ordinary woolen undershirt and a lithograph depicting a young woman pulling up her stocking, and a dandy with an open vest and a small beard peeking at her from behind a tree—a picture that had been hanging in the same place for over ten years. He walked away and said with annoyance: "How can such foolish and unlikely rumors confuse people?"

Then the rumor circulated that Major Kovalyov's nose was not strolling along Nevsky Prospect, but in the Tavrichesky Gardens, and that he had been there for a while; that even when Khozrev Mirza° was staying there, he had been very surprised by this strange freak of nature. Some students from the Surgical Academy set off to see it. One venerable aristocratic lady requested in a special letter to the keeper of the garden to show her children this rare phenomenon and, if possible, to provide an instructive and edifying explanation for the young people.

All of the men about town, who necessarily attend receptions and love to amuse ladies, were extremely glad for all these events, because their repertoire of anecdotes was already depleted. A small segment of respectable and well-intentioned people was extremely displeased. One gentleman said with indignation that he didn't understand how such absurd ideas could circulate in this enlightened age, and he was astonished that the government wasn't paying any attention to it. This gentleman, apparently, belonged to that group who wished the government would become involved in everything, even in their everyday quarrels with their wives. After this . . . but here again the entire episode becomes enveloped in fog, and it's absolutely unknown what occurred subsequently.

3

The most *absurd* things occur in the world. Sometimes there's no semblance of truth whatsoever: all of a sudden that very same nose who was going around with the rank of a state councilor and making so much noise in town, turned up in its rightful place once again, that is, between Major Kovalyov's two cheeks, as if nothing untoward had even happened. This occurred on April 7. After waking up and happening to glance in the mirror, he sees: a nose! He grabs hold of it in his hand—a nose, precisely! "Hey!" said Kovalyov and almost let loose dancing barefoot a trepak° all around the room in his joy, but Ivan's entrance stopped him. He ordered him to help him wash at that very moment, and while doing so he looked into the mirror once again and saw: a nose! Wiping his face with a towel, he looked into the mirror once more: a nose!

"Look here, Ivan, I seem to have a pimple on my nose," he said, and meanwhile he thought: "It would be awful if Ivan said, 'No, sir, there is no pimple there, nor is there even a nose!'"

But Ivan said:

"Nothing, sir, no pimple: your nose is clear!"

"That's good, damn it!" said the major to himself and snapped his fingers. Just then the barber Ivan Yakovlevich peeked in through

the door, but timidly, like a cat who'd just been swatted for steal-
ing the lard.

"Tell me in advance: are your hands clean?" Kovalyov shouted
from afar.

"Clean."

"You're lying!"

"So help me God, sir, they're clean."

"Well, you'd better watch out if it isn't true."

Kovalyov sat down. Ivan Yakovlevich covered him with a cloth
and the next moment, with the aid of his brush, had covered
Kovalyov's beard and a part of his cheeks with cream, the kind
served at merchants' name-day celebrations.

"Just look here!" said Ivan Yakovlevich to himself after he saw
the nose, and then he turned Kovalyov's head and looked at it from
the side. "So that's it! My, my, my! Who would've thought?" he
continued and stared at the nose for a long time. At last very gently,
with great care that you could only imagine, he raised two fingers to
take hold of the nose by the tip. Such was Ivan Yakovlevich's system
of shaving.

"Now, now, now. Be careful!" cried Kovalyov.

Ivan Yakovlevich lowered his fingers, was flabbergasted and
confused, as never before. Finally he cautiously began tickling him
with the razor beneath his beard; and although it was awkward and
difficult to shave him without holding on to the olfactory part of
his body, somehow he managed, pressing his rough thumb into his
cheek and his lower jaw; overcoming all obstacles, he finally finished shaving him.

When everything was ready, Kovalyov hastened to get dressed
that very minute, took a cab, and drove to the confectioner's. As he
entered, he cried out from afar, "Boy, bring me a cup of chocolate!"
And he himself glanced into the mirror: he had a nose! He turned
around cheerfully and, with a satirical expression, he looked,
slightly squinting, at two soldiers, one of whose noses was only
slightly bigger than a button on a vest. After that he set off for the
office of the department where he was contending for a position as
vice-governor, and in case he didn't get that post, then as an administrator. As he made his way through the reception room, he glanced
into the mirror: he had a nose! Then he went to see another collegiate

assessor, or a major, a great lover of sarcasm, to whose nagging remarks he often replied by saying, "Oh, you. I know you, you're a scoffer!" Along the way he thought: "If the major doesn't burst out laughing when he sees me, then that's a sign that everything is in its rightful place." But the Collegiate Assessor had no reaction. "Fine, fine, damn it all!" Kovalyov thought to himself. Along the road he met Madame Podtochina with her daughter; he bowed to them and was met with joyful exclamations: therefore, there was nothing wrong with him. He chatted with them for a long time and, intentionally taking out his snuffbox, purposefully filled each nostril with tobacco, saying to himself: "So much for you, you women, you birdbrains! I still won't marry your daughter. It's simply *par amour*,° if you please."

And from that day forward Major Kovalyov would stroll around on Nevsky Prospect, in the theater, and everywhere else as if nothing had happened. And his nose, too, as if nothing had happened, stayed in his usual place, without any indication of coming off at the sides. And after that, Major Kovalyov was always seen to be in a good mood, smiling, resolutely following all pretty women, and even pausing once in front of a window in the Shopping Arcade and purchasing a ribbon of some honorary order; it was unclear for what reason, since he wasn't a cavalier of any order himself.

That's the sort of story that occurred in the northern capital of our capacious empire! Only now, when we think about the whole episode, do we see that there is much that is implausible about it. Not to mention the fact of the strange, supernatural separation of the nose and its appearance in various places in the guise of a state councilor—how was it that Kovalyov never realized that it was impossible to place an advertisement in the newspaper about a missing nose? I'm not saying that I consider it too expensive to place an ad: that's nonsense and I'm not one of those mercenary-minded people. But it's indecent, inappropriate, incorrect! And once again: how did the nose turn up in a loaf of fresh bread, and how about Ivan Yakovlevich himself? No, I don't understand that, not at all! But what is strangest, most incomprehensible of all—is how authors can choose such subjects. I confess this is beyond understanding; it's just . . . No, no, I just don't understand it. In the first place, there's definitely no benefit from it to the fatherland; in the second place . . . in the second place, there is also no benefit to it. I simply don't know what it is. . . .

But still, having said all this, although, of course, you can posit the first thing, the second, and the third; one can even . . . but where do absurd things not occur? Yet, when you think it all over, in all this business, there really is something. No matter what anyone says, such things do occur—rarely, but they do.

The Carriage

The small town of B. was much enlivened when the cavalry regiment was stationed there. Before then it was terribly boring. When you happened to pass through and glance up at the low, badly painted buildings that looked out sourly onto the street, then . . . it's impossible to describe the feeling that came over one's heart: such melancholy as if you'd just lost a game of cards, or you had committed some blunder—in a word, it wasn't good. The clay, with which the houses were plastered, had been washed away by the rain; instead of white, the walls had become mottled; the roofs were largely thatched with reeds, as is usually the case in our southern towns; the mayor had long ago ordered the little garden orchards to be cut down to improve the look of the place. You don't meet a soul on the street, except perhaps a rooster who scurries across your path, soft as a pillow from the layer of dust, which, with the slightest amount of rain, turns into mud; then the streets in the town of B. are filled with those plump animals that the current mayor likes to refer to as "Frenchmen." Poking their humorless snouts out of their mud baths, they raise such an uproar with their grunting that the traveler has no choice but to drive his horses on faster.

However, it was difficult to find a traveler in the little town of B. Rarely, very rarely did a landowner wearing a nankeen coat, who owned eleven serfs, rumble across the cobblestones in some half-carriage/half-cart, peeking out from behind a pile of flour sacks; he would urge on his bay mare, behind which galloped her foal. Even the market square had a somewhat dismal appearance: the tailor's house looked out onto the street foolishly, not facing it, but at an angle. Across from it some stone building with two windows had been in the works for the last fifteen years; further on there stood all by itself a fashionable wooden fence, painted gray, just like the mud; it had been built by the mayor in his youth as a model for other structures; this was before he had the habit of taking a nap right after dinner or before sleep drinking a strange concoction made from dried gooseberries. In other places the fences were made of wattle; the smallest shops stood in the middle of the market square; there one could always find strings of bagels, a woman in a red kerchief, a pile of soap, several pounds of bitter almonds, gunshot for flintlocks, some *demi-coton*, and two assistants who spent all their time pitching horseshoes in front of shop doors.

But as soon as the cavalry regiment was stationed in the little provincial town, everything changed. The streets livened up and became colorful—in a word, they took on a completely different appearance. The squat houses would often see some stately, agile officer pass by with a plume on his hat; he would be going to visit a friend to chat about some business, or some superb tobacco, or sometimes to place a wager on a carriage, which could be called the regimental carriage, because it stayed within the regiment and circulated among all the officers: today a major would be riding in it; tomorrow it would show up in a colonel's stable; a week later, it was back at the major's, where his orderly was greasing its axles with lard.

The wooden fence between the houses was covered with soldiers' caps hanging in the sun; a gray overcoat was also invariably hanging on some gate; soldiers with mustaches as wiry as shoe brushes turned up in the side streets. These mustaches were evident everywhere. If market wives would congregate at the market with their scoops, mustaches would undoubtedly turn up behind their shoulders. Next to the town scaffold, a soldier with a mustache could be seen reprimanding some country lad, who merely snorted and gaped in reply. The officers breathed some life into society, which until that time had consisted solely of a judge, who lived in the same house as the deacon's widow, and the mayor, an intellectual, but who slept away the whole day, from dinner until evening, and from evening until dinner. Society became even more populous and entertaining when a brigadier general was transferred to town. The landowners from the surrounding area, about whose existence no one had previously guessed, began coming into town more frequently to spend time with the officers, sometimes to play a game of faro, the rules of which they could only dimly recall, in part because their minds were filled with sowing crops, hunting rabbits, and various commissions from their wives.

It's a pity that I can no longer recall what the occasion was when the Brigadier General threw a large dinner; the preparations for this event were enormous; the clatter of the chefs' knives in the general's kitchen could be heard as far away as the town gates. The entire market was stripped of produce for this event; the result was that the judge and the deacon's widow had to eat buckwheat rolls and jelly made of potato starch. The general's small courtyard was filled with carts and carriages. Society consisted of men: officers and a few landowners from the surrounding estates. Of the landowners, the most notable was Pifagor Pifagorovich Chertokutsky, one of the principal figures in the local aristocracy of the district, and one of the most vocal during the elections, who always arrived in a very stylish carriage. He had served previously in a cavalry regiment, where he was one of the most significant and prominent officers. At least he had been seen at many fashionable balls and various meetings, wherever his regiment was quartered; however, one should ask the young women of Tambovsk and Simbirsk provinces about this. It's very likely that he would also have earned similar acclaim in other provinces, if he hadn't been forced to retire as a result of one occurrence, which is usually described as an unfortunate episode: whether he boxed someone's ears, or had his ears boxed, I can't quite recall; but the fact of the matter was that he was asked to resign. However, in no way was his importance diminished: he wore a frock coat with a high waist that resembled a military uniform, spurs on his boots, and a mustache under his nose, because without these things, the nobles might think he was serving in the infantry, to which he sometimes referred with contempt. He visited all the crowded country fairs, where the quintessence of Russia, consisting of mothers, daughters, and fat landowners, came for entertainment; they arrived in carts, wagons, and carriages, such as no one has ever seen even in a dream. He sniffed out the place where the cavalry regiment was stationed, and always came to visit the officers. He would jump down very nimbly in front of them from his cart or carriage, and would soon get to know them. During the last elections, he hosted a magnificent dinner for the nobility, at which he declared that if they were to elect him marshal, he would do his best to improve their lot. In general, he behaved himself like a gentleman, as they say in the district and provinces; he married a rather attractive woman with a dowry of some two hundred serfs and a capital of several thousand rubles. This money was immediately used to purchase six really fine horses, gilt locks for his doors, a tame monkey for his house, and to hire a French butler. Two hundred serfs together with two hundred of his own were mortgaged to finance some sort of commercial venture. In a word, he was a landowner as to be expected . . . an exemplary landowner.

In addition to him, there were several other landowners at the general's dinner, but there's nothing more to be said about them. The rest were members of the same regiment and two staff officers: a colonel and a rather portly major. The general himself was a strapping, stout fellow, but a good commander, according to his officers. He spoke with a rather deep, ponderous bass voice.

The dinner was extraordinary: sturgeon, beluga, starlet, bustards, asparagus, quails, partridges, and mushrooms demonstrated that the chef had had nothing to eat for the last two days; four soldiers wielding knives had worked through the night preparing *fricassées* and *gêlées*. The abundance of bottles, tall ones with Château Laffite, and squat ones with Madeira, the splendid summer's day, the windows open to the fresh air, platters of ice on the table, the bottom buttons on the officers' vests left unfastened, the crumpled shirtfronts of the owners' oversized frock coats, the lively crossfire of conversation, drowned out by the general's voice and loosened by the champagne—all contributed to the harmony. After dinner, everyone rose from the table with a pleasant heaviness in their stomachs, and, after lighting their long- or short-stemmed pipes, retired to the porch with cups of coffee in hand.

The general, the colonel, and even the major had all unbuttoned their uniforms, displaying their aristocratic suspenders of fine silk; but the officers observed proper decorum and kept their uniforms fastened, except for the three bottom buttons.

"Now you can take a look at her," announced the general. "Please, my good man," he said, turning to his adjutant, a rather clever young man with a pleasing appearance—"have the bay mare brought over here! You'll see for yourselves."

At this point the general drew on his pipe and released a plume of smoke.

"She's still not properly groomed: there's no decent stable in this accursed backwater. But this horse," *puff, puff,* "is first-rate!"

"And, Your Excellency," *puff, puff,* "have you had her for a long time?" asked Chertokutsky.

Puff, puff, puff, pu-u-uff. "Not that long. It's only been two years since I got her from the farm."

"And was she already broken in, Your Excellency, or did you have to break her in here?"

Puff, puff, puff, pu-, pu-, pu-, puff. "Here." Saying that, the general disappeared in a cloud of smoke.

Meanwhile, a soldier came rushing up from the stable, the sound of hooves could be heard, and at last there appeared another soldier wearing a capacious white cloak and sporting a large black mustache, leading by her bridle a trembling, terrified horse, which, suddenly raising her head, almost lifted the soldier, including his mustache, clear off the ground.

"Now, now, Agrafena Ivanovna!" he said, leading her up to the porch. The mare was named Agrafena Ivanovna; she was headstrong and a bit wild, just like a southern beauty; she stepped up noisily onto the wooden porch and then suddenly stopped. The general, lowering his pipe, began examining Agrafena Ivanovna with a satisfied look. The colonel, getting off the porch, took hold of the horse by the muzzle. The major patted Agrafena Ivanovna's flank, and the others clicked their tongues in approval.

Chertokutsky also came down from the porch and walked behind the mare. The soldier who had led her out and who was holding the bridle looked directly at the visitors, as if he wanted to jump at them.

"Very fine, fine!" said Chertokutsky. "A splendid horse! May I ask, Your Excellency, how she rides?"

"Her stride is very good; only . . . the devil knows why . . . that idiot vet gave her some sort of pills, and for the last two days all she's been doing is sneezing."

"Very, very fine. And do you, Your Excellency, have a suitable carriage?"

"A carriage? But this horse is for riding."

"I know; but I asked Your Excellency if you have a suitable carriage for your other horses."

"Well, I don't have enough carriages. I must confess that I've wanted to acquire an up-to-date carriage. I wrote about this to my brother, who's now living in Petersburg, but I don't know if he's planning to send me one or not."

"I think, Your Excellency," observed the colonel, "that the best carriages come from Vienna."

"You're absolutely right," *puff, puff, puff.*

"Your Excellency, I have a splendid carriage made specifically in Vienna."

"Which? The one you came in?"

"Oh, no. That's just my everyday carriage, for my own outings, but my other one . . . it's astonishing, light as a feather; and when you sit in it, it's just as if, I hope Your Excellency will pardon the expression, your nanny was rocking you in a cradle!"

"It must be comfortable."

"Very, very comfortable; the cushions, the springs—all first-rate."

"That's good."

"And it's so roomy! That is, Your Excellency, I've never seen one like it. When I was still in the service, I could fit ten bottles of rum and twenty pounds of tobacco in the trunk; besides that, I had around six uniforms, linen, and two tobacco pipes, Your Excellency, such long pipes called, if you'll allow me to say, 'tapeworms,' and you could still fit a whole bull into the side pockets."

"That's good."

"I paid, Your Excellency, four thousand rubles for it."

"Judging from that price, it must be a very fine one. And did you buy it yourself?"

"No, Your Excellency; it came to me by chance. My friend purchased it, an exceptional fellow, a comrade from my youth, with whom you would really get along; what's mine is his, and what's his is mine, it makes no difference. I won the carriage from him in a card game. Would you care, Your Excellency, to do me the honor of dining with me tomorrow, and we could inspect the carriage together?"

"I don't know what to say. It would be awkward for me to come alone. . . . Might I bring along some of my fellow officers?"

"I also invite your fellow officers. Gentlemen, I would consider it a great honor if I had the pleasure of seeing you all in my home!"

The colonel, the major, and the other officers thanked him with polite bows.

"Your Excellency, I myself am of the opinion that if you buy an item, it should be of good quality; if it's not, then it's not worth purchasing. Now tomorrow, when you honor me with a visit, I will show you some of the objects that I've acquired on my estate."

The general looked at him and released a puff of smoke from his mouth.

Chertokutsky was extremely satisfied that he had invited the officers to his house; he was already planning which pâtés and sauces to serve; with great merriment he regarded the officers, who, for their part, somehow doubled their respect for him; he could tell by their looks and their small gestures resembling half-bows; Chertokutsky himself became more relaxed with them, and his voice assumed a tone of torpor: he was a man burdened with pleasure.

"In addition, Your Excellency, you'll become acquainted with the lady of the house."

"With great pleasure," said the general, stroking his mustache.

After this Chertokutsky wanted to leave for home immediately, in order to prepare in good time to welcome his guests to tomorrow's dinner; he was just about to pick up his hat, but in some strange manner, he wound up staying a little longer. Meanwhile, card tables had been set up in the general's room. Soon everyone there divided into groups of four to play whist and spread out to various corners around the general's rooms.

Candles were brought in. For a long time Chertokutsky didn't know whether to sit down to play cards or not. But when the officers began to encourage him, he considered it would be very impolite to refuse. He took his seat. Without his thinking about it, a glass of rum punch turned up in front of him, which, without thinking, he drank at once. After playing two rounds, Chertokutsky once again found a glass of rum punch in front of him, which, without thinking, he downed, after saying, "It's time for me to go home, gentlemen, really, it is." But he sat down once more and played a second round.

Meanwhile, private conversations were taking place in various corners of the room. The card players were rather taciturn; but those who weren't playing, sitting on sofas to the side, were deep in conversation.

In one corner a staff captain, who'd placed a pillow under his one side, holding a pipe in his teeth, was recounting in a rather free and easy manner his amorous adventures to a circle of listeners paying full attention. One extremely corpulent landowner with short arms resembling two overgrown potatoes was listening with an unusually sweet expression on his face, and only from time to time trying to extend one stunted arm behind his broad back to extract his snuffbox. In another corner a rather heated discussion had flared up about a cavalry drill; and Chertokutsky, who by this time had twice thrown out a jack instead of a queen, kept intervening in other conversations by shouting from his corner, "What year was that?" or "Which regiment did you say?"—without noticing that his questions sometimes bore no relation to the ongoing discussion.

Finally, a few minutes before supper, the card games ended, but the officers carried on the conversation; it seems that all heads were still occupied with whist. Chertokutsky vividly recalled that he had won a great deal, but he didn't take away any winnings when he left the table; he stood for a long time in the position of a man who discovers that he has no handkerchief in his pocket. Meanwhile, supper was served. It goes without saying that there was no lack of wines, and that Chertokutsky almost unwillingly had to refill his own glass because there were full bottles on both sides of him.

The conversation at the table seemed endless; however, it was conducted in a rather strange way. One landowner, who had served in the campaign of 1812, recounted a battle that had never taken place; and then, though it's not known why, he removed the stopper from the decanter and thrust it into the cake. In a word, when people began to disperse, it was already three o'clock in the morning, and the coachmen had to gather up some of the guests in their arms, as if they were parcels just purchased in a shop; Chertokutsky, in spite of his aristocratic manner, sitting in his carriage, kept bowing so low and swinging his head around that he returned home with two thistles caught in his mustache.

Everyone was asleep in his house; the coachman could hardly rouse the valet, who led his master through the living room and turned him over to the young housemaid, behind whom Chertokutsky somehow made it to his bedroom and lay down next to his pretty, young wife, who looked so lovely in her snowy white nightgown. The upheaval produced by her husband as he collapsed into bed woke her. She stretched, raised her eyelashes, and blinked her eyes quickly three times; then she opened them with a half-angry smile; but seeing that this time her husband didn't want to offer up any signs of affection, she turned onto her other side in annoyance; resting her fresh cheek on her hand, she fell fast asleep soon after he did.

It was at a time that, in the countryside, is no longer called "early" when the young mistress awoke next to her snoring husband. Recalling that he had returned home after three in the morning, she decided to spare him; putting on her slippers, which her husband had ordered for her from Petersburg, and wearing a white dressing gown draped around her like flowing water, she went into her dressing room, washed her face with water as fresh as she was, and sat down at her dressing table. Glancing twice at her face in the mirror, she saw that today she looked not bad at all. Apparently, this insignificant circumstance made her remain seated in front of the mirror exactly two extra hours. At last, she got dressed very nicely and went out to the garden for some fresh air.

As if on purpose, the day was splendid, as only a summer day in the south can be. The sun, which was high in the sky, shone with all its might; nevertheless, it was still cool to stroll under the thick shade of the garden paths; the flowers, warmed by the sun, tripled their fragrance.

The pretty young mistress completely forgot that it was already twelve noon and her husband was still asleep. She could already hear the after-dinner snores of two coachmen and the postilion, asleep in the stable behind the garden. But she sat in the shady alley, where she had a view of the open road beyond; she was idly regarding the empty, deserted space when suddenly a cloud of dust appearing in the distance caught her attention. Looking more closely, she could soon make out a line of carriages. In front came an open, light two-seater; in it sat a general with large epaulets glistening in the sunlight, and next to him was a colonel. Behind it came another carriage, a four-seater; in it sat a major with the general's adjutant and two more officers sitting opposite them; behind them came the familiar regimental cart, which this time was being driven by the stout major; behind it, another four-seater carriage in which sat four officers with a fifth squeezed in . . . and behind she could see three more officers on splendid bay horses with dark markings.

"Is it possible they're coming to visit us?" the mistress of the house wondered. "Ah, my God, they've turned in at the bridge!"

She shrieked, wrung her hands, jumped over the flowerbeds, and ran straight to her husband's bedroom. He was sleeping like a log.

"Wake up, wake up, wake up immediately!" she yelled, pulling him by the arm.

"Ah?" Chertokutsky said, stretching, but not opening his eyes.

"Get up, sweetie! Do you hear? We have guests!"

"Guests? What guests?" After saying this he made a sound like a calf mooing when he searches its mother's udder for her teat. "Mmm," he muttered, "stretch out your neck, my dear, and I will give you a nice kiss."

"Dearie, get up, for God's sake, quickly. It's the general with his officers. Ah, my God, you have thistles in your mustache."

"The general? So he's on his way here? Why the hell didn't anyone wake me up? What about the dinner? Is everything ready for it?"

"What dinner?"

"Didn't I order it?"

"You? You came home at four in the morning, and no matter how many times I asked you, you didn't tell me anything. I didn't wake you, sweetie, because I felt sorry for you: you didn't get much sleep. . . ." She said the last words in an extremely languorous and imploring tone.

Chertokutsky, his eyes staring wildly, lay in bed for a minute as if he'd been thunderstruck. At last, wearing only his shirt, he jumped up from the bed, forgetting that this was most improper.

"Ah, what a jackass I am!" he said, slapping his forehead. "I invited them to dinner. What shall I do? Are they far away?"

"I don't think so. They'll be here any minute."

"Hide, my dear! Hey! Who's out there? You, girl, come in here! What are you afraid of, you fool? The officers will be here any minute. Tell them that the master's not at home, and won't be here all day; tell them that he left home early this morning. Do you hear? And tell all the servants. Go at once!"

After saying this, he grabbed his dressing gown and ran out to hide in the carriage barn, thinking that there he would be completely safe. But, standing in a corner of the shed, he realized that he could still somehow be seen.

"Ah, this will be better," flashed through his head, and in a minute he pulled down the steps of the carriage that was next to him and jumped up into it, closed the doors behind him, and, for greater security, covered himself with a coverlet and sheepskin. He lay very quiet, wrapped up in his dressing gown.

Meanwhile, the carriages had arrived at the porch. The general got out and shook himself off; after him came the colonel, adjusting the plume on his hat. Then the fat major jumped down from his cart, holding his sabre under his arm. Then the slender second lieutenants hopped down from their cart with the ensign who'd been squeezed between them; and finally, the officers, who were showing off their riding skills, dismounted their horses.

"The master's not at home," said the footman who came out onto the porch.

"Not at home? How can that be? He'll be back for dinner, won't he?"

"Not at all. He's away for the whole day. He'll only be back tomorrow at about this same time."

"How about that?" said the general. "How can this be?"

"That's quite something, I must say," said the colonel, laughing.

"Surely not! How can he do this?" continued the general with discontent.

"Damn it. Hell! If he couldn't receive us, why did he invite us?"

"I don't understand, Your Excellency, how he could have done this?" said one young officer.

"What?" said the general, who had the habit of always uttering this interrogative when he was conversing with a lower-ranking soldier.

"I said, Your Excellency: how could he behave in this fashion?"

"Indeed. . . . Well, perhaps something came up—if so, then at least let people know or don't invite them."

"There's nothing to be done, Your Excellency. Let's go back," said the colonel.

"Naturally, there's no other course of action. However, we can have a look at his carriage even if he's not here. Undoubtedly, he didn't take it with him. Hey, who's there? Come over here, my good man!"

"Yes, sir. What would you like?"

"Are you the stable-hand?"

"I am, Your Excellency."

"Show us the new carriage, which your master's just acquired."

"Yes, sir. Right this way to the barn."

The general set off together with the other officers to the barn.

"Let me first bring it out for you; it's so dark in here."

"Never mind, never mind; it's fine where it is!"

The general and the other officers walked around the carriage and carefully examined its wheels and springs.

"It's nothing special," said the general. "It's a most ordinary carriage."

"Perfectly plain," said the colonel, "not much to look at."

"It seems to me, Your Excellency," said one of the young officers, "that it isn't worth four thousand rubles."

"What?"

"I said, Your Excellency, that it doesn't seem worth four thousand rubles."

"Four thousand rubles? It's not even worth two thousand. It's simply not worth it. Perhaps there's something special about its interior. . . . Please, my good man, pull back the cover. . . ."

And there, right before the eyes of the officers, lay Cherto-kutsky in his dressing gown and hunched up in a most unusual position.

"Ah, here you are!" said the astonished general.

After saying this, the general covered Chertokutsky again, slammed the carriage door shut, and left together with the other officers.

The Portrait

1

Nowhere did people stop more often than in front of the little picture shop on Shchukin Court. This shop offered the most diverse collection of marvels; the majority of the pictures were painted in oil, coated in dark green varnish, set in tasteless, dark yellow frames. Winter with white trees, a completely red evening resembling the glow of a great fire, a Flemish peasant with a pipe and a broken arm, looking more like a turkey-cock in cuffs than a person—those were the usual subjects. In addition, one had to add several engravings: a portrait of Khozrev-Mirza in a sheepskin cap, portraits of some generals with crooked noses, wearing three-cornered hats. The doors of such a shop are usually hung with bunches of paintings that bear witness to the original talent of Russian artists. On one of them was a portrait of the Tsarevna Miliktrisa Kirbitievna,° on another, the city of Jerusalem, where the houses and churches were unceremoniously splattered with red paint, covering part of the ground, with two Russian peasants praying in their mittens. There were few buyers of these works of art; on the other hand, there were crowds of spectators. Some sort of lowlife footman was already yawning in front of them, holding in his hands covered dishes from the inn for his master, who, without doubt, would be having his soup served lukewarm today. There's also probably a soldier standing in front of them, a cavalier of flea markets, selling a few penknives, and a peddler from Okhta with a box filled with shoes. Everyone expresses his admiration in his own way: peasants usually prod the paintings with their fingers; cavaliers examine them seriously; the young footmen and servant boys laugh and tease each other with their caricatures; the old footmen in their heavy wool coats simply stare to have something to gawk at; and the young Russian peddler women hasten instinctively to listen to what the people are saying and to see what they are looking at.

At about this time the young artist Chertkov paused in front of the shop as he was passing by. His old overcoat and his unfashionable attire attested to the fact that he was a man who was selflessly devoted to his work and who didn't have time to worry about his clothes, which is always a source of mysterious attractiveness for young people. He stopped in front of the shop and at first laughed inwardly at these ugly paintings; then he was overcome involuntarily by reflection: he began thinking about who might need these works. That Russians could stare at these paintings of *Yeruslan Lazarevich*, or *He ate and drank a great deal, Foma*, and *Yeryoma*°—that didn't seem surprising to him: the subjects depicted were very accessible and comprehensible to the common people; but where were the buyers of these motley, dirty daubs in oil? Who needed all these Flemish peasants, these red and blue landscapes, which revealed some pretensions to a higher level of art, but which expressed art's profound degradation? If these had been the works of a child, yielding to some involuntary desire, if they had contained no precision whatever, but if they had preserved even the basic conventions of mechanical drawing, if only everything in them was done as caricature, but with some apparent effort, some attempt to produce a likeness of nature—but nothing of the kind could be seen in them. Some kind of obtuseness of old age, some senseless desire, or, better to say, some whim, had guided the hand of their creators. Who labored over them? Without doubt, it was one and the same person who had agonized over them because it was all the same colors, the same style, the same skilled, experienced hand belonging to a crudely made automaton, rather than to a human being.

Nevertheless, he continued to stand in front of these grimy pictures and stare at them, but failed to notice how the owner of the picture shop, a grayish man aged about fifty with a long, unshaven chin, wearing a woolen overcoat, was telling him: "These pictures are all *first-class*, just arrived from the market, the varnish hasn't dried yet, and they're not yet framed. *Have a look for yourself, I can assure you that you'll be satisfied.*" All these deceptive words flew right past Chertkov's ears. Finally, to reassure the proprietor somewhat, he picked up a few dusty paintings from the floor. They were old family portraits of people whose descendants were scarcely likely to be traced. He began almost mechanically wiping the dust from one of them. A light flush appeared on his face, a flush that indicates secret satisfaction at something unexpected. He began to rub his hand impatiently and soon beheld a portrait that bore the strokes of a master's brush, although the colors seemed a bit faded and darkened. It was a picture of an old man with some sort of disturbed, even malicious expression: there was a smile on his face, sharp and biting, together with some horror; the flush of illness was subtly discernible in his wrinkled and distorted expression; his eyes were large and dark; but at the same time some strange animation was evident in them. This portrait seemed to depict some sort of miser who had spent his life guarding his chest of money, or one of those unfortunate types whose life was tormented by other people's good fortune. In general his face preserved the clear indication of southern physiognomy. His dark complexion, hair black as coal but streaked with gray—all of this was not characteristic of inhabitants of northern provinces. In the entire portrait there was evidence of some sort of incompleteness, but if it had been fully finished, an expert would have lost his mind trying to guess how a splendid work by Van Dyck had turned up in a little shop on Shchukin Court in Russia.

With a pounding heart, the young artist placed the portrait to one side and began to sort through the others to see if he might find a similar work, but all the rest made up a completely different world and merely showed that this guest had turned up among them by dumb luck. At last Chertkov inquired about the price. The sly merchant, seeing from his attention that the portrait was worth something, scratched behind his ear and said:

"Well, ten rubles would be too little to ask."

Chertkov reached his hand into his pocket.

"I'll pay eleven!" said someone standing behind him.

He turned around and saw that a crowd had gathered and that one man in a raincoat had been standing in front of this painting, just like him. Chertkov's heart started racing and his lips began twitching quietly, like those of a man who feels that the object he has been searching for is about to be stolen away from him. Examining the new buyer carefully, he was somewhat consoled when he noticed his clothes were no better than his own; he said in a trembling voice:

"I'll pay twelve rubles; the picture is mine."

"Proprietor! The picture is mine; here's fifteen rubles!" said the buyer.

Chertkov's face convulsed feverishly, he gasped for breath, and said involuntarily:

"Twenty rubles."

The proprietor rubbed his hands with glee, seeing that the buyers were doing the bargaining themselves in his favor. People surrounded the buyers more closely, sniffing out that an ordinary sale had turned into an auction, which was always of strong interest, even to onlookers. The price was finally bid up to fifty rubles. Almost in despair Chertkov cried out, "Fifty," recalling that fifty rubles was all he had, out of which he had to pay a part for his apartment, and besides that, he had to buy paints and some other necessary items. At this time his opponent conceded: that amount, it seemed, exceeded his means—and the picture went to Chertkov. Taking a bank note out of his pocket, he threw it into the proprietor's face and seized his picture greedily, but he suddenly backed away from it, struck by fear. The dark eyes of the old man gazed in so life-like, yet such a deathly manner that it was impossible not to experience fear. A part of real life seemed to have been preserved in them by some inexplicable force. The eyes had not been merely painted; they were alive; they were human. They were immobile, but could not have been more frightening if they'd moved. Some sort of primeval feeling—it was not fear, but that inexplicable feeling we experience at the appearance of something strange that indicates a disorder of nature, or, better to say, some insanity of nature—that very feeling that caused almost everyone to let out a scream.

Chertkov ran his hand timidly over the canvas, but the canvas was smooth. The effect produced by the painting was universal; people rushed away from the shop, horror-stricken; the man who had bid against him retreated fearfully. At that time the twilight grew darker, seeming to render this incomprehensible occurrence even more terrifying. Chertkov wasn't able to stay any longer. Without even thinking about taking the picture with him, he ran out into the street. The fresh air, the noise on the pavement, the chatter of people seemed to revive him for a moment, but his soul remained in the grip of some oppressive sensation. No matter how much he looked at surrounding objects on each side, his thoughts were occupied by one unusual phenomenon. "What's this?" he wondered: "art or some supernatural magic that flouts the laws of nature? What a strange, ineffable riddle! Or is there a line for a man to which higher knowledge leads, but once having crossed it, he grasps something not created by human labor, and tears something vital from life, which had animated the original? Why is this crossing the line, this border of the imagination, so terrifying? Or does reality finally follow the imagination, the impulse, that terrifying reality which displaces imagination from its axis by some external shove, that awful reality which presents itself to a man thirsting after it when, wishing to understand that which is beautiful in man, he arms himself with a surgeon's scalpel, opens up the inner self, and sees that which is abhorrent in man? It's incomprehensible! So astonishingly, horrifyingly life-like! Or is too close an imitation of nature just as false as a dish that has too much sugar?" With such thoughts he entered his little room in a small wooden house on the Fifteenth Line of Vasilievsky Island; there, scattered in all corners of the room, were his student sketches, copies from the classics, careful, precise, a demonstration of the artist's efforts to understand the fundamental laws and internal dimensions of nature. He examined them for a long time; finally his thoughts flowed one after another and began to express themselves almost in words—he was so acutely aware of what he was thinking!

"It's been a year since I've been slaving away over this dry, skeletal work! I've been trying with all my might to find out what it is that artists can do so miraculously and that seems to be the result of a moment's swift inspiration. They merely touch their brush to the canvas and a man appears, headstrong and free, such as he was created by nature; his movements are dynamic, unforced. They do it quickly, while I have to work at it my whole life; all the time I search for boring principles and elements, devoting my entire life to colorless work that doesn't represent my feelings. Such is my daubing! They're faithful copies of the originals; but if I want to paint something original—it doesn't turn out well at all: the leg isn't accurate and unforced; the arm doesn't raise lightly and freely; a turn of the head will never be as natural as theirs; and the ideas, those indescribable scenes. . . . No, I'll never be a great artist!"

His reflections were interrupted by the entrance of his servant, a lad of about eighteen, with a pink face and red hair, wearing a Russian shirt. He began to remove Chertkov's boots without a fuss, while Chertkov was sunk into his reflections. This lad in the red shirt was his footman and his model; he cleaned his boots, loafed about in his small hallway, ground his paints, and soiled the floor with his filthy shoes. After he took off Chertkov's boots, he tossed him a dressing gown; as he was leaving the room, he turned his head and said in a loud voice:

"Sir, should I light a candle or not?"

"Yes," Chertkov replied distractedly.

"And the landlord stopped by," said the grubby servant in passing, following the praiseworthy habit of all such people of his calling to add the most important thing in a P.S. "The landlord came by and said that if you don't pay him his money, he'll throw all your paintings out the window together with your bed."

"Tell the landlord not to worry about the money," replied Chertkov, "I've got it."

Saying this, he reached into his coat pocket, but suddenly remembered that he had given all his money to the shopkeeper for the portrait. He began reproaching himself silently for running out of the shop without any reason, frightened by some insignificant occurrence, taking neither the portrait nor his money with him.

He decided to return to the merchant tomorrow to get his money back, considering that he was completely justified in refusing his purchase, all the more so since his domestic circumstances didn't allow him to make any unnecessary expenditures.

The moonlight spread across his floor like a bright white window, enveloping part of his bed and ending at the wall. All of the objects and pictures hanging in the room seemed to be smiling, their edges catching at times a part of that eternally beautiful brilliance. At that moment he somehow inadvertently glanced at the wall and saw the very same strange portrait that had so struck him in the shop. At this moment a light tremor ran through his body. The first thing he did was summon his servant and model and ask who had brought him this portrait and by what means; but the servant-model swore that no one had come, except for the landlord, who had stopped by that morning and had nothing in his hands except a key. Chertkov felt his hair stand up on end. Sitting down next to the window, he tried to convince himself that there couldn't be anything supernatural about this, that the lad might have dozed off, and that the proprietor of the portrait could have sent it, having learned somehow where his apartment was located. . . . In a word, he began to adduce all these banal explanations that we use when we want to believe that everything occurred just as we thought it would. He resolved not to look at the portrait, but his head inadvertently turned toward it, and his glance was captivated by the strange picture. The immobile gaze of the old man was unbearable; his eyes were absolutely glowing, absorbing the moonlight, and their life-likeness was so terrifying that Chertkov inadvertently covered his own eyes with his hand. A tear seemed to be quivering on the old man's eyelashes; the bright twilight into which the sovereign moon transformed the night increased the effect; the canvas seemed to be disappearing, and the old man's terrible face moved forward and glared out of the frame, as if through a window.

Ascribing this supernatural effect to the moon, the miraculous light of which contains the secret ability to convey to objects a part of the sounds and colors of another world, he asked for the candle that his servant was using to rummage around; but the old man's expression in the portrait was in no way diminished; the moonlight, merging with the candlelight, lent it a more incomprehensi-

ble and, at the same time, strangely life-like quality. Grabbing a
sheet, he set about covering the portrait; he wrapped it around three
times so that it wouldn't shine through; nevertheless, either as a
result of his own severely distraught imagination, or because his
own eyes, exhausted by considerable strain, had retained some
fleeting, moving skill—for a long time it seemed to him that the old
man's stare was shining right through the canvas.

At last he decided to blow out the candle and get into bed,
which was separated from the portrait by a screen. In vain he waited
to fall asleep: the most distressing thoughts dispelled that peaceful
condition which leads to the onset of sleep. Anguish, annoyance,
the landlord who was demanding money, his unfinished paintings—
the creations of an impotent impulse, his poverty—all of these
thoughts swirled around him, one after another. And when he managed to drive them away for a moment, the extraordinary portrait
forcefully invaded his imagination, and its murderous eyes seemed
to shine through a gap in the screen. His soul had never experienced such heavy oppression. The moonlight, which contains so
much music when it intrudes into a poet's lonely bedroom and
hangs child-like, enchanting half-dreams over the head of his bed—
this moonlight didn't bring him any musical musings; his dreams
were morbid. Finally he fell not into sleep, but into some kind of
semi-unconsciousness, into that painful condition when, with one
eye, we see approaching visions of a dream, and with the other, surrounding objects in an indistinct cloud. He saw how the old man's
external form detached itself and left the portrait, just as the surface foam separates from boiling liquid; it floated into the air and
drew closer and closer to him, finally approaching his bed. Chertkov felt his breathing stop; he tried to get up—but his arms were
unmoving. The old man's eyes shone faintly and pierced him with
all their hypnotic strength.

"Don't be afraid," the strange old man was saying; Chertkov
noticed a grin on his lips, which seemed to sting him with disdain
and light up the dark wrinkles of his face with brilliant life-likeness.
"Don't be afraid of me," the strange apparition kept saying. "You
and I will never part. You came up with an extremely foolish
approach: why did you choose to spend years poring over the alpha-
bet, when you could already read lofty works? Do you think that

with prolonged efforts you'll be able to create real art, that you'll win and receive something in return? Yes, you will." As he said this, his face was strangely contorted and some sort of immobile laughter appeared on all his wrinkles: "You'll receive the enviable right to throw yourself off the Isakievsky Bridge into the Neva, or else, winding a scarf around your neck, you'll hang yourself on the first available nail; the first dauber who buys your works for a ruble will cover them with primer, before painting someone's red mug on your canvas. Get rid of that foolish idea! Everything on earth is done for some good. Pick up your brush now and paint portraits of the whole town! Take whatever work is commissioned; but don't fall in love with your own paintings; don't labor over them day and night; time is passing swiftly and life doesn't pause. The more portraits you paint in a day, the more money you'll have in your pocket and the more fame you'll achieve. Give up this attic and find an expensive apartment. I like you; that's why I'm giving you such advice; I'll also give you some money, but you must come to me." While he was saying this, the old man's face once again expressed that horrible, immobile laughter.

An incomprehensible shudder seized Chertkov and a cold sweat broke out on his face. Gathering all of his strength, he raised his arm and finally got out of bed. But the old man's image was becoming faint, and he merely observed how he returned to his picture frame. Chertkov got up in agitation and began pacing. To revive himself a little, he went over to the window. The moonlight still enveloped the rooftops and white walls of the houses, although small clouds had begun to move across the sky more frequently. Everything was quiet: every now and then the distant sound of a carriage could be heard, in which a drowsy coachman was asleep in some remote lane, lulled by his lazy nag, awaiting a late-night passenger. Chertkov finally convinced himself that his imagination was too distraught and was presenting him with the product of his disturbed thoughts in his dreams. He went up to the portrait once more: the sheet completely hid it from view, yet it seemed that a small glimmer of light was shining through from time to time. Finally he fell asleep and slept through until morning.

Upon waking, he felt for a long time the unpleasant sensation that overcomes a person after being overpowered by fumes: his

head ached unpleasantly. It was hard to see in his room; a disagree-
able dampness hung in the air and seeped through the cracks in
his windows, plastered with pictures or splattered with primer.
Soon he heard the sound of knocking at his door; the landlord
entered with a police superintendent, whose appearance was as
unpleasant for people of modest means as the obsequious face of a
petitioner is for the wealthy. The landlord of the small house in
which Chertkov lived was one of those creatures who are the usual
owners of houses on the Fifteenth Line of Vasilievsky Island, or on
the Petersburg districts, or in a remote corner of Kolomna; there
are many such creatures in Russia, and their character is as hard
to describe as the color of a worn out frock coat. In his youth he
had been a captain and a loudmouth; he'd been employed for civil-
ian affairs; he was a master with the whip, quick-witted, a dandy,
and stupid, but in his old age he combined all these forceful characteristics into some vague indeterminacy. He was already a wid-
ower, and already retired; he was no longer a dandy, a boaster, or a
fighter; he merely loved to drink tea and spout all kinds of nonsense; he would walk around his room and adjust a candle end;
precisely at the end of each month he would make the rounds of
his lodgers to collect the rent; he would go outside carrying his key
in his hand to check the roof of his house; several times he had to
chase the servant away from his burrow where he had hidden to
sleep—in a word, he was a man in retirement, who, after leading a
dissolute life and bobbing up and down in a carriage, had been left
with only trivial habits.

"Take a look yourself," said the landlord, turning to the police
superintendent and spreading his arms, "please deal with this
matter and explain it to him."

"I must inform you," said the police superintendent, placing
one hand under the lapel of his uniform, "that you must pay the
rent for this apartment for the last three months."

"I would be glad to pay, but what's to be done? I have no money,"
said Chertkov coolly.

"In that case, the landlord must take your property equal in
value to the amount you owe, and you must vacate the premises
immediately."

"Take whatever you like," replied Chertkov, almost reflexively.

"Many of the pictures have been done with some skill," continued the superintendent, looking through several of them. "It's a pity that they're not finished and that the colors are not that lifelike. . . . No doubt your lack of funds didn't allow you to purchase paints. What's this picture wrapped up in a piece of canvas?"

At this point the policeman abruptly approached the picture and removed the sheet from it, because these gentlemen always allow themselves some freedom whenever they see either vulnerability or poverty. The portrait seemed to surprise him because the unusual life-likeness of the eyes produced the same impression on everyone. Examining the picture, he seized the frame somewhat roughly, since the hands of policemen are always associated with harsh manual labor, and the frame suddenly broke; a small piece of wood with a small sack of gold fell with a clink on the floor; several shiny round objects rolled away in all directions. Chertkov greedily rushed to collect them and grabbed a few from the hands of the policeman, who had picked them up.

"How can you say that you don't have the means to pay," observed the policeman, smiling pleasantly, "when you have so many gold coins?"

"This money is sacred to me!" cried Chertkov, avoiding the policeman's dexterous hands. "I must keep it; it was left to me by my late father. However, to satisfy you, take this for the apartment rent!" Saying this he tossed a few gold coins at the landlord.

The expression and manners of the landlord and the worthy guardian of the rights of drunken coach drivers changed immediately.

The policeman began to apologize and assure him that he was only fulfilling his lawful duties, and, moreover, he had no right whatever to compel him; to convince Chertkov of this, he effusively offered him a pinch of snuff. The landlord assured him that he was only joking, and further assured him with such swearing and impudence that one expects from the merchants at the Shopping Arcade.

But Chertkov ran out and resolved not to remain in that apartment any longer. He didn't even have the time to consider the strangeness of this occurrence. When he examined the sack, he found more than a hundred gold pieces. The first thing he did was to rent a fashionable apartment. The apartment he happened to find seemed to have been made just for him: four tall rooms in a row, large windows, all the advantages and conveniences for an artist! Lying on a Turkish divan and looking through the unbroken windows at the growing and rushing waves of people, he was overwhelmed by a feeling of self-satisfied oblivion and astonished at his own fate, which only yesterday had crept up on him in his attic. Both unfinished and finished pictures were hung on the enormous, elegant walls; among them hung the mysterious portrait, which had come to him in such a unique manner. Once again he began thinking about the reason for the unusual life-likeness of the portrait's eyes. His thoughts returned to the semi-dream he had experienced, and finally to the miraculous treasure hidden in the frame. Everything led him to the conclusion that there was some kind of story connected with the existence of this portrait, and that perhaps even his existence was somehow linked with it. He jumped up from his divan and began examining it closely: there was a small drawer contained within the frame, enclosed by a very thin piece of wood, but executed so skillfully and matched with the surface in such a way that no one would have known of its existence, if it weren't for the policeman's heavy finger pressing on it. He returned it to its place and looked at it once again. The life-like quality of the eyes didn't seem quite so terrifying amid the bright light filling his room through the huge windows and the noise of the crowds in the street that reached his ears, but there was still something unpleasant about its gaze, so that he tried to avert his eyes as soon as he could.

Just then his doorbell rang and a respectable lady of advanced years entered; she had a narrow waist and was accompanied by a young girl about eighteen years old; a footman wearing expensive livery opened the door and waited in the hallway.

"I've come to you with a request," the lady said in a sweet voice, the tone used when speaking to artists, French hairdressers, and others born to provide pleasure to others. "I've heard of your talents. . . ." (Chertkov was surprised at how quickly his fame had spread.) "I would like you to paint a portrait of my daughter."

At this point, the pale face of her daughter turned toward the artist; had Chertkov been skilled in matters of the heart, then he would have read her brief history at once: her childish passion for society balls, her misery and boredom during extended periods before and after dinner, her desire to run around in a fashionable dress at a crowded affair, her impatient eagerness to see her girl-friend in order to say: "Ah, my dear, I'm so bored," or else to com-ment on what flounces Madame Sichler had put on Princess B.'s dress. . . . All that was expressed by the young visitor's face, pale, almost expressionless, but with a tinge of some sickly sallowness.

"I would like you to set to work on the portrait immediately," continued the lady. "We can give you an hour."

Chertkov rushed to pick up his paints and his brushes, took up the prepared stretched canvas, and got down to work.

"I should tell you a bit beforehand," said the lady, "about my Annette, and by doing so facilitate your work. In her eyes and in all her features there has always been a certain languor; my Annette is very sensitive, and I confess that I never allow her to read mod-ern novels!" The artist looked closely at the young lady and didn't observe any languor. "I would like for you to depict her simply in a family setting, or even better, alone in the fresh air, in green shade, with no suggestion that she is on her way to a ball. Our balls, I should admit, are so boring and so soul-destroying that, to tell the truth, I myself derive no pleasure from attending them."

But the features of her daughter and even of the respectable lady clearly indicated that they hardly missed one ball.

Chertkov reflected for a moment about how to reconcile these little contradictions, and finally decided to take a sensible middle road. Besides, he felt a desire to overcome the difficulties and carry the day with his art, preserving the ambiguous expression of his portrait. His brush applied the first misty layer on the canvas, artis-tic chaos; from that, shapes slowly began to develop and emerge. He dove deep into the traits of his model and had begun to capture those elusive features which convey some character to the most col-orless model in a realistic copy, comprising the sublime triumph of truth. Some sort of sweet agitation began to affect him, and he felt that at last he grasped and perhaps would express that which rarely manages to be expressed. Only someone with genuine tal-ent can know that pleasure, both inexpressible and intensifying gradually. Under his brush the face of the portrait involuntarily seemed to acquire the coloration, which was the most unexpected discovery even for him; but the model began to fuss so much, and yawn in front of him, that the artist, still inexperienced, found it difficult to capture her constant expression in fits and starts and brief moments.

"That seems to be enough for the first sitting," said the respectable lady.

Good Lord, how awful! His soul and his strength had been stimulated and desired to spread their wings. Hanging his head down and putting aside his palette, he stood before his painting.

"They told me that you'd finish the portrait in two sittings," the lady said, approaching the picture, "but so far you have only the rough contours. We'll come to see you tomorrow at the same time."

The artist escorted his guests in silence and remained in a state of unpleasant rumination. In his crowded attic no one ever disturbed him as he sat over his uncommissioned work. With annoyance he moved aside the incomplete portrait and wanted to get to work on other unfinished paintings. But how can thoughts and feelings, once they've penetrated the soul, be replaced by new ones, with which our imagination has not yet fallen in love? Throwing down his brush, he left the house.

Youth is fortunate that many different roads lie before it, that its fresh soul is open to a thousand varied pleasures; therefore, Chertkov was instantly distracted. Having a few gold coins in his pocket—what lies beyond the power of forceful youth? Besides, Russians, especially gentry and artists, have a strange quality: as soon as any money lands in their pocket—it's all the same to them and the sky's the limit. He still had some thirty gold pieces left after his payment in advance for the apartment. And he managed to squander all thirty during the course of one evening. First, he ordered a splendid dinner, drank two bottles of wine, and didn't ask for the change; he rented a fashionable carriage merely to attend the theater located a stone's throw from his apartment, treated three of his friends at a café, dropped by somewhere else,° and returned home without a kopeck in his pocket. Throwing himself on his bed, he fell fast asleep, but his dreams were so incoherent, and his chest felt constricted as on the first night, as if there were some heavy weight pressing down on him; through the crack in his screen he saw the image of the old man detach itself from the canvas and,

with an anxious expression, count piles of money, gold coins spill-
ing from his hands. . . . Chertkov's eyes burned; it seemed that he
recognized in that gold the indescribable delight that he'd previously been unable to comprehend. The old man beckoned to him
with his finger and showed him a whole pile of gold coins. Chertkov feverishly extended his hand and woke up. When he was awake,
he approached the portrait, shook it, and cut all around the frame
with a knife, but nowhere did he find any hidden gold; finally he
waved his arm dismissively and decided to get to work, giving himself his word that he wouldn't labor for long and wouldn't be
tempted by the seductive paintbrush.

Just at that time the woman who had come the day before
arrived with her pale daughter, Annette. The artist placed the portrait on his easel, and this time his brush moved more quickly. The
sunny day and the clear light imparted a particular expression to
his model; a number of hitherto unnoticed subtleties were revealed.
His soul was inspired by determination once more. He attempted
to capture the smallest point or line—even her yellow pallor and
the uneven coloration in the face of this yawning and exhausted
young beauty—with the precision that inexperienced artists allow
themselves, imagining that truth might please other people the
same way it pleases them. His brush was just about to capture the
general expression of the whole portrait when the annoying word
"Enough" rang out just over his ears and the lady approached the
portrait.

"Oh, my God! What have you done?" she cried with annoyance. "Annette is all yellow; she has some dark spots under her
eyes; it looks like she's just swallowed several vials of medicine. No,
for heaven's sake, correct your portrait: it's not her face at all. We'll
come again tomorrow at the same time."

Chertkov threw down his brush in annoyance; he cursed himself, his palette, the courteous lady, her daughter, and the whole
world. The hungry artist sat in his magnificent room and didn't
have the strength to set to work on any pictures. The next day, waking early, he seized upon the first work that came to hand: it was a
picture of Psyche that he had begun a long time ago; he placed it
on his easel intending to continue work on it. Just then the lady
from yesterday came in.

"Ah, Annette, look, come here and see!" cried the lady with a joyful look. "Ah, how it resembles you! Delightful, just delightful! The nose, the mouth, and the eyebrows! How can we thank you for this splendid surprise? How sweet! How nice it is that this hand is raised slightly. I can see that you are indeed that great artist that I've heard so much about."

Chertkov stood there dumbfounded, seeing that the lady mistook his picture of Psyche as a portrait of her daughter. Like a novice, he bashfully began to explain to her that this rough sketch was intended to portray Psyche; but the daughter took this as a compliment and smiled rather sweetly, as did her mother. A diabolical thought flashed through the artist's mind; a feeling of annoyance and rage strengthened it, and he resolved to take advantage of it.

"Allow me to ask you to sit for me a little while longer," he said, turning to the fair-haired woman who was so pleased. "You see that I haven't painted her dress at all, because I wanted to capture it from real life."

He quickly dressed his Psyche in a nineteenth-century costume, slightly touched up the eyes and lips and lightened the hair a bit, and turned the portrait over to his visitors. His reward was a pile of bank notes and a warm smile of gratitude.

But the artist stood there, as if rooted to one spot. His conscience bothered him; he was overcome by that scrupulous, fleeting fear for his unsullied name that a young man experiences, bearing in his soul the nobility of talent, which forces him to destroy or, if not, then at least to conceal from the world those works in which he himself sees imperfections, which compel him to suffer the contempt of the masses, rather than that of the true connoisseur. It seemed to him that a stern judge already stood in front of his painting; shaking his head, he was reproaching him for lack of shame and lack of talent. What he wouldn't have given to get that portrait back! He was about to go running after the lady, to rip the portrait out of her hands, tear it up, and stamp on it with his feet, but how could he do this? Where should he go? He didn't even know his visitors' surname.

From this time onward, however, a happy change took place in his life. He expected that his name would be covered in infamy, but it was just the opposite. The lady who ordered the portrait spoke

enthusiastically about this unusual artist, and our Chertkov's workshop was filled with visitors, wishing to double their likeness and,
if possible, to increase it by tenfold. But the fresh, still innocent
Chertkov, feeling in his soul that he was unworthy of undertaking
such a feat, in order to somehow expiate and atone for his crime,
resolved to devote himself to his work with all possible determination, and decided to redouble his efforts; this alone would produce
miracles. But his intentions met with unexpected obstacles: his visitors, whose portraits he was painting, were for the most part
impatient, occupied, and in a hurry; and therefore, as soon as his
brush began to depict something not quite in the ordinary vein, a
new visitor would appear, stick out his head imposingly, burning
with a desire to see his likeness on canvas as soon as possible, and
the artist would hasten to complete his work. His time, finally, was
so filled that he didn't have any time at all to devote to reflection;
inspiration, constantly extinguished at its very inception, finally
stopped visiting him. At last, to speed up his work, he began to con-
fine himself to known, definite, monotonous, well-worn forms.
Soon his portraits began to resemble those family portraits of the
old masters that one can see in all the countries of Europe, and even
in all corners of the world, where ladies are depicted with their
hands folded across their bosom, holding a flower in one hand, and
their cavaliers are dressed in uniform, one hand tucked into their
jacket. Sometimes he wanted to depict some new pose, not yet worn
out, set apart by its originality and informality; but, alas, all that is
informal and light in the work of a poet or artist appears too formal, and is the result of great effort. In order to yield a new and bold
expression, to discover a new secret in painting, he had to think
long and hard, turning his eyes away from his surroundings, from
everything worldly and from life. But he had no time for that, and
besides, he was too exhausted by his daily work to be prepared to
receive inspiration; the world he depicted in his works was too ordinary and monotonous to rouse and incite his imagination. The
motionless face of a department head deep in thought; the handsome, but uniform expression of an Uhlan captain; the pale face
but with a forced smile of a Petersburg beauty; and many others,
all extremely ordinary—such were the subjects that presented
themselves to our artist every day. Finally, his paintbrush seemed

to acquire the colorlessness and absence of energy that characterized his models.

At last, the bank notes and gold coins that constantly flashed
before his eyes undermined the innocent impulses of his soul. He
shamelessly took advantage of people's weakness; for an extra trait
of beauty added by the artist to their depiction, they were ready to
forgive him all the faults, even though that beauty contradicted the
likeness.

Chertkov, in the end, became a completely stylish painter. The
entire capital turned to him; his portraits were hung in all the studies, bedrooms, living rooms, and boudoirs. Genuine artists
shrugged their shoulders, as they glanced at the works of this favorite of formidable fortune. They searched in vain for even one indication of real truth, displayed by keen imagination: there were
correctly depicted faces, almost always handsome because the artist still maintained his sense of beauty; but there was no knowledge
of the heart, passions, or even the habits of men—nothing of the
sort that would have indicated the clear development of refined
taste. A few people, who knew Chertkov, were surprised at this
strange turn of events, because they had seen signs of talent in his
first efforts, and they tried to resolve this perplexing riddle: how
could talent vanish in the full bloom of one's strengths, instead of
developing into full brilliance?

But the self-satisfied artist paid no heed to these discussions
and exulted in his general renown, jingling his gold coins, and
beginning to believe that everything in the world was ordinary and
simple, that no such thing as revelation from above existed, and that
everything necessary had to be brought under the severe order of
accuracy and uniformity. He was already nearing that stage in life
when everything inspired by impulse begins to lessen, when the
powerful bow of a violin has less effect on the soul and its shrill
notes don't envelope the heart, when the touch of beauty no longer
transforms the virginal power into fire and flame, but all the burnt-
out feelings become more responsive to the sound of gold, heeding
more attentively its seductive music, gradually and imperceptibly
allowing them to undermine them completely. Fame can't satisfy
and provide pleasure to someone who's stolen it, instead of earning it; it produces a constant excitement only in someone worthy

of it. And therefore all of his feelings and impulses focused on gold. Gold became his passion, his ideal, his fear, his pleasure, and his goal. Piles of bank notes accumulated in his chests. And just like everyone to whom this awful gift is given, he began to become boring, inaccessible to everything, and indifferent to all. It seemed that he was ready to turn into one of those strange creatures who sometimes turn up in the world, whom an energetic and passionate man regards with horror, and who appear to be no more than live bodies enclosing a corpse. However, one event struck him brutally and provided him with a completely different direction in his life.

One day he found on his table a note in which the Academy of Arts asked him, as a respected member, to come and offer his opinion of a newly arrived picture completed by a Russian artist living in Italy. This artist was one of his former comrades, who from his earliest years had nourished in himself a passion for art; with the zealous strength of a true worker, he had devoted himself to it with all of his soul, and for it he had torn himself away from friends, family, and his usual habits, and set out without any means of support to an unknown land; he suffered poverty, humiliations, even hunger, and with rare self-sacrifice, he scorned everything and was oblivious of everything, except for his beloved art.

Upon entering the hall, he found a crowd of spectators gathered in front of the picture. The deepest silence, such as is rarely experienced among a large crowd of critics, predominated on this occasion. Chertkov assumed the profound expression of an expert, approached the picture—but, good Lord, what he beheld!

Pure, chaste, beautiful as a bride—the artist's work stood before him. Not one indication of a desire to shine, not one trace of excusable vanity, not a thought of showing off to the crowd—nothing of the sort, not a single thing! It aspired to humility. It was simple, innocent, divine, the talent of genius. The astonishingly splendid figures were grouped naturally, easily, not touching the canvas; startled by so many glances being directed at them, they seemed to lower their beautiful eyelashes bashfully. In the features of their divine faces there breathed the secret phenomena that the soul doesn't grasp and cannot communicate to another person; the inexpressible was placidly expressed on them; and everything was depicted so easily, so modestly, that it seemed to be the product of the artist's momentary inspiration, suddenly entering his thoughts. The entire picture was a moment, but that moment toward which all human life is merely the preparation. Involuntary tears were about to run down the faces of the visitors gathered around the painting. It seemed that all tastes, all impudent, incorrect deviations of taste, merged in some sort of silent hymn to the divine work of art. Chertkov stood there immobile in front of the painting, his mouth gaping, and at last, when the spectators and critics gradually began to stir and discuss the merits of this work of art, and when, at last, they turned to him with the request to share his thoughts, he recovered his senses; he wanted to assume an indifferent, normal appearance; he wanted to pronounce the usual, banal judgment of hackneyed artists: that the work was adequate, the artist had some talent, but that it was to be desired that the artist had implemented his idea and design more skillfully in many places—but those words died on his lips, tears and sobs awkwardly emerged as his answer, and he ran out of the hall like a man deranged.

For a minute he stood stock-still and devoid of feelings in the middle of his majestic workshop. His entire being, his whole life was aroused in that one moment, as if his youth had returned to him, as if his extinguished sparks of talent had flared up once more. Good Lord! To have destroyed all the best years of his youth so mercilessly, to have quenched the fire that had perhaps glowed in his breast, and might by now have developed into greatness and beauty, and have occasioned tears of astonishment and gratitude! To destroy all this, to destroy all this without a trace of regret! It seemed as if in that one moment there revived in his soul those efforts and impulses which at one point he knew so well. He grabbed his paintbrush and approached a canvas. The sweat of great effort appeared on his face, and he was completely transformed into one desire; one could say that he was aflame with one idea: he wanted to depict a fallen angel. This idea more than any other corresponded to his frame of mind. But, alas! His figures, poses, groups, and ideas turned out to be forced and incoherent. His brush and his imagination had already been too occupied with one theme, and the impotent impulse to break free of the boundaries and restraints that he had imposed on himself was characterized by error and imprecision. He had ignored the exhausting and long ladder of gradual learning, and the basic principles of future greatness. In anger he eliminated from his room all his works that revealed the deathly pallor of superficial fashion, locked the door, ordered that no one be admitted, and began to work like a passionate youth. But, alas! At every stage he was stopped by his ignorance of the most basic elements; the simple, insignificant mechanism had frozen all his impulses and stood like an insuperable barrier to his imagination. From time to time the ghost of an unexpected great thought occurred to him; his imagination saw in dark perspective something that, if seized and thrown onto the canvas, could have become extraordinary and at the same time accessible to every soul; some sort of star of the miraculous sparkled in the unclear fog of his thoughts, because he really did harbor within himself the ghost of talent. But, God! Some sort of insignificant condition, familiar to every student, some dead rule of anatomy—and the thought would vanish, the impulse of impotent imagination would freeze, unspoken, unexpressed; his brush involuntarily turned to routine forms, hands folded in the same studied manner, a head unable to assume any unusual turn; even the folds of the clothes didn't want to hang or be draped on unfamiliar body poses. And he felt this, he did, and he saw this himself! Sweat poured down his face, his lips quivered, and after a long pause, during which all of his feelings inside were rebelling, he set to work again; but at thirty plus years, it was more difficult to learn the boring ladder of strict rules and anatomy, even more difficult to understand suddenly that which develops slowly and takes long years of effort, great striving, and profound self-sacrifice. At last he came to know the awful torment that sometimes occurs as a striking exception in nature, when a weak talent struggles to express itself within the bounds of its limits, but is unable to do so; the torment that in a youth gives birth to something great, but that in someone who has crossed the boundaries of dreams turns into fruitless longing; the awful torment that makes a man capable of committing horrible crimes. He was overcome with terrible envy, one not unlike madness. Bitterness crossed his face when he saw a work bearing the imprint of talent. He gnashed his teeth and devoured it with a monstrous glance. At last there was conceived in his soul the most wicked intention that any man ever nourished, and with mad fury he hastened to implement his plan. He began to hoard all the best works of art that were produced. After buying a picture for a large price, he carefully carried it back to his room; he would hurl himself at it with the force of a tiger, ripping and tearing it to shreds, stamping on it, accompanied by horrible laughter expressing diabolical pleasure. As soon as any new work of art appeared somewhere, breathing the fire of new talent, he expended all his efforts to purchase it no matter what. The vast amount of money he had earned provided him with the means of satisfying his fiendish desire. He untied all his bags of gold and opened all his chests. Never had a monster of ignorance destroyed as many magnificent works of art as did this ferocious avenger. And people who carried within them a spark of divine knowledge, people who thirsted for greatness, were pitilessly, inhumanly deprived of those holy, splendid works, in which great art raised the veil of heaven and revealed to man a part of the inner world, so full of sounds and sacred secrets. Nowhere, not in a single corner, could they hide from his rapacious passion, which knew no mercy. His attentive, fiery gaze penetrated everywhere and located even amid the forgotten dust any trace of the artist's brush. At all the auctions that he happened to attend, everyone else would despair in advance of being able to procure any work of art. It seemed as if the enraged heavens had intentionally sent this terrible scourge into the world to abolish all its harmony. This terrible passion cast some sort of nasty color on his face; his face had a bilious look almost all the time; his eyes shone almost like a madman's; his furrowed eyebrows and the constant wrinkles on his forehead conveyed a ferocious expression to his face and distinguished him completely from the peaceful inhabitants of the earth.

Fortunately for the world and for art, such an intense and violent life couldn't continue for long; the dimensions of his passion were too abnormal and colossal in size for his weak strength. Attacks of madness and insanity began to occur more frequently, and, at last, all of this turned into the most terrible illness. Acute fever, together with severe galloping consumption, overpowered him so ferociously that in three days all that was left of him was a mere shadow of his former self. All the traits of hopeless insanity were added to this. At times several men were unable to restrain him. He began to imagine the long-forgotten, life-like eyes of that unusual portrait, and then his fury was really terrifying. All the people surrounding his bed seemed to him to be terrible portraits. This portrait doubled, then redoubled in his eyes, and finally it seemed to him that all the walls were hung with these terrible portraits, casting their fixed gaze at him. Terrible portraits looked at him from the ceiling, the floor, and in addition he saw his room expand in all directions to accommodate even more of these immobile eyes. The doctor, who took upon himself the obligation to treat him and who had already heard something about this strange case, tried as best he could to isolate the secret relationship between the visions that plagued his patient and the events of his life, but he was unable to do so. The patient understood and felt nothing except for his torments; he cried out in a piercing, inexpressibly heartrending voice, imploring them to remove the irresistible portrait with the life-like eyes, whose location he described in such strange detail for a madman. They expended all efforts in vain to find that incredible portrait. Everything was searched in his apartment, but the portrait was nowhere to be found. Then the patient managed to raise himself up a bit and describe its whereabouts with a precision that indicated the presence of a clear and perceptive mind; but all searching was to no avail. The doctor finally concluded that it was no more than a peculiar symptom of his insanity. Soon his life was terminated by a last, silent attack of suffering. His corpse was terrifying. Moreover, they could find no trace of his vast wealth, but, seeing the shreds of so many great works of art, the price of which exceeded millions of rubles, they understood the horrible use to which the money had been put.

2

A large number of carriages of different shapes and sizes stood in front of the entrance to a house where an auction was taking place of the effects of one of those wealthy patrons of the arts, who slumbered their whole lives sweetly, enveloped by zephyrs and cupids, who were innocently reputed to be as rich as Maecenas, and who had naively expended millions on their passion, money amassed by their founding fathers, and often even by their own previous labors. The long hall was filled with the most motley crowd of visitors, who had flocked like birds of prey to an abandoned body. There was a full flotilla of Russian merchants from the Shopping Arcade and even from the flea market, wearing blue German frock coats. Their appearance and expression were more severe, more open, and did not reflect that false obsequiousness which is so apparent in Russian merchants. In general they didn't stand on ceremony, in spite of the fact that this hall was populated by a majority of those notable aristocrats before whom, in another setting, they were prepared with their bows to wipe off the dust brought in by their own boots. Here they were completely relaxed, pawing unceremoniously at books and pictures, wishing to determine the quality of the items, and boldly outbidding the prices offered by the aristocratic experts. Here were many visitors essential at these auctions, who made it their business to attend one every day instead of having lunch; aristocratic experts who considered it their duty not to miss an opportunity to increase their collections, and who had nothing better to do between the hours of noon and 1 p.m.; and finally, those noble gentlemen whose clothes and pockets were so badly lined, who appear every day without any goal of profit, but merely to see how this all will end, to see who will offer more, who, less, who will outbid whom, and who will carry away the item in the end. There was a great number of paintings scattered around without any order; pieces of furniture were mixed in with them, as well as books with crests of their previous owners, who probably never possessed the commendable curiosity to glance inside them. Chinese vases, marble tabletops, new and antique furniture with curved lines, griffins, sphinxes, lion paws, some gilded, others not, chandeliers, oil lamps—everything was piled up, without any order, as one might find in shops. It all resembled a kind of artistic chaos. In general our reactions to an auction are strange: there's some resemblance to a funeral procession. The hall in which it occurs is somehow always gloomy; the windows are hidden by furniture and pictures, and allow in little light; silence is spread over everyone's face, and the voices—"One hundred rubles!" "One ruble, twenty kopecks!" "Four hundred rubles, fifty kopecks!"—burst forth from people's lips in a way that's somewhat shrill to the ear! But an even greater impression is made by the auctioneer's sepulchral voice, banging his gavel and chanting the funeral service over the poor works of art grouped here so strangely.

But the auction had not yet begun; the visitors were examining various items, tossed into a pile on the floor. Meanwhile, a small crowd had gathered in front of one portrait: it depicted an old man with particularly strange, life-like eyes, which involuntarily attracted their attention. It was impossible not to accord the painter some genuine talent; even though the work was unfinished, it still indicated the presence of a powerful brush; but having acknowledged that, the supernatural life-likeness of the eyes had aroused some sort of unintentional reproach to the artist. People felt that there was something here that was the apex of truth that only a genius could depict to such a degree, but that this genius had boldly overstepped the boundaries of human will. Their attention was suddenly interrupted by the exclamation of one older visitor. "Ah, that's him!" he cried with a powerful gesture, his eyes fixed on the painting. Such an exclamation naturally aroused everyone's curiosity, and several of those looking at the picture couldn't refrain from observing, as they turned to him:

"You probably know something about this portrait?"

"You're not mistaken," replied the visitor who had issued the inadvertent exclamation. "As a matter of fact, I know the history of this portrait better than anyone else. Everything assures me that it must be the same picture that I wish to speak about. Since I see that you're all interested in knowing more about it, I'm now ready to satisfy your curiosity somewhat."

The visitors with nods of their heads indicated their gratitude and prepared to listen with great attentiveness.

"Without doubt a few of you," he began, "know well that part of town called Kolomna. Its character is quite distinct from other parts. Customs, occupations, conditions, and the residents' habits are entirely different. Here nothing resembles the capital, but it's also nothing like a provincial town because the fragmentation of multifaceted and, if one may say, civilized life has also penetrated here and is evident in such subtle details as only a densely inhabited city can produce. It's quite a different world here, and if you venture into some of the remote streets of Kolomna, you'll feel how your youthful desires and impulses seem to forsake you. There's no life-giving, optimistic future here. All is silence and retreat. Here is everything that has settled out from the lively capital. In fact, retired civil servants move here with their pensions of no more than five hundred rubles a year; widows who were living previously on their husbands' labors; people of modest means who enjoy a pleasant acquaintance with the Senate, and therefore have condemned themselves to live out the rest of their lives here; retired cooks who spend the whole day elbowing each other at the markets, spouting nonsense with peasants in a small shop, and buying five kopecks' worth of coffee and four kopecks' worth of sugar every day; and finally, there is that entire group of people whom I refer to as ashen, who, with their clothes, faces, and hair have some sort of dusky, ashen appearance. They resemble a gray day, when the sun doesn't blind you with its bright light, when a storm isn't howling, accompanied by thunder, rain, and hail, but simply when the sky is neither one thing nor another; a fog descends and blurs the outline of objects. These people's faces are of a somewhat rusty-reddish color, and their hair is also reddish; their eyes have almost no luster at all; their clothing is very drab and suggests that dull shade that comes when you mix all the different colors together; and in general their whole appearance is completely dreary. This includes retired theater ushers, fifty-year-old dismissed titular councilors, retired children of Mars° with pensions of less than two hundred rubles a year, a missing eye, and a swollen lip. These people are totally lacking in passion: it's all the same to them; they walk along in silence, paying no attention to anything, thinking about nothing at all. In their room they have a bed and a bottle of pure Russian vodka, which they guzzle drearily all day, without any daring surge in their head caused by the strong dose, such as that young German craftsman usually likes to treat himself to on Sunday, or that student on Meshchanskaya Street, that ruler of the pavement after twelve midnight.

"Life in Kolomna is always the same: a carriage rarely rolls down the peaceful streets, except perhaps for one with actors aboard, which, with its jingling bells, thunder, and rattles, disturbs the general silence. Here almost everyone goes on foot. A cab infrequently, lazily, and almost always without a passenger, crawls along, dragging a load of hay for its scraggly nag. The price of an apartment rarely exceeds a thousand rubles; there are more of them that cost fifteen, twenty, or thirty rubles a month, not counting the large number of corners that rent for four and a half rubles, including heat and coffee. Widows of civil servants receiving a pension are the most respectable inhabitants of this district. They behave very well, keep their rooms clean, and converse with their neighbors and acquaintances about the high cost of beef, potatoes, and cabbage; often they have a young daughter, a withdrawn, silent creature, though sometimes rather nice-looking; they also have a rather nasty dog and a very old clock with a pendulum. These widows live in the best rooms, paying from twenty to thirty rubles a month, and sometimes as much as forty. The actors come after them, whose salaries don't allow them to move out of Kolomna. They're free and easy people, like all artists, living only for their own enjoyment. Sitting in their dressing gowns, they either carve some small items out of bone or clean their pistols, or else assemble some useful household item out of cardboard and glue, or play a game of checkers or cards with a visiting friend, and thus they spend their mornings; they do the same thing in the evening, often accompanied by a glass of punch. After these big shots, this aristocracy of Kolomna, comes an unusual assortment of small fry; for the observer it's as difficult to assemble a list of all the inhabitants of the various nooks and corners of one room as it is to name the variety of insects who reside in a jar of old vinegar. You meet all sorts of people here! Old women who pray, old women who drink, old women who both drink and pray together, old women who manage in some incomprehensible manner to survive like ants who drag old rags and linen from Kalinkin Bridge to the flea market to sell them there for fifteen kopecks. In a word, all the pitiful and wretched dregs of humanity.

"It's natural that these people sometimes experience great shortages, which deny them the possibility of leading an ordinary, poor life; they must often request emergency loans to disentangle themselves from their obligations. Then there are among them those people referred to as powerful capitalists, who can make loans at various rates of interest, almost always exorbitant, of sums between twenty and a hundred rubles. These people gradually amass sufficient funds to enable them to purchase their own little homes.

"But there was one strange creature named Petromikhali who was unlike all other usurers. Whether he was Greek, Armenian, or

Moldovan, no one knew for sure, but at least his facial features were entirely southern. He always wore an ample Asian coat; he was rather tall, olive-skinned, with large black eyebrows and a mustache streaked with gray, all of which conveyed to him a rather threatening appearance. It was impossible to detect any particular expression on his face: it was almost always immobile and his southern physiognomy presented a sharp contrast to the ashen look of the other residents of Kolomna. Petromikhali was not at all like the other usurers mentioned above who lived in this lonely part of town. He could lend whatever sum of money was asked for: naturally, the interest he charged was also unusual. His dilapidated house with numerous outbuildings was located on the Goats' wetland. It wouldn't have been so run-down if its owner would agree to spend any money on repairs, but Petromikhali simply refused to spend any money at all. All the rooms, except for the small hut where he himself lived, were cold storerooms in which he had amassed porcelain, gold, jasper vases, and all sorts of junk, even furniture that debtors of various ranks and titles brought as pledges, because Petromikhali didn't reject anything; and in spite of the fact that he loaned hundreds of thousands of rubles, he was also willing to provide a sum less than one ruble. Old, useless linen, broken chairs, even worn-out boots—he was ready to accept all of it for his storerooms; beggars approached him brazenly with bundles in their hands. Expensive pearls, which perhaps once surrounded the most splendid necks in the world, were contained in his dirty iron chest together with an antique snuffbox belonging to a fifty-year-old lady, a diamond jewel that had once graced the alabaster forehead of some beauty, and a diamond ring of a poor civil servant, who had received it as a reward for his tireless labors. But it must be noted that it was only dire poverty that drove people to seek him out. His conditions were so harsh that they repelled every desire. But the strangest thing of all was that at first his interest rates didn't seem so high. By means of his strange and unusual accounting, he arranged things in such a complicated manner that the interest grew at a frightening rate, and even the auditors couldn't fathom this incomprehensible rule, all the more so since it seemed to be based on the laws of mathematics; they saw the obviously inflated total, but also knew that there was no error in these calculations.

Pity, like all other human passions, never touched him, and no pleading could ever incline him to cancel someone's debts or reduce someone's payments. Several times unfortunate old women, stiff from the cold, were found on his doorstep; their blue faces, frozen limbs, and deathly outstretched hands still seemed to be pleading for mercy, even near death. This situation often aroused general indignation, and several times the police wanted to investigate more carefully the actions of this strange man, but the superintendents always managed under some pretext to dissuade them and present the matter in a different light, in spite of the fact that they never received even a kopeck from him. But wealth has such a strange power that people have as much faith in it as they do in government bank notes. Without appearing to do so, it can exert as much influence invisibly on everyone as if they were wretched slaves. This strange creature would sit there on a divan that was blackened with age, his legs curled under him, receiving his petitioners without moving, with only a slight sign of greeting in his eyebrows; and one could never hear him say anything that was superfluous or tangential. However, there were rumors to the effect that he sometimes gave away money for free, without demanding its return, but setting such conditions that everyone ran away from him in fear, and even the most talkative of landladies lacked the strength to move their lips and convey them to someone else. Those who had the fortitude to accept his proffered funds turned yellow, wasted away, and died, without daring to reveal the secret.

"In this part of town there lived an artist in a small house; he was known at that time for his really magnificent works of art. That artist was my father. I can show you several of his works, which demonstrate his indisputable talent. His life was the most serene. He was a modest, devout artist, the sort who used to live during the religious era of the Middle Ages. He could have had great fame and earned a considerable income had he dared to accept the many offers that he had received from all sides, but he preferred to work on religious subjects; for an insignificant fee he agreed to paint the whole iconostasis of his parish church. Often he found himself in need of funds, but he never had the courage to resort to the awful usurer, even though he would always have the opportunity to repay the debt, because all he would have to do would be to sit down and paint a few portraits—and the money would be in his pocket. But he was so reluctant to tear himself away from his project, so sad to separate himself even for a short time from his beloved idea, that he was sitting in his room hungry; and he would have done so if he hadn't had a much-beloved wife and two children, one of whom you see before you now. However, one time his need became so great that he was ready to resort to the Greek, when suddenly the news spread that the terrible usurer was on the verge of death. This struck him, and he was already prepared to interpret it as a sign from above to prevent him from carrying through on his intention, when on his porch he met an old woman all out of breath, who served in three different capacities for the usurer: she was his cook, servant, and valet. The old woman, who worked for this strange master, had fallen out of the habit of speaking, muttered a few indistinct, incoherent words, from which my father could only deduce that her master needed him urgently and requested that he come and bring his paints and brushes. My father was unable to imagine why he was so necessary at such a time, especially with his paints and brushes, but, roused by curiosity, he grabbed the case with his supplies and set off following the old woman.

"He could scarcely make his way through the crowd of beggars surrounding the house of the dying usurer, nourishing the hope that perhaps, before death, the sinner would repent and give away a small part of his enormous wealth. He entered a little room and saw stretched out almost to his full length the body of the Asiatic man, who he thought was already deceased, since it lay so straight and still. At last he raised his emaciated head, and his eyes stared so chillingly that my father began to tremble. Petromikhali let out a hollow cry and finally uttered, 'Paint my portrait!' My father was surprised at such a strange request; he began to make clear to him that this was not the time to think about such things; that he should renounce all earthly desire, that he had only a very short time to live, and therefore it was time to think about his former deeds and repent in the presence of the Almighty. 'I don't want anything; paint my portrait!' Petromikhali said in a stern voice; at which point his face was covered with such convulsions that my father would certainly have left if he hadn't been stopped by a certain feeling, excusable in an artist who's struck by an unusual subject for his brush. The usurer's face was one of those that constitute a treasure for an artist. With fear as well as some secret desire, he placed a canvas on his lap, since he didn't have an easel, and began to paint. The idea of using this face later in his work when he wanted to depict a man possessed by demons, driven out by the powerful words of the Savior—this idea provided strength for his resolve. With haste he sketched an outline and the first shades, fearing that at any moment the life of the usurer would suddenly end, because it seemed that death was already hovering on his lips. From time to time he merely snorted and anxiously directed his terrifying stare at the portrait; finally something resembling joy flashed in his eyes at the sight of his own likeness emerging on the canvas. Fearing for the usurer's life at every moment, my father decided to finish work on the eyes first of all. This was the most difficult aspect, because the feeling conveyed in them was the most extraordinary and inexpressible. He worked on them for about an hour, and at last managed to capture that fire that was already fading in the original. With secret pleasure he moved slightly back from his portrait to get a better look at it; but he jumped back from it with horror, seeing the life-like eyes glaring back at him. Incomprehensible fear overcame him to such a degree that he threw down his palette and paints and was about to rush for the door; but the terrible, almost half-dead body of the usurer rose up from his bed, seized him with his scrawny hand, and ordered him to continue his work on the portrait. My father kept crossing himself and swearing that he would not continue painting. Then that awful creature rolled out of bed and his bones began to rattle; he gathered his last strength, his eyes shone with life-like energy, and his arms encircled my father's legs; crawling on all fours, he kissed the hem of my father's clothes and begged him to complete the portrait. But my father was implacable and was merely astonished at the old man's strength of will, which had overcome even the approach of death. At last the desperate Petromikhali with extraordinary strength pulled out an old chest from beneath his bed, and a huge pile of gold coins fell on the floor; seeing my father's powerful determination, the old man groveled at his feet and a whole stream of incantations flowed from his previously silent lips. It was impossible not to feel some sort of terrible, and if one may say so, repulsive compassion. 'Good sir!

God-fearing man! Man of Christ!' cried the living skeleton with a voice of despair. 'I implore you in the name of your little children, your lovely wife, the grave of your father, to finish my portrait! Spend only one more hour working on it! Listen, I'll reveal a secret to you.' While he was saying this, the deathly pallor began to spread across his face even more quickly. 'But you mustn't tell anyone this secret—not your wife, nor your children, otherwise you will die and they will die, and all of you will be miserable. Listen, if you won't feel any pity for me now, I won't ask you any more. After I die, I have to go to the one whom I would rather not see. There I will have to undergo torments that you have never even dreamed of; but I can postpone that for a long time, even to the end of the world, if only you will complete my portrait. I learned that half my life will go into the portrait, but only if it is painted by a skilled artist. You can see that a part of my life has already gone into the eyes; it will also go into the features of the portrait if you complete work on it. And although my body will perish, half my life will remain on earth and I will avoid those torments for a very long time. Finish it! Finish it! Finish it!' this strange creature cried in a heart-rending, failing voice. My father was even more overcome with horror. He felt his hair stand on end from learning this terrible secret, and he dropped his paintbrush, which he had just picked up, touched as he was by the old man's entreaties. 'Ah, so you don't want to finish my portrait?' Petromikhali said in a hoarse voice. 'Well, then take the portrait away with you: I give it to you.' At those words something like a terrible laugh burst forth from his lips; life seemed to shine in all his features once more, and a minute later all that remained of him was a bluish corpse. My father didn't want to touch the brushes and paints that he had used to capture those apostate features, and went running out of the room.

"To dispel the unpleasant thoughts occasioned by these events, he walked around town for a long time and returned home toward evening. The first object he encountered when he entered his workshop was the portrait he'd painted of the old usurer. He asked his wife, his cook, and his servant, but all of them gave the same definitive answer: that no one had brought the portrait and no one had even come during his absence. This forced him to reflect for a minute. He approached the portrait and averted his eyes involuntarily, so filled was he with disgust for his own work. He ordered that it be taken down and carried up to the attic, but even so he felt some strange, oppressive anxiety and the presence of frightening thoughts. But most of all what astonished him was, even after he had gone to bed, the following, almost unbelievable occurrence: he clearly saw how Petromikhali entered his room and stood in front of his bed. He stared at my father for a long time with his life-like eyes, and then began to make such awful suggestions, wanting to put his art to such diabolical purposes, that with a moan of anguish, in a cold sweat, and feeling unbearable oppression in his soul and, at the same time, fiery indignation, the artist jumped up from bed. He saw how the wonderful likeness of the deceased Petromikhali returned to the portrait frame, which once again was hanging on the wall in front of him. He resolved that very day to burn the cursed work of his own hands. As soon as the fire was lit in the hearth, he threw the portrait into the raging flames and with secret pleasure saw how the frame, over which the canvas had been stretched, exploded and how the paints, which had not yet dried completely, began to sizzle; at last only a pile of ashes remained from its existence. And when it began to fly up the chimney as a light dust, it seemed that the hazy image of Petromikhali left with it. He experienced a sense of relief in his soul. With a feeling of recovery from a prolonged illness, he turned to the corner of his room, where an icon he had painted used to be displayed, to express his repentance; and he saw with horror that the very same portrait of Petromikhali was hanging there, the eyes of which seemed to be even more life-like, so even his children let out a cry when they saw it. This turn of events astonished my father a great deal. He decided to confess everything to the priest of our parish and to ask his advice as to how to proceed after this extraordinary occurrence. The priest was a sober-minded man, and also devoted with warm affection to his calling. He came immediately upon the summons from my father, whom he respected as a worthy parishioner. My father didn't even consider it necessary to take him aside; he decided, in the presence of my mother and their children, to recount the unbelievable events. But he had barely uttered the first word when my mother suddenly cried out softly and fell down on the floor unconscious. Her face was covered with a terrible pallor, her mouth was still, wide open, and all of her features were distorted by convulsions. My father and the priest ran to her and with horror saw that she had accidentally swallowed a dozen needles that she had been holding in her mouth. The doctor who arrived declared that the case was hopeless: some needles remained stuck in her throat, others had passed into her stomach and insides, and my mother died a horrible death.

"This occurrence had a powerful impact on my father's entire life. From this time forth a kind of gloom took possession of his soul. He rarely engaged in his work, almost always remained silent, and avoided all society. Meanwhile, the awful portrait of Petromikhali with its life-like eyes began to haunt him even more often; frequently my father experienced a rush of such fierce, desperate thoughts that they forced him to shudder. Everything that settles like a black residue in the depth of a human being, everything that is wiped away and dispelled by education, noble deeds, and imitation of what is beautiful—all this was stirring within him, trying to emerge and develop in all of its evil perfection. The bleak state of his soul was such that it compelled him to grab hold of this dark side of man. But I must note that my father's strength of character was immeasurable; the power that he exerted over himself and his passions was extraordinary, his convictions were harder than granite, and the worse the temptation became, the more he attempted to resist it with all the indestructible strength of his soul. At last, weakened by this struggle, he resolved to relieve and bare his soul in relating the entire tale to the same priest, who had almost always been able to provide him with reprieve with his wise words.

"This happened at the beginning of autumn; the day was magnificent, the sun shone with some sort of fresh, autumnal light; the windows of our rooms were open; my father was sitting with the worthy priest in his workshop; my brother and I were playing in the next room. Both of these rooms were on the second floor, in the attic of our little house. The door to the workshop was slightly open; I happened to glance into the opening and saw that my father had moved closer to the priest and I even heard what he was saying: 'At last I will reveal this whole secret. . . .' All of a sudden a momentary cry forced me to turn around: my brother had vanished. I went over to the window and—my God! I'll never forget what happened: the body of my brother lay covered in blood on the pavement below. While he was playing, he must have inadvertently leaned out of the window too far and fallen, without doubt head-first, because his head was smashed to pieces. I'll never forget this awful incident. My father stood motionless in front of the window, his arms crossed and his eyes looking to the sky. The priest was seized with fear, recalling my mother's terrible death, and demanded that my father keep the awful secret to himself.

"After this my father sent me away to a military school where I received my education, while he himself retired to a monastery in a remote town, surrounded by desert, where the bleak north offers only harsh nature; there he solemnly took his vows as a monk. He fulfilled all the duties of this calling with such obedience and humility, he led a life of toil with such humility, combined with enthusiasm and the fervor of his faith, that apparently the criminal force was powerless to touch him. But the terrible image he had painted with its life-like eyes pursued him even in his almost sepulchral isolation. The abbot, having learned of my father's unusual artistic talent, commissioned him to adorn the church with several icons. One had to see the extraordinary degree of religious humility that he brought to this task: he prepared himself for it with strict fasting and prayer, in profound meditation and solitude. He constantly spent his nights over his sacred images and, as a result, perhaps, you will rarely find works even by famous artists that reflect such genuinely Christian emotions and thoughts. There was such heavenly serenity in his saints, such spiritual anguish in his repentant sinners, which I have encountered so infrequently in the works of acknowledged masters. Finally, all his thoughts and desires aspired to depict the holy Mother of God, gently extending her arms over the praying people. He worked on this icon with such self-sacrifice and with such unawareness of himself and the entire world that a part of the tranquility conveyed by his brush to the features of the heavenly Protectress of the world seemed to have entered into his own soul. At last the terrible image of the usurer ceased visiting him and the portrait vanished to no one knows where.

"Meanwhile, my education at military school ended. I was commissioned as an officer, but to my greatest regret, circumstances did not allow me to see my father. At the time we were dispatched to active service in the army; as a result of the ongoing war with the Turks, I was sent to the border. I won't burden you with stories of my life spent in campaigns, bivouacs, and heated battles; it's enough to say that hard work, dangers, and the hot climate changed me completely, so that those who had known me previously no longer recognized me at all. My suntanned face, my enormous mustache, and my loud, hoarse voice lent me a completely different appearance. I was a convivial fellow, without a thought for tomorrow, and loved to uncork an extra bottle with a comrade, chat nonsense with dark-skinned young women, fool around—in a word, I was a carefree soldier. However, as soon as the campaign ended, I considered it my duty to visit my father.

"When I approached the isolated monastery, I was overcome by a strange feeling that I had never experienced before; I felt that I was still connected with one creature, that there was still something incomplete about my existence. The secluded monastery amid nature, pale and bare, caused me to feel some sort of poetic oblivion and afforded a strange, vague direction to my thoughts, the kind we usually experience in late autumn, when the leaves rustle under our feet and there's not a single leaf overhead, when black branches are wound into flimsy nets, ravens cackle in the distant sky, and we quicken our step involuntarily, as if trying to collect our scattered thoughts. A large number of blackened wooden buildings surrounded the stone structure. I entered under long galleries, rotten in some places, overgrown with moss at others, surrounding the monks' cells; I asked to see the monk Father Gregory. That was the name my father had assumed when he entered the monastic order. They showed me to his cell.

"I will never forget the impression he made on me. I saw an old man whose pale, exhausted face seemed to lack all features, all thoughts of earthly life. His eyes, accustomed to being directed toward heaven, had assumed that dispassionate look, infused with otherworldly fire, which visits an artist only during a moment of inspiration. He sat before me motionless, like a saint staring out from a canvas that an artist's hand had captured for the praying people; he seemed not to notice me at all, although his eyes were directed to that part of the room where I had entered. I still didn't want to make myself known to him, so I merely asked for his blessing as a traveling pilgrim; but I was astonished when he said, 'Greetings, my son, Leo!' This amazed me: I had parted with him when I was ten years old; besides, people who had seen me more recently didn't recognize me. 'I knew that you would come to see me,' he continued. 'I asked the Holy Virgin and a saint for this, and have been waiting for you hour by hour, because I feel that my end is near and I want to reveal an important secret to you. Come with me, my son, and let us pray beforehand!' We entered the church and he led me up to a large image depicting the Mother of God blessing the people. I was struck by the profound expression of godliness in her countenance. He lay there prostrate before the image for a long time; after a very extended period of silence and meditation, he left the church with me.

"Subsequently, my father told me everything that you've just heard from me. I believed in the truth of what he said because I myself was a witness to many of the sad events of our life. 'Now I will tell you, my son,' he added after this story, 'what was revealed to me by a saint, recognized by no one else in the crowd but me, to whom the merciful Creator delivered his ineffable blessing.' Saying this, my father crossed his arms and raised his eyes to the heavens, to which he was completely committed with all of his being. And, at long last, I heard what I am now prepared to relate to you. You mustn't be surprised by the strangeness of his account: I saw that he was in that condition of the soul which overtakes a man when he experiences powerful, unbearable misfortunes; when, wishing to gather all his strength, all the iron might of his soul, and not finding it strong enough, he turns entirely to religion; and the stronger the yoke of his misfortunes, the more fervent are his spiritual meditations and prayers. He no longer resembles a quiet, contemplative hermit, anchored in his own desolate wasteland as if to a favorite harbor, with the desire to rest from life and to pray to Him, to whom he felt closest and most accessible, with Christian humility; on the contrary, he becomes something enormous. The ardor of his soul is not extinguished in him; on the contrary, it gushes forth and emerges with great strength. Then he turns to one great burst of flame of religious fervor. His head is always filled with miraculous dreams. He sees visions at every step and hears revelations; his thoughts are kindled; his eye no longer sees anything belonging to this earth; all his movements, as a result of his eternal striving for one thing, are filled with enthusiasm. From the first, I noticed this condition in him and mention it so that the words I heard from him won't seem so astonishing to you.

"'My son!' he said after a long, almost motionless stare into the heavens: 'the time is fast approaching when the tempter of the human race, the Antichrist, will be born on the earth. That time will be terrible: it will occur just before the end of the world. He will come riding in on a giant steed, and the torments of those who remain faithful to Christ will be terrible indeed. Listen, my son: the Antichrist has been wanting to come for a long time, but he can't because he must be born in a supernatural manner; but in our world everything is organized by the Almighty in such a way that everything occurs in a natural order; therefore, no power, my son, can help him break into our world. But our world is mere dust before the Creator. By His laws, it must be destroyed, and with every day the laws of nature will become weaker, and therefore the borders restraining the supernatural are becoming easier to overcome. He is already being born now, but only a certain part of him is breaking into and appearing in this world. He chooses man himself for his dwelling-place and appears in those people who seem to have been abandoned by their angel at birth; they are cursed by a terrible hatred of mankind and everything else that was made by the Creator. Such a creature was that amazing usurer whom I, a sinner, dared to depict with my own sinful paintbrush. It was he, my son; it was the Antichrist himself. If my sinful hand hadn't dared to depict him, he would have retreated and vanished, because he couldn't have lived any longer than the body that had contained him. A diabolical presence was preserved in those repulsive, life-like eyes. Marvel, my son, at the terrible power of the devil. He tries to infiltrate all of our actions, our thoughts, and even an artist's inspiration. The number of victims of this demonic spirit will be countless; he is able to live invisibly, without any image, on this earth. He is that black spirit who invades us even in moments of the purest and holiest meditation. Oh, if my brush had not stopped its wicked work, he would have committed even more evil deeds, and there are no human forces that could oppose him. For he chooses precisely that moment when the greatest misfortune befalls us. Woe to poor humankind, my son! But listen to what the Mother of God herself revealed to me during a holy vision. When I was working on the holy countenance of the Virgin Mary, I wept tears of repentance over my past life; I spent a long time in fasting and prayer, in order to be more worthy of depicting her sacred features; then I was visited by inspiration, my son, and felt that a higher power had come over me and that an angel was guiding my sinful hand; I felt how my hair stood on end and my soul began to tremble. Oh, my son! For that minute I would undergo a thousand torments. I myself was surprised at what my brush was painting. Then I saw the face of the Virgin in a dream and found out that as a reward for my labors and prayers, the supernatural existence of this demon in the portrait would not be eternal; that if someone solemnly related this tale, after fifty years had passed, at the first new moon, its power would vanish and disperse like dust; and that I could convey all this to you before my death. Thirty years have now elapsed since he was alive; twenty more lie ahead. Let us pray, my son!' Saying this, he fell to his knees and became absorbed in prayer.

"I confess I attributed all of these words to his heated imagination, heightened by his constant fasting and prayer, and therefore out of respect I didn't want to make any remarks or observations. But when I saw him raise his withered arms to heaven and noted the profound silence of this inwardly damaged man; the inexpressible humility with which he prayed for those who lacked the strength to oppose the demonic tempter and had thus destroyed all that was sublime in their souls; the passionate grief displayed as he prostrated himself; and how his revealing tears flowed down his face, how all his features displayed only his mute anguish—oh! then I lacked the strength to delve into cold reflection and to analyze his words.

"Several years passed after his death. I didn't believe in this tale and didn't even think about it very much; but I was unable to relate it to anybody. I don't know why that was, but I always felt that something was restraining me from doing it. Today, without any set goal, I dropped in on the auction and for the first time told the story of this extraordinary portrait—so that I am even beginning to wonder if there was a new moon today, about which my father had spoken, because twenty more years have actually passed since that time."

Here the narrator stopped and the listeners who had been giving him their undivided attention unintentionally turned their eyes to the strange portrait; to their astonishment, they noticed that its eyes no longer possessed that strange life-likeness which had so struck them at first. Their astonishment increased when the features of the strange picture began to disappear almost gradually, as one's breath vanishes from the surface of cold steel. Some obscure outline remained on the canvas. When they went up closer to take a look, they saw there some unfamiliar landscape. Thus the visitors, as they left, were puzzled for a long time: had they really seen the mysterious portrait, or was it all a dream, for a moment appearing before their eyes, which were exhausted from staring too long at old pictures?

The Overcoat

In a certain department ... but it's better not to say which department. Nothing can get more irritating than departments, regiments, offices—in a word, all sorts of official bodies. Now every private individual considers a personal insult an insult against society. They say that not long ago there was a request from a police commissioner, I don't recall from what town, in which he stated clearly that governmental institutions were perishing and that his sacred name was being taken in vain. As proof he attached to his petition an enormous volume of some romantic composition, where every ten pages or so there appeared a police commissioner, at times even completely drunk. And so, to avoid any unpleasantness, it's better to call the department with which we're concerned a *certain department*. And so, in a *certain department* there worked a *certain civil servant*; it can't be said that the civil servant was remarkable; he was short, somewhat pock-marked, somewhat red-headed, even somewhat shortsighted, with a small bald patch on his forehead, wrinkles on both cheeks, and a complexion that can best be described as hemorrhoidal. . . . What's to be done? The Petersburg climate is to blame. As far as his rank is concerned (because in Russia one's rank has to be specified first of all), he was what's called a perpetual titular councilor, about which rank, as is well known, various writers, who have the admirable habit of attacking those who can't fight back, have offered all sorts of jeers and mockery.

The civil servant's surname was Bashmachkin. From his name alone it's obvious that at some time in the past it was derived from the word *bashmak* [shoe]; but when, at what time, and how it came from the word *bashmak* isn't known at all. Both his father and his grandfather, and even his brother-in-law, as well as all the other Bashmachkins, used to wear boots, having them resoled only some three times a year. His name and patronymic was Akaky Akakievich. Perhaps it might seem a bit unusual and artificial, but one can be sure that no time was wasted in searching for that name; events occurred in the most natural way; it was impossible to give him any other name; here is how it happened.

Akaky Akakievich was born toward evening, if memory serves me right, on the twenty-third day of March. His late mother, the wife of a civil servant and a very good woman, made arrangements, as was appropriate, to have the child christened. His mother was still lying in bed facing the door; his godfather, an excellent man, Ivan Ivanovich Yeroshkin, who served as head clerk in the Senate, stood on the right with his godmother, the wife of the district police inspector, a woman of rare virtue, Arina Semyonovna Belobryush-kova. They presented the mother with a choice of three names, whichever she wished to pick: Mokiy, Sossiy, or else to name the child after the martyr Khozdazat.° "No," thought the poor woman, "those names are all so strange." To satisfy her, they opened the calendar to another place; three more names emerged: Trifiliy, Dula, and Varakhasiy. "That's quite a punishment," said the old woman. "What names they are: I've never heard anything like that. If only it was Varadat or Varukh, but not Trifiliy and Varakhasiy." They turned to another page—and found: Pavsikakhiy and Vakhtisiy. "Well, I can see," said the old woman, "that such is his fate. If that's the case, let him be called like his father. His father was Akaky, and let his son also be Akaky." This was how he came to be named Akaky Akakievich. They christened the child, at which time he began to cry and made such a face, as if he had a premonition that he would become a titular councilor. And so, that's how it all transpired. We recounted all this so the reader could see for himself that this happened absolutely of necessity and that it was completely impossible to give him any other name.

When and at what time he joined the department and who appointed him, no one can recall. No matter how many directors served and how they varied, he could be seen sitting in one and the same place, in the same position, doing the same thing, that is, copying official documents, with the result that afterwards everyone was convinced that he had been born into the world fully prepared for his job, wearing his uniform, and with a bald patch on his head.

No respect was ever shown to him in the department. The porters not only didn't get up from their places when he arrived, but didn't even look at him, acting as if a common fly had flown through the waiting room. His superiors treated him with cool despotism. An assistant to the chief clerk would shove some documents right under his nose without even saying, "Copy these," or "Here's a nice, interesting little case," or some other pleasantry, as is customary in well-bred departments. And he took them, seeing only the documents, without looking up to see who had given them to him and whether that person had any right to do so. He accepted the documents and immediately settled down to copy them.

The young civil servants laughed and made fun of him, as much as their clerkly wit would allow, telling various fictitious stories about him to his face; they would say that his landlady, a seventy-year-old woman, used to beat him; they would ask when their wedding would be, and would scatter scraps of paper on his head, calling it snow. But Akaky Akakievich didn't reply with a single word, as if there was no one in front of him at all; and this behavior didn't have any impact on his work: amid all this teasing, he didn't make even one mistake in his copying. Only if the joke became too intolerable, when they would shove his arm, preventing him from doing his work, would he say: "Leave me alone. Why are you treating me like this?" And something strange could be heard in these words and in the tone in which they were uttered. There was something in it that elicited compassion, such that one young man, recently appointed, who, following the example of the other clerks, was about to allow himself to laugh, stopped suddenly, as if stabbed through the heart; since then everything seems to have changed before him and now appears in a different light. Some sort of unnatural force alienated him from his comrades with whom he had become acquainted, having taken them for decent, well-bred people. And for a long time afterwards, amid the merriest moments, he would see before him the little civil servant with the bald patch on his forehead, with his poignant words, "Leave me alone. Why are you treating me like this?" In these touching words he heard others: "I am your brother." And the poor young man would cover his face and many times later in his life would shudder at seeing how much inhumanity there was in man, how much fierce boorishness was hidden behind refined, cultured good manners, and, good Lord, even in a man the world regarded as noble and honest.

One could hardly find a person who lived so much for his work. It is not enough to say that he served with zeal—no, he served with love. There, in his copying, he would imagine his own diverse, pleasant world. Enjoyment was expressed in his face; some letters were his favorites, such that, when he reached them, he was beside himself with joy; he would chuckle, wink, and shape his lips, so that it seemed you could read in his face every letter formed by his pen. If rewards were granted according to his zeal, he, to his own astonishment, might even be promoted to state councilor; but, as his comrades, the office wits, used to say, he served long enough to receive a badge in his buttonhole and hemorrhoids on his rear. However, it's impossible to maintain that there was no attention showed to him. One director, who was a good man and wished to reward him for his long service, ordered that he be given something more important than the usual copying; that is, from a completed case, he was instructed to make a report for another department; all he had to do was change the title of the document and alter some verbs from the first person to the third person. This proved to cause him so much exertion that he broke out in a sweat, wiped his forehead, and finally said: "No, you'd better give me something to copy instead." Since then they had left him alone to carry on with his copying forever.

Besides this copying, it seemed, nothing else existed for him. He didn't think about his apparel at all: his uniform was no longer green, but some sort of rusty-muddy color. Its collar was narrow and short so that his neck, in spite of the fact that it wasn't very long, appeared to be extremely long as it stuck out of the collar, like those plaster kittens with heads that dozens of foreign street-peddlers carry about on their heads. And there was always something sticking to his uniform: either a little piece of straw or some thread; in addition, as he walked along the street, he had the special skill of winding up under a window at the same time as all sorts of rubbish was being tossed out, so he was always wearing on his hat bits of melon, watermelon rind, and similar items. Not once in his life did he pay any attention to what was happening every day on the street, which, as is well known, his comrades, young civil servants, always regard, using the perspicacity of their bold vision to notice even on the other side of the street someone whose lower trouser strap has come undone—which calls forth a malicious grin on their faces.

But if Akaky Akakievich ever looked at anything, he saw only his clean, neatly written words, and only if a horse, coming from God knows where, put his muzzle on his shoulder and from its nostrils blew a strong breath on his cheek, only then did he notice that he wasn't in the middle of a line, but rather in the middle of a street. Upon arriving home, he would sit down at his table at once, quickly gulp down his cabbage soup, eat a piece of beef with onion, without noticing the taste whatsoever, eat everything, flies and all, whatever God sent to him at that time. Having noticed that his belly had started to swell, he would get up from the table, take out a bottle of ink, and begin copying documents that he had brought home. If he had nothing to copy from work, he would make a copy for himself, for his own enjoyment, especially if the document was remarkable, not in its style, but in being addressed to some new or important person.

Even at those hours when the gray Petersburg sky fades completely, and all other civil servants have eaten their fill and finished their dinner, as best each could, given their salary and desire—when all have had their rest after the scraping of pens in the department and the press of necessary business, their own and other people's, and everything else that an indefatigable man takes on himself, even more than is necessary—when civil servants hasten to enjoy their remaining hours: the more adventurous going to the theater; others to stroll along the street, looking at some women's hats; some to a gathering—to spend it complimenting some pretty girl, the star of a small circle of civil servants; some, and this happens most of all, to call on one of their comrades on the third or fourth floor, in two small rooms with an entrance hall or kitchen, and fashionable pretensions, a lamp or another item that cost a great deal of sacrifice, refusing dinner or an outing—in a word, even at the time when all civil servants disperse to their friends' small apartments to play a fiery game of whist, slurping tea from a glass with inexpensive rusks, or inhaling smoke from long pipes, relating while dealing the cards some scandal occurring in high society, which a Russian can never resist under any circumstances, or even, when there's nothing to talk about, repeating the old anecdote about the commandant who was informed that the tail of Falconetti's monument had been docked—in a word, even when everyone strives to enjoy himself—Akaky Akakievich didn't indulge in any amusement. No one could ever say that they had ever seen him at a gathering. After copying to his heart's content, he would go to bed, smiling beforehand at the prospect of the next day: what would God send him to copy tomorrow? Thus passed the peaceful life of a man who, with a salary of some four hundred rubles, could be content with his lot; perhaps it would have continued into his old age, if it hadn't been for various misfortunes strewn along the way, misfortunes not only of titular councilors, but also of privy, actual, court, and any other councilors, even those who provide no counsel to anyone, and do not accept counsel from anyone.

There is in Petersburg a powerful enemy of all those earning four hundred rubles or thereabouts a year in salary. This enemy is none other than our northern climate, although people say that it's good for one's health. At nine o'clock in the morning, precisely the time when the streets are filled with people going to their departments, it begins to impart such mighty and stinging blows to all noses, without exception, with the result that the poor civil servants simply don't know what to do. At this time, when even those occupying higher ranks suffer from aching foreheads and tears forming in their eyes, the poor titular councilors are sometimes defenseless. Their only salvation consists in running as fast as they can in their flimsy overcoats for five or six blocks and then stamping their feet briskly in the porter's lodge until such time as they can thaw out all of their abilities and talents for their various jobs, which were frozen along the way.

For some time Akaky Akakievich had been feeling that the cold had begun to penetrate his back and shoulders, in spite of the fact that he tried to run the required distance as quickly as possible. He began to wonder, at last, if there might not be some deficiencies in his overcoat. Having examined it carefully at home, he discovered that in a few places, precisely on the back and shoulders, it had begun to resemble a piece of cheesecloth: the fabric had worn so thin that it let the wind in, and the lining had fallen apart. It should be stated that Akaky's overcoat had come to serve as the butt of jokes made by the other civil servants: they had even withdrawn the noble designation of "overcoat" from it and referred to it as a "dressing gown." As a matter of fact, it had a rather strange appearance: its collar had shrunk with each passing year, since it served as the source of patches for the coat itself. The repairs didn't attest to the tailor's art, and they turned out awkward and unattractive indeed. Having seen what the problem was, Akaky Akakievich decided that he would have to take his overcoat to Petrovich, the tailor, who lived somewhere on the fourth floor up a back staircase, and who, in spite of the fact that he had only one eye and had pockmarks all over his face, was engaged successfully in repairing the trousers and frock coats of civil servants and various others—naturally, when he was sober and didn't have any other scheme in mind. Of course, it's unnecessary to say very much about this tailor, but since it's already well established that the character of every person mentioned in a story must be described fully, then there's nothing to be done: let's bring forward Petrovich.

At first he was called simply Grigory and was a serf belonging to some gentleman or other; he began to be known as Petrovich when he received his freedom and began to drink rather heavily on most holidays, at first on the major ones and then, without exception, on all church holidays, wherever there was a cross indicated on his calendar. So from that point of view he was true to his forebears' customs; arguing with his wife, he would call her a secular woman and a German. Since we just mentioned his wife, we have to say a few words about her; but unfortunately, very little is known about her, except for the fact that Petrovich had a wife, and that she wore a cap instead of a kerchief; but it seems she couldn't brag about her beauty; at least, in meeting her, only guardsmen were known to peer under her cap, tugging their mustaches and emitting some strange sounds.

As he was climbing the stairs to Petrovich's apartment—which, to give them their due, were soaked with water and slops, and saturated with the smell of ammonia, which burns the eyes and, as is well known, is regularly present on all the back staircases in Petersburg houses—as he was climbing the stairs, Akaky Akakievich was already thinking about how much Petrovich would charge, and he resolved not to pay more than two rubles. The door was open because the tailor's wife had been cooking some fish and had produced so much smoke in the kitchen that it was impossible to see even the cockroaches. Akaky Akakievich went through the kitchen, not even noticed by Petrovich's wife, and entered a room where he saw Petrovich sitting on a large unpainted wooden table, with his legs crossed underneath him like a Turkish pasha. His feet, as is the custom of tailors who are sitting over their work, were bare. The first thing that caught his eye was Petrovich's big toe, well known to Akaky Akakievich, with its misshapen toenail, thick and hard, just like the shell of a turtle. A hank of silk and thread hung around Petrovich's neck, and on his lap lay some worn piece of clothing. For several minutes he had been trying to thread a needle and been unable to do so; consequently, he was very angry at the darkness in the room and at the thread itself, muttering under his breath: "It won't go in, dammit; you'll wear me out, you bitch!" Akaky Akakievich wasn't pleased that he had come at such a moment when Petrovich was angry; he preferred to come with an order when Petrovich was already somewhat tipsy or, as his wife used to say, "Been guzzling his raw vodka, that one-eyed devil." In that state Petrovich would usually concede and agree very willingly, usually even bowing and thanking him. Then, it's true, his wife would come to Akaky Akakievich in tears, saying that her husband had been drunk and settled for too little; so he would add ten kopecks, and then everything was fine. Now it seemed that Petrovich was sober and, therefore, stern, uncommunicative, and liable to charge any price. Akaky Akakievich realized this and was, as they say, about to beat a hasty retreat, but things had already gone too far. Petrovich screwed up his one eye and glared at him. Akaky Akakievich said reluctantly:

"Hello, Petrovich!"

"How do you do, sir," replied Petrovich and he squinted at Akaky Akakievich's hands, wishing to see what he'd brought to offer him.

"I've come to see you, Petrovich, about a . . ."

One should know that Akaky Akakievich expressed himself for the most part with prepositions, adverbs, and, lastly, such particles that categorically have no meaning at all. If the matter at hand was very difficult, he even had the habit of not finishing his sentences, so that very often, after beginning with the words "It's really, don't you know . . . ," nothing would follow, and he himself would forget, thinking that he had already said all he had to say.

"What is it?" asked Petrovich, at the same time examining with his one eye Akaky's whole uniform, beginning with the collar and the sleeves, the back, the tail, and the buttonholes—all of which he knew very well, because it was his own work. Such is the custom of tailors: it's the first thing they do upon meeting.

"I've come, Petrovich, about . . . my overcoat. The material, you see, is in good condition all over; it's a bit dusty, and it seems a little old, but it's new, only in one place it's a little . . . on the back, and a little worn on one of the shoulders, and on the other shoulder, too, you see, that's all. Not much work needed. . . ."

Petrovich took the "dressing gown," spread it out at first on the table, looked at it carefully for a long time, shook his head, reached out his hand to the window for his round snuffbox with the portrait of some general, it's unknown which one, because the place where his face was supposed to be had been poked in by a finger and covered over with a square bit of paper. After taking a pinch of snuff, Petrovich picked up the dressing gown and held it up to the light and once more shook his head. Then he turned it with the lining up and shook his head again; he took the lid with the general's portrait covered in paper and, filling his nose with snuff, closed and hid the snuffbox, and announced at last:

"No, it's impossible to repair it. It's a wretched piece of clothing."

At these words Akaky Akakievich's heart sank.

"Why is it impossible, Petrovich?" he said in almost the imploring voice of a child. "It's only a little worn on the shoulders, and you must have some patches. . . ."

"Patches I can find, and patches there are," said Petrovich, "but there's nothing to sew them onto: it's all rotten; you touch it with a needle—and it'll fall apart."

"If it falls apart, then you can patch it again."

"There's nothing to sew the patches onto, there's nothing for the patch to hold onto; it's all worn out. It's not really cloth anymore; if the wind blows at it, it will fly away."

"You can attach it somehow. How can it be, you know, really . . . ?"

"No," said Petrovich decisively. "It's impossible to do anything. It's in poor shape. What you should do is this: when cold winter comes, make some leg wrappings out of it for yourself, because socks won't keep your feet warm. It's the Germans who thought up socks to make more money" (Petrovich loved to taunt the Germans on any occasion); "as for your overcoat, you'll have to get a new one made."

At the words "new one," Akaky Akakievich's eyes began to grow misty, and everything in the room began to swim. The only thing he saw clearly was the general with the paper patch on the cover of Petrovich's snuffbox.

"What do you mean, 'a new one'?" he said, as if he were still dreaming. "But I don't have the money for it."

"Yes, a new one," Petrovich said with dreadful serenity.

"And if I had to get a new one, I mean, how much would . . . ?"

"That is, how much would it cost?"

"Yes."

"I suppose you'd have to pay a hundred and fifty rubles or more," said Petrovich, pursing his lips meaningfully. He really was fond of strong effects, he loved to confound someone suddenly and then steal a glance to see what sort of a face the person would make as a result of his words.

"A hundred and fifty rubles for an overcoat!" poor Akaky Akakievich cried out, perhaps for the first time in his life, because he was always known for the softness of his voice.

"Yes, sir," said Petrovich, "and that depends on what kind of overcoat. If you have marten fur for the collar and a silk lining for the hood, it could cost up to two hundred rubles."

"Please, Petrovich," Akaky Akakievich kept saying in an imploring voice, not hearing or wishing to hear Petrovich's words and all of his effects, "repair it somehow, so that I can wear it a bit longer."

"No, it will be a waste of my labor and a waste of your good money," said Petrovich, and after these words Akaky Akakievich left feeling completely overwhelmed.

And Petrovich, after his departure, remained in the same place, his lips pursed meaningfully, not getting back to work, feeling satisfied that he hadn't demeaned himself, nor had he betrayed the tailor's art.

After going out to the street, Akaky Akakievich felt as if he were dreaming. "So that's how it is, is it?" he kept saying to himself. "I really didn't think that it would be like this. . . ." And then, after a silence, he added, "So that's what! That's how it finally turned out, but I never supposed that's how it would be." There followed another very long silence, after which he said: "So that's what it is! Well, it's really so completely unexpected. . . . I never would have . . . such a situation!" After saying this, instead of heading home, he turned in the exact opposite direction, not even noticing where he was going. Along the way a chimney sweep brushed his sooty side up against him and blackened his shoulder; a hatful of plaster fell on him from the top of a house that was being built. He didn't notice any of this, and only later, when he bumped into a policeman who, placing his halberd next to him, was sprinkling some tobacco from a horn on his calloused fist, only then did he return to his senses somewhat, and that was because the policeman said: "Why are you crawling up into my face? Isn't the sidewalk big enough for you?" That forced him to look around and return home. Only then did he begin to collect his thoughts, regard his situation in a clear and genuine light, and begin to talk to himself not in broken phrases, but rationally and honestly, as if conversing with a sensible friend, with whom one can share one's most intimate and heartfelt matters.

"Well, no," said Akaky Akakievich, "there's no dealing with Petrovich now: he's, you know, a little . . . His wife must have given him a beating. It's better if I go to see him Sunday morning: after drinking on Saturday night, he'll be screwing up his one eye, and still half asleep, eager for another drink; his wife won't give him any money, and then I can slip ten kopecks into his hand, and he'll be more reasonable and the overcoat will be, you know . . ." That's how Akaky Akakievich reasoned with himself, cheered himself up, and waited until the first Sunday. Seeing from afar that Petrovich's wife left to go somewhere, he went right in to see him. Petrovich, after the previous night's drinking, had screwed up his one eye, hung his head to one side, and was very sleepy; but, in spite of all that, as soon as he realized what was happening, it seemed that the devil had gotten into him. "It's impossible," he said; "you'll have to order a new one." That's when Akaky Akakievich slipped him the ten kopecks. "Thank you, sir, I'll fortify myself a bit and drink to your health," said Petrovich, "but you ought to stop worrying about that overcoat: it's good for nothing at all. I'll make you a fine new coat, I swear I will."

Akaky Akakievich wanted to say something more about a repair, but Petrovich didn't listen to him and said: "I'll make you a new one for sure, you can be certain, I'll do my best. It could even be like the fashion now: the collar can have a silver-plated clasp."

At this point Akaky Akakievich realized that it would be impossible to avoid getting a new overcoat, and he fell into total despair. How, indeed, with what money could he do it? Of course, he could count in part on the holiday bonus he would receive, but that money had already been divided up and apportioned a long time ago. He had to get a new pair of trousers, to pay his old debt to the cobbler for fixing new tops to some old boots, and he had to order three shirts from the seamstress, as well as two pairs of underwear that are improper to mention in print—in a word, all of that money would have to be spent on other things; and even if the director were to be that generous, and instead of forty rubles for his bonus, were to appropriate forty-five or fifty, all that would be left would amount to no more than a drop in the ocean for building the capital for an overcoat. Although, of course, he knew that Petrovich had the habit of naming the devil knows what sort of price, so that it sometimes happened that his wife couldn't restrain herself and would shout, "Have you lost your mind or what, you fool! Sometimes he takes on work for next to nothing, and now the devil makes him ask a price that's more than he himself is worth." Although, of course, he knew that Petrovich would do it even for eighty rubles; but where would he get eighty rubles? He might be able to find half that sum; half could be found, perhaps even a little more than half; but where would he find the other half? But first the reader needs to know where the first half would come from. Akaky Akakievich had the habit of putting aside two half-kopeck pieces from every ruble spent into a small box, locked with a key, with a slit in the top where money could be deposited. At the end of every six months he counted up the accumulated copper coins and replaced them with silver. He had been saving like that for a long time and thereby, in the course of several years, had accumulated the sum of more than forty rubles. So, he had half the needed amount in hand; but where would he find the other half? Where would he find the other forty rubles? Akaky Akakievich thought and thought, and decided that it would be necessary to reduce his customary expenses, at least in the course of the next year: forgo drinking tea in the evening, stop lighting candles in the evening, and if he had to do something, he would go into the landlady's room and take advantage of her lighted candles; walking along the street, he would step as lightly and carefully as possible on stones and cobbles, almost on tiptoe, so as not to wear out the soles of his boots too soon; he would give his linen to the laundress less often, so that it wouldn't wear out; each time he came home, he would take it off and remain in his dressing gown made of cotton twill, a very old garment that even time itself had spared. Truth be told, at first he found it difficult to get used to such limitations; but then he somehow became accustomed to them and things went smoothly; he even learned to go hungry in the evening; on the other hand, he was nourished spiritually, bearing in mind the constant thought of his future overcoat. From that time forward it was as if his very existence had become fuller, as if he had gotten married, as if some other person were present with him, as if he weren't alone, but some pleasant helpmate had agreed to travel life's path with him—and this helpmate was none other than the overcoat with its thick padding and sturdy lining that would last forever. He became somehow more alive, even stronger in character, like a man who had determined and posited a goal. Doubt and uncertainty disappeared on their own from his face and his actions—in a word, all his indeterminate and vacillating character traits faded. At times a gleam would appear in his eyes; indeed, even the boldest and most daring ideas flashed through his mind: should he have a fur collar of marten after all? These reflections almost resulted in distraction. Once, copying a document, he almost even made a mistake, such that he almost cried aloud: "Oh!" and crossed himself. During the course of every month he would pay at least one visit to Petrovich to talk about the overcoat, where best to buy the cloth, of what color, and at what price; and, although he was a little worried, he would always return home satisfied, thinking that at last the time would come when it would all be purchased and his new overcoat would be ready. The matter proceeded even faster than he had hoped. Contrary to all expectations, the director awarded Akaky Akakievich a bonus of not forty or forty-five rubles, but the sum of sixty rubles; whether he knew that Akaky Akakievich needed a new overcoat, or whether it happened on its own, the fact was that he had an extra twenty rubles in hand. This circumstance hastened the process. Still some two or three more months of mild privation—and Akaky Akakievich had managed to save up about eighty rubles. His heart, in general very calm, began to beat faster. The very next day he went to a few shops with Petrovich. They purchased some very fine cloth—and it's no wonder they did, because they had been thinking about it for the six months before, and it was the rare month that they didn't drop into the shops to ask the price; but then Petrovich himself said that better cloth couldn't be found. They chose calico for the lining, but such high-quality and durable calico that, according to Petrovich, it was even better than silk, and looked even more attractive and shinier. They didn't buy marten because it really was expensive; but they chose cat fur instead, the best they could find in the shop: cat fur which from a distance could be taken as marten. Petrovich worked on the overcoat for two whole weeks because there was so much quilting to be done; otherwise it would have been done earlier. For the labor Petrovich asked twelve rubles—it couldn't possibly be any less: he used only silk thread to sew it, with double seams throughout, and Petrovich tightened every seam afterwards with his own teeth, leaving various tooth marks on the cloth.

It was . . . it's hard to say exactly on which day, but, no doubt, it was the most glorious day of Akaky Akakievich's life, when at long last Petrovich delivered the overcoat. He brought it in the morning, just before Akaky Akakievich had to leave home to go to the department. The overcoat could not have come at a better time, since rather hard frosts had begun, and the weather was predicted to become even colder. Petrovich arrived with the overcoat, just as a good tailor should. His face expressed solemn significance, such as Akaky Akakievich had never seen before. It seemed that he absolutely felt that he had accomplished no mean feat and had suddenly exposed the gulf that existed between those tailors who merely repair linings and mend coats, and those who create something new. He took the overcoat out of a large handkerchief in which he had carried it; the handkerchief had just come back from the laundress; then he folded it and put it into his pocket for future use. After taking out the overcoat, he looked very proudly around and, holding it in both hands, threw it very deftly over Akaky Akakievich's shoulders; he pulled it down and smoothed it out with his own hands; then he draped it around Akaky Akakievich and left it open a bit in the front. Akaky Akakievich, like a man getting on in years, wanted to put his arms into the sleeves; Petrovich also helped him put his arms through the sleeves—it turned out that the sleeves also fit well. In a word, it turned out that the overcoat was just right. Petrovich didn't miss the chance to say that this was because he lived on a small street without a signboard, and that he had known Akaky Akakievich for so long that he had asked so little for his labor; and that on Nevsky Prospect they would have asked at least seventy-five rubles for the labor alone. Akaky Akakievich didn't want to talk about all this with Petrovich, and he was afraid of large sums, such as those Petrovich was fond of tossing around for effect. He paid him, thanked him, and headed off to the department in his new overcoat. Petrovich went out after him and stood on the street looking at the overcoat from a distance for a long time; then he turned to one side on purpose and took a shortcut so that he could get another look at his overcoat from the other side, that is, from the front.

Meanwhile, Akaky Akakievich walked along in a most festive mood. He felt at every second of every minute that he was wearing a new overcoat; several times he even chuckled to himself from his inner satisfaction. And in fact there were two advantages: the first was that it was warm, and the second, that it was good. He didn't notice his path at all and suddenly found himself at the department; he took off his overcoat in the porter's lodge, looked it over, and entrusted it to the special care of the porter. It's not known how everyone in the department suddenly found out that Akaky Akakievich had a new overcoat, and that the "dressing gown" no longer existed. They all rushed out immediately to the porter's lodge to have a look at Akaky Akakievich's new overcoat. They began to greet him and congratulate him, so that at first he just smiled, and then even felt embarrassed. When everyone surrounded him and began saying that he really ought to celebrate his new overcoat and should host a party for them, Akaky Akakievich was completely flustered and didn't know what to do, what to say, and how to extricate himself. After a few minutes, he blushed from ear to ear, and simply began to assure them that it wasn't a new overcoat at all, but really it was just, you know, really his old coat. At last, one of the officials, an assistant head clerk, no less, no doubt to show that he was not a proud man and didn't spurn people even lower than himself, said, "So be it; I will give a party instead of Akaky Akakievich and invite everyone to come for tea this evening; as a matter of fact, today happens to be my name-day." The civil servants, naturally, began to congratulate the assistant head clerk and eagerly accepted his invitation. Akaky Akakievich started to make excuses, but everyone began saying that it was impolite, and that he should be ashamed of himself, and that he simply couldn't refuse to attend. However, afterwards he felt rather pleased when he remembered that it would be a reason to go out in the evening in his new overcoat.

That entire day was like a great holiday for Akaky Akakievich. He returned home in the happiest frame of mind, took off his overcoat, and hung it up carefully on the wall, admiring the material and the lining once more, and then pulled out his old dressing gown, which had fallen apart by then, for comparison. He regarded it and even started to chuckle: there was such a huge difference between them! And for a long time after, during his dinner, he kept smiling to himself as soon as he recalled the condition of his old dressing gown. He enjoyed his dinner a great deal and afterwards didn't do any copying, not one document; instead he lay on his bed for a little while like a sybarite, until it grew dark. Then, not to linger, he got dressed, put on his overcoat, and went out into the street.

Unfortunately, we can't say precisely where the official who had invited people to tea lived: memory has started to betray us so severely that everything in Petersburg, all the streets and houses, has blurred and merged in our head, and it's very difficult to make sense of it. Be that as it may, at least it's certain that the civil servant resided in the better part of town—which means that it was far from where Akaky Akakievich lived. At first he had to pass through some deserted streets with bad lighting; but as he drew closer to the civil servant's apartment, the streets became livelier, more crowded, and better lit. Pedestrians began to appear more often, well-dressed women appeared, and men sporting beaver collars; there were fewer poor cabbies with wooden railed sleighs studded with brass nails—on the other hand, there were more fine cabmen wearing crimson velvet hats, driving lacquered sleighs, with bear-skin blankets, and decorated boxes, dashing swiftly through the streets, their wheels crunching the snow.

Akaky Akakievich regarded all of this as a novelty. It had been several years since he had left his apartment in the evening. He stopped with curiosity in front of a lighted shop window to look at a picture in which a beautiful woman was removing her shoe, showing her whole leg, which was very attractive; and behind her back, from the door to another room, a man with side-whiskers and a handsome pointed beard on his chin was poking his head. Akaky Akakievich shook his head, grinned, and then continued on his way. Why did he grin? Was it because he had encountered something totally unfamiliar, but about which everyone retains a certain feeling, or was it that he thought as follows, like many other civil servants: "Oh, those Frenchmen! What can I say, if they want something like that, exactly like that. . . ." But perhaps he didn't think that at all—after all, it's impossible to delve into another man's soul and to know everything he's thinking.

At last he reached the house where the assistant head clerk lived. He lived in the grand style: a lamp was lit on the staircase; the apartment was on the second floor. Having entered the hallway, Akaky Akakievich saw a whole row of galoshes lined up on the floor. Among them, in the midst of the room, stood a samovar, hissing and releasing clouds of steam. All the overcoats and cloaks were hanging on the wall, among which were some even with beaver collars or velvet lapels. From the other side of the wall came the sounds of noise and conversation, which suddenly became clear and loud when the door opened and a footman emerged with a tray full of empty glasses, a jug of cream, and a basket of rusks. It was obvious that the civil servants had gathered a while ago and had already drunk their first glass of tea. Akaky Akakievich, after hanging up his overcoat, entered the room; before his eyes candles, clerks, pipes, and card tables all flashed at the same time, and his ears were struck with the sound of conversations rising up all around him and the sound of moving chairs. He stopped in the middle of the room, feeling very awkward, seeking and trying to think of what he should do next. But he had already been noticed, greeted with shouting, and everyone immediately filed out to the porter's lodge to have another look at his new overcoat. Although Akaky Akakievich was a little embarrassed, being a sincere person, he couldn't help from feeling glad, seeing how everyone praised it. Then, naturally, everyone forsook both him and the overcoat, and returned, as people do, to the card tables set up for a game of whist.

All of this, the noise, the conversation, and the crowd of people—all of this seemed somehow strange to Akaky Akakievich. He simply didn't know what to do, where to put his hands, feet, and his entire body; he finally sat down next to the card players, looked at the cards, glanced from one face to another, and in a short while began to yawn and to feel bored, all the more so since his usual bedtime had long since passed. He wanted to say goodbye to the host, but they wouldn't let him go, saying that they would have to drink a glass of champagne in honor of his new overcoat. An hour later supper was served, consisting of vegetable salad, cold veal, meat pies, sweet pastries, and champagne. They insisted that Akaky Akakievich drink two glasses, after which it seemed to him that the room was merrier; however, he was still unable to forget that it was past midnight and high time for him to go home. To make sure that the host would not detain him for any reason, he left the room quietly and looked for his overcoat in the hall, which he found, not without regret, lying on the floor; he brushed it off, removing from it any dust, put it on, and went down the stairs and out onto the street.

It was still light outside. Some little shops were open, these per-petual clubs for servants and all sorts of people; others, however, which were closed, displayed a long strip of light from under their doors, indicating that there were still people inside, most likely maids and servants who were finishing their conversations and gos-sip, who were leaving their masters at a complete loss as to their whereabouts. Akaky Akakievich walked along in a good mood, and was even just about to run after some lady suddenly, for some rea-son or other, who rushed past him like lightning, every part of whose body was in extraordinary motion. But he stopped almost at once and continued at his previous slow pace, even wondering where that sudden burst of speed had come from. Soon there stretched before him those deserted streets that even during the day were not very animated, even less so at night. Now they seemed even more desolate and lonely: there were fewer streetlamps and the oil in them, apparently, was running low; there were only wooden houses and fences; there was not a soul to be seen; snow glistened on the streets, and lowly, somnolent huts with their closed shutters stretched sadly before him. He drew near to a place where the street was intersected by an enormous square, houses barely vis-ible on the opposite side, which resembled a dreadful desert.

In the distance, God knows where, there was a gleam of light in a sentry booth, which appeared to stand at the end of the earth. Akaky Akakievich's good cheer was significantly reduced. He entered the square not without some involuntary dread, as if his heart sensed something bad. He looked back and to his sides: it was just like a sea surrounding him. "No, it's better not to look," he thought and walked on with his eyes closed; when he opened them to see if the end of the square was nearby, he suddenly saw that right in front of him, almost in his face, stood some men with mustaches, but who or what they were, he was unable to determine. His eyes grew dark and his heart began pounding. "Why, that's my overcoat!" said one in a thunderous voice, seizing him by the collar. Akaky Akakievich wanted to shout, "Help!" when the other man shoved a fist the size of an official's head in his face, and uttered: "Just you try to scream!" Akaky Akakievich merely felt how they took off his over-coat and gave him a swift kick with a knee, and he fell face-first into the snow; he didn't feel anything more. In a little while he recovered and stood up, but there was no one to be seen. He felt that it was terribly cold in the square and his overcoat was gone; he started to shout but there was no way his voice could reach the end of the square. Desperate, and not stopping his shouting, he set off running across the square straight to the sentry booth, next to which stood a policeman who was leaning on his halberd, watching, it seems, with curiosity, hoping to find out who the devil was running toward him from the distance and shouting as he ran. Akaky Akakievich, having run up to the policeman, began shouting at him; he was gasping for breath and charged that he was asleep and not keeping watch at all, and didn't he see how a man had been robbed. The policeman replied that he hadn't seen anything, that he had observed how two men stopped Akaky Akakievich in the middle of the square, and thought that they were his acquaintances; he advised him that instead of wasting his time shouting, he should go see the police inspector the next day and he would find out who took his overcoat.

Akaky Akakievich ran home in complete disarray: his hair, which barely grew on his temples and the back of his head, was completely tousled; his side, his chest, and his trousers were covered in snow. The old woman, his landlady, heard a terrible knocking at the door; she jumped hastily out of bed and, wearing only one shoe, ran to open the door, modestly clutching her nightshirt to her bosom; but, after opening it, she stepped back, seeing the state Akaky Akakievich was in. When he told her what had happened, she threw up her hands and said that he had to go right to the district superintendent, because the local police officer would dupe him, make promises, and lead him around by the nose; the best thing would be to go right to the superintendent; she even knew him personally, because Anna, a Finnish girl, who used to work as her cook, now served as a nanny for the superintendent. She said that she saw him frequently because he drove past their house, and that he went to church every Sunday, praying and looking cheerfully at everyone, and therefore must of course be a good-natured man. After hearing this advice, a saddened Akaky Akakievich trudged to his room; how he spent the night there will be left to those who can somehow imagine what another person experiences.

Early the next morning he went to see the superintendent; but they said that he was asleep; he came back at ten o'clock, and they said the same thing; he returned at eleven, and they said he wasn't at home; he came back at dinnertime, but the clerks in the hall didn't want to admit him and demanded to know what his business was, what brought him there, and what had happened. The result was that Akaky Akakievich at last, for once in his life, wanted to show his character and declared point-blank that he definitely needed to see the district superintendent personally, that they didn't dare refuse to admit him, that he came from the department on official business, that he would lodge a complaint against them, and then they would see what was what. The clerks were unable to object to any of this and one of them went to summon the superintendent. He came and took an extremely strange view of the story of the theft of the overcoat. Instead of focusing on the main point, he began to interrogate Akaky Akakievich: why was he returning home so late? Had he not visited and spent time in some house of ill repute? As a result Akaky Akakievich became very embarrassed and left not knowing whether the necessary steps would ever be taken to return his overcoat.

He didn't go the department all that day (for the only time in his life). The next day he appeared all pale, in his old "dressing gown," which was in an even sorrier state. The tale of the theft of the overcoat, in spite of the fact that there were a few clerks who couldn't refrain from making fun of him even about this incident, touched many of them. It was decided then and there to take up a collection for him, but they managed to gather a very small sum because they had already spent a great deal, having contributed to a fund for the director's portrait and for a book, at the suggestion of the department head, who was a friend of the author; so, the amount collected was very insignificant indeed. One person, moved by compassion, decided at least to help Akaky Akakievich by giving him some good advice, telling him not to go to the superintendent, because it might happen that he would somehow manage to find the overcoat, but, desiring to please his superior, the overcoat would remain with the police if Akaky Akakievich couldn't provide legal proof that the coat belonged to him; that the best thing would be for him to appeal to a certain *Very Important Person;* and that this *Very Important Person*, by writing and contacting the appropriate people, could expedite the whole matter. There was nothing else to be done. Akaky Akakievich decided to go to see the *Very Important Person*. What exactly the *Very Important Person* did remains unknown up to this moment. It should be noted that the *Very Important Person* had only recently become Very Important, and that previously he had been an unimportant person. However, even now his position wasn't considered very important, when compared with others who were even more important. But one can always find a group of people for whom an unimportant person seems to be an important person. However, this person tried to increase his importance by many different means, to wit: he insisted that lower-ranking civil servants meet him on the staircase when he arrived at the office; that no one dare approach him directly, but that everything be done in the strictest order: the collegiate registrar should report the matter to the provincial secretary, the provincial secretary to the titular councilor or to whomever it might be; and in such a way the matter would come to him. Thus it is in Holy Russia that everyone has a craze for imitation, and that each person copies and imitates his superior. They even say that some titular councilor, when he was promoted to be the head of some separate small office, immediately sectioned off a special area for himself, calling it the "audience room," and positioned some sort of valets with red collars and braids by the door, who took hold of the handles and opened the doors to any person who had come to see him, although in the "audience room" there was barely enough room to fit an ordinary writing desk.

The habits and customs of the *Very Important Person* were grand and majestic, but not very subtle. The basis of his system was strictness. "Strictness, strictness, and—strictness," he used to say, and as he uttered the final word, he would always look meaningfully into the face of the person with whom he was speaking. Although, however, there was really no reason for this, since the dozen or so clerks who made up the administrative machinery of the office were in a proper state of fear even without that: seeing him from afar, they would stop work and stand at attention until the head of the department passed through the room. His usual conversation with inferiors was marked by strictness and consisted of only three phrases: "How dare you? Do you know with whom you're speaking? Do you realize whom you're standing before?"

However, he was a good man in his soul, pleasant with his friends, obliging, but the rank of general had gone completely to his head. After receiving that promotion, he became confused, lost his way, and simply didn't know how to behave. If he happened to be with people of equal rank, he behaved appropriately; he was a decent fellow, in many respects not a stupid man; but if he found himself in society, where there were people even one rank lower than his, he seemed to be completely at a loss; he remained silent and his situation aroused pity, all the more so since he himself felt that he could be spending his time so much more enjoyably. Sometimes his eyes revealed a strong desire to participate in some interesting conversation or circle, but he was always stopped by the thought: might it be too much from his side, too familiar? Might he lower his dignity by doing so? As a result of such considerations, he always remained in the very same silent situation, uttering from time to time some monosyllabic sounds; therefore he acquired the reputation of being a most boring person.

It was this *Very Important Person* that Akaky Akakievich went to see, and went to see at a most inopportune time, very unfortunate for him, although it was most opportune for the *Very Important Person*. He was in his study and was talking very, very cheerily to an old friend who had recently arrived, a comrade from his childhood whom he hadn't seen in many years. At that time he was informed that a man by the name of Bashmachkin had come to see him. He asked abruptly: "Who's that?" They replied, "Some civil servant." "Ah! Let him wait. I don't have time," said the *Very Important Person*. Here it must be said that the *Very Important Person* was telling a baldfaced lie: he did have time. He had been talking about everything with his friend and for some time their conversation had been punctuated by extremely long silences, interrupted only by one of them patting the other on the knee and saying, "That's how it is, Ivan Abramovich!" or "Yes, indeed, Stepan Varlamovich!" Nevertheless, he made the civil servant wait to show his friend, who had retired from the civil service a long time ago and spent all his time at home in the country, how long civil servants have to wait for him in his entrance hall. At last they had talked themselves out, or been silent for so long, and after smoking a cigar in very comfortable armchairs with reclining backs, the *Very Important Person* seemed to remember something all of a sudden and said to the secretary who was standing next to the door with some documents in hand, waiting to report: "Isn't there some civil servant waiting to see me? Tell him to come in."

Seeing Akaky Akakievich's humble appearance and his very old uniform, he turned to him and said suddenly, "What do you want?" in an abrupt and firm voice, which he had intentionally rehearsed earlier in solitude in front of a mirror in his room, a week before he had received his current position and the rank of general.

Akaky Akakievich had been feeling appropriately timid well in advance; he became somewhat confused, and as best he could, as much as his tongue would allow, he explained with the addition even more often than at other times of the phrases "well" or "you know" that his overcoat was brand new, and that it had been stolen in a monstrous manner, and that he was appealing to him so that with his intervention, writing to the police superintendent, or someone else, he would locate the overcoat. For some reason or other, it seemed to the general that such behavior was too familiar.

"What do you mean, sir," he continued in an abrupt voice, "don't you know the correct order? Where have you come? Don't you know how these things are done? First you should have sent a petition to the office; it would have been passed along to the head clerk, then to the head of the department, then passed to the secretary, and then the secretary would have given it to me. . . ."

"But, Your Excellency," said Akaky Akakievich, trying to summon all possible courage that he had in him, and feeling at the same time that he was horribly drenched in sweat, "I dared trouble you because secretaries are such . . . unreliable people. . . ."

"What? What? What?" said the *Very Important Person.* "Where did you get that attitude? Where did you get that idea? What sort of insubordination has spread among young people against their superiors and their chiefs?"

It seems that the *Very Important Person* failed to notice that Akaky Akakievich was already over fifty years old. Therefore, if he could be called a young person, then it was only relative, compared to those who were already seventy years old.

"Do you know to whom you're speaking? Do you understand who's standing before you? Do you understand this? Do you understand? I'm asking you!"

Here he stamped his foot and raised his voice so loud that Akaky Akakievich wasn't even the only person to be frightened. He was horrified, staggered, and trembling all over, barely able to stand: if the guards hadn't come running to support him, he would have collapsed on the floor; he was almost unconscious as they escorted him out. And the *Very Important Person*, satisfied that the effect even exceeded his expectation, and completely charmed by the idea that his words could even deprive a person of his consciousness, glanced sideways at his friend to see how he regarded this scene. He noticed with some delight that his friend was experiencing vague unease and that he, too, was even beginning to feel afraid.

How he went down the stairs, how he made it out to the street Akaky Akakievich didn't recall. He couldn't feel either his hands or his feet. In his whole life he had never been so severely reprimanded by a general, and from another department at that. He walked along in a snowstorm that was whistling in the streets, his mouth gaping, almost stumbling off the pavement; the wind, as it usually does in Petersburg, blew on him from all four sides, from all the little lanes. In an instant his throat became inflamed, and he made it home, unable to utter even one word; he was all swollen and went right to bed. That's how powerful an official reprimand can be!

The next day he had a high fever. Thanks to the generous assistance of the Petersburg climate, his illness proceeded more rapidly than could have been expected. When the doctor arrived, after taking his pulse, he could do nothing other than prescribe a moist compress, if only for the reason that the patient shouldn't forgo the benefits of medical treatment; however, he told him that his end would come in about two days. After that, he turned to the landlady and said, "And you, dear lady, so as not to lose any time, should order a pine coffin for him, because an oak coffin would be too expensive." It's not at all known whether Akaky Akakievich heard these fatal words spoken about him, and if he did hear them, whether they produced a shattering effect on him, and whether he regretted his ill-starred life—because he was constantly in delirium and running a high fever. Apparitions, each one stranger than the last, were appearing to him constantly: first he saw Petrovich, and he was ordering him to make an overcoat with some sort of traps for robbers who, he thought, were constantly swarming under his bed; he kept summoning his landlady to remove a robber who was even under his blanket; then he was asking why his old dressing gown was still hanging next to him when he had a new overcoat; then he dreamt that he was standing before the general, listening to a proper reprimand, and was saying, "I'm sorry, Your Excellency"; then finally he even started using foul language, uttering the most horrible words, so that his old landlady even crossed herself, never having heard such language from him before, the more horrible because these words followed immediately after the phrase "Your Excellency." Afterwards he uttered such terrible nonsense that it was impossible to make anything out of it; one could only see that all his chaotic words and thoughts concerned nothing but his overcoat.

At last Akaky Akakievich gave up the ghost. Neither his room nor his belongings were sealed, in the first place because there were no heirs, and in the second, because there were very few items left, to wit: a bundle of quills, a packet of white government paper, three pairs of socks, two or three buttons that had come off his trousers, and the "dressing gown," already familiar to the reader. God knows who got all these things: the teller of this tale had no interest in that question.

They carried Akaky Akakievich away and buried him. And Petersburg remained without Akaky Akakievich, as if he had never even lived there. A creature had departed and disappeared, defended by no one, dear to no one, interesting to no one, not even attracting the attention of a naturalist, one who wouldn't miss the chance to put a pin into an ordinary fly and examine it under his microscope; a creature who patiently endured mockery at the office, and who, without any extraordinary incident, went to his grave, but for whom, nevertheless, right before the end of his life, there had appeared a bright visitor in the form of an overcoat, enlivening his poor life even for an instant, and on whom afterwards unbearable misfortune fell, as it also does to tsars and to the mighty of this world. . . .

A few days after his death an emissary was sent from the office to his apartment, to order him to appear in the department at once:

his superior was demanding it; but the emissary had to return without him, reporting that he was no longer able to come, and in reply to the question, "Why?" he expressed himself with the words, "He can't come, sir, you see, because he's dead. He was buried three days ago." That was how they learned in the department about Akaky Akakievich's passing; the next day a new clerk was already sitting in his place, who was much taller and whose letters were not as straight as his, but much more slanted and crooked.

But who could have imagined that this was still not everything about Akaky Akakievich, and that he was fated to live on sensationally a few days after his death, as if as to make up for a life that passed completely unnoticed? But that's just what happened, and our sad story unexpectedly has a fantastic ending.

In Petersburg rumors suddenly started circulating that near the Kalinkin Bridge and for a ways beyond, a corpse in the guise of a clerk was appearing at night, searching for a stolen overcoat, and, under the pretext of recovering his coat, was stripping all sorts of overcoats from the shoulders of passersby, without regard for rank or standing: those with cat fur or beaver trim, wadded, or made of raccoon, fox, or bear—in a word, all sorts of furs and skins, which people used to cover themselves. One of the clerks in the department saw the corpse with his own eyes and immediately recognized Akaky Akakievich; but that inspired such fear that he set off running as fast as he could and consequently couldn't get a good look at him and merely saw how the corpse was threatening him by wagging his finger from a distance.

Complaints were constantly arriving from all sides that backs and shoulders, not merely those of titular councilors, but even those of privy councilors, were subject to catching cold as a result of being stripped of their overcoats. The police were given orders to apprehend the corpse as soon as possible, dead or alive, and to punish it severely as an example to others, and they almost managed to do so. Namely, the policeman of one district in Kiryushkin Lane almost succeeded in grabbing the corpse by the collar at the very location of the crime of trying to snatch a frieze wool overcoat from some retired musician, who at one time used to play the flute. After seizing him, he summoned his two other comrades and ordered them to keep hold of the corpse, while he leaned down for a moment to extract from his boot his snuffbox to revive his nose which, some six times in his life, had been nipped by the frost; but the tobacco was so strong that probably even the corpse couldn't stand it. Hardly had the policeman covered his right nostril with his finger and taken some snuff into his left nostril than the corpse sneezed so violently and sprayed the eyes of all three of them. While they were using their fists to wipe their eyes, the corpse disappeared without a trace, so that they didn't even know for sure whether he had been apprehended or not. Since then, policemen had had such fear of corpses that they even refrained from seizing the living, and would merely shout from a distance: "Hey you! Keep moving!" The clerk's corpse began to appear even beyond the Kalinkin Bridge, inspiring terror in all timid folk.

However, we have completely abandoned the *Very Important Person*, who, as a matter of fact, was the real cause of the fantastic direction taken by this otherwise truthful tale. First of all, fairness demands that it be said that the *Very Important Person* experienced something like compassion after Akaky Akakievich left following his crushing reprimand. Such compassion was not foreign to him; his heart was open to many generous impulses, in spite of the fact that his rank hindered him to a great extent from expressing them. As soon as his friend left his office, he even began thinking about Akaky Akakievich. From that time forward almost every day he pictured the pale clerk, who was unable to withstand the requisite reprimand. The thought of him was so troubling that a week later he decided to send a clerk to inquire how he was faring and whether in fact there was something he could do to help; and when they informed him that Akaky Akakievich had died suddenly in a fever, he was even struck, felt twinges of conscience, and was in a bad mood all that day. Wishing to amuse himself somehow and to forget the unpleasant impression, he went to spend the evening at the home of one of his friends, where he could find respectable society, and where, best of all, everyone there was almost of the same rank, so that he could feel unconstrained. This had an astonishing effect on his spiritual state of mind. He opened up, became good-natured in his conversation, genial—in a word, he spent a very pleasant evening.

At supper he drank two glasses of champagne—a recognized remedy for improving one's mood. The champagne inspired him to various unusual actions, namely: he decided not to go home just yet, but to pay a visit to a certain lady, Karolina Ivanovna, a lady of German extraction toward whom he harbored entirely amicable feelings. One must mention that the *Very Important Person* was no longer a young man; he was a good husband and a respected head of his family. He had two sons, one of whom already served in an office, and a pretty daughter of sixteen with a slightly turned-up but nice little nose, who came every day to kiss his hand and say, "*Bonjour, Papa.*" His wife, who still retained her freshness and who was not at all bad-looking, let him kiss her hand first, and then, turning over his hand, would kiss it. But the *Very Important Person*, though completely satisfied with these domestic family displays of affection, found it appropriate to have a lady friend in another part of town for affable relations. This lady was by no means prettier or younger than his wife; but such puzzles do exist in this world and it's not our business to judge them.

And so, the *Very Important Person* went downstairs, got into his sleigh, and said to the driver: "To Karolina Ivanovna's." Meanwhile, he wrapped himself up very sumptuously in his warm overcoat, and remained in that pleasant state, nicer than any that could be imagined by a Russian, that is, when you're not thinking about anything in particular, while thoughts come to mind on their own, each one nicer than the last, without the work of having to search or follow them. Full of satisfaction, he easily recalled the most pleasant parts of the evening, all the words that had caused the small circle to laugh; he even repeated many of them to himself in a whisper, and found that they were still as amusing as they were before, and therefore it was no wonder that he laughed heartily at them again. From time to time, however, a gust of wind annoyed him, which, coming suddenly God knows from where and for what reason, would tear at his face, hurling clumps of snow at him, filling his overcoat's collar like a sail, or suddenly, with unnatural strength, forcing it over his head, so that he had trouble finding his way out of it.

All of a sudden the *Very Important Person* felt that someone grabbed him very firmly by the collar. Turning around, he noticed a short man in an old worn-out uniform, and, not without horror, recognized Akaky Akakievich. The clerk's face was as white as snow and looked exactly like a corpse. But the *Very Important Person's* fear exceeded all bounds when he saw the corpse's mouth distorted, and, breathing on him the terrible chill of the grave, the clerk uttered the following words: "Ah! So here you are at last! I finally, you know, have nabbed you by the collar! Now I need your overcoat! You didn't concern yourself with mine, and you even reprimanded me—so now give me yours!"

The poor *Very Important Person* almost died. As strong-willed as he was in the office and with his underlings, and although, after glancing at his manly appearance and his figure, everyone would say, "What a strong character he has!" here, just like very many people who have a heroic exterior, he experienced such terror that he, not without reason, began to fear that he would have some sort of painful attack. He even stripped his own overcoat off his shoulders and shouted to his driver in an unnatural voice, "Head for home as quickly as possible!" The driver, after hearing a voice that was familiar only from the most critical moments, and was even accompanied by something much more physical, hunched up his shoulders, brandished his whip, and flew like an arrow.

In just a little over six minutes the *Very Important Person* was already in front of his own door. Pale, panicky, and without his overcoat, he arrived home instead of at Karolina Ivanovna's; he dragged himself to his own room and there spent the night in great distress, with the result that the next morning at tea his daughter said right to him, "Papa, you look so pale today." But Papa remained silent and said not a word to anyone about what had happened to him, where he was, and where he had wanted to go afterwards. This even made a very strong impression on him. He even began to say less often to his subordinates, "How dare you? Do you understand who's standing before you?" And if he did say it, he first waited until he'd heard what the business was about.

But, what was more remarkable was that from that time forward appearances of the clerk's corpse ceased completely: it seems that the general's overcoat fit him perfectly; at least after this no more incidents occurred where someone's overcoat was snatched away. However, many energetic and thoughtful people refused to be comforted and used to say that in remote corners of the town the clerk's corpse was still making appearances. And, as a matter of fact, one policeman in Kolomna saw with his own eyes a ghost who appeared from behind one house; but, being a bit frail by nature, such that once an ordinary mature suckling pig, after darting out of someone's house, knocked him off his feet, to the great amusement of those cabmen standing around, whom he fined two kopecks each for showing him such disrespect—and so, being somewhat frail, he dared not detain the ghost, but rather followed him at a distance until such time as, finally, the ghost suddenly turned around, stopped, and demanded: "What do you want?"— and showed him such a large fist as you never can see among the living. The policeman said, "Nothing," and turned back at once. That ghost, however, was much taller, had a huge mustache, was heading, it seems, toward the Obukhov Bridge, and vanished completely into the dark night.

Notes

IVAN FYODOROVICH SHPONKA AND HIS AUNTIE

p. 4 *the Jewish tax-farmer*: In Russia, tax farming (*otkup*) was introduced in the late fifteenth or early sixteenth century. It was used especially for the collection of customs duties and salt and liquor revenues.

p. 4 *Nikifor Timofeevich Deeprichastie*: "Deeprichastie" means "gerund" in Russian.

p. 5 *in order to induce the monitor to write* scit: "He knows [it]" (Latin).

p. 6 *Yids*: Yid (*zhid*) is a derogatory term for a Jewish person; the neutral form in Russian is *evrei*.

p. 20 *Korobeinik's* Journey to Holy Places: Trifon Korobeinikov was a sixteenth-century Moscow merchant and traveler. He made two visits to Palestine, Mount Athos, and İstanbul, in 1582 and 1594, on assignments for Tsars Ivan IV and Fyodor I. His account of his travels was first published in 1594 and reprinted many times during the eighteenth and nineteenth centuries.

p. 22 *she thought to herself*: When his aunt thinks to herself, she does so in Ukrainian, not Russian.

NEVSKY PROSPECT

p. 29 *a sleepy Ganymede*: According to Greek mythology, Ganymede is the most beautiful of mortals; Zeus falls in love with his beauty and abducts him to serve as cupbearer on Olympus.

p. 33 *painted by Perugino*: Pietro Perugino (c. 1446/1452–1523) was an Italian Renaissance painter of the Umbrian school.

p. 51 *remarks about A. A. Orlov*: A. A. Orlov (1791–1840) was the author of moralistic tracts for the masses. Alexander Pushkin (1799–1837) is sandwiched between two mediocre authors, F. V. Bulgarin (1789–1859) and N. I. Grech (1787–1867).

p. 51 *a vaudeville like* Filatka: *Filatka and Miroshka*, a popular vaudeville by P. G. Grigoriev (1807–1854), also known as Grigoriev the Younger, first staged in 1831. See also note to p. 67 below, "They were presenting . . ."

p. 51 Dmitry Donskoi *and* Woe from Wit: *Dmitry Donskoi* is a tragedy by V. A. Ozerov (1769–1816) and *Woe from Wit* is a famous comedy by A. S. Griboedov (1795–1829).

p. 53 *the Schiller who wrote* William Tell *and* The History of the Thirty Years' War: Friedrich von Schiller (1759–1805), a German poet, philosopher, physician, historian, and playwright. *William Tell* was a drama written in 1804. Schiller also wrote a history of the Thirty Years' War.

p. 53 *the writer Hoffmann*: E. T. A. Hoffmann (1776–1822), a German Romantic author of fantasy and Gothic horror, a jurist, composer, music critic, draftsman, and caricaturist.

p. 53 *on holidays I take some rapé*: A strong snuff made from the coarser, darker tobacco leaves.

p. 53 *I'm a Swabian German*: An ethnic German people who are native to the cultural and linguistic region of Swabia, which is now mostly divided between the modern states of Baden-Württemberg and Bavaria.

p. 56 "Mein Frau!" . . . "Was wollen Sie doch?" . . . "Gehen Sie . . .": "My wife!" . . . "What do you want?" . . . "Go . . ." (Ger.).

p. 60 *read something out of the* Northern Bee: A semi-official Russian political and literary newspaper published in St. Petersburg from 1825 to 1864. It was an unofficial organ of the Third Section, the secret police.

p. 60 *the College of Inspectors*: State body in charge of accounting and statistics.

p. 61 *he is talking about Lafayette*: Marquis de Lafayette (1757–1834), a French aristocrat and military officer who fought in the American Revolutionary War. He was also a key figure in the French Revolution of 1789 and the July Revolution of 1830.

NOTES OF A MADMAN

p. 66 *It must be something Pushkin wrote*: Actually, the preceding lines are from a lyric by the minor poet and playwright Nikolai Nikolev (1758–1815).

p. 67 *They were presenting the Russian fool Filatka*: The stock character in the vaudeville *Filatka and Miroshka* by the actor and playwright P. G. Grigoriev (1807–1854).

p. 75 *some* donna: Lady (Sp.).

p. 76 *all the kings of Spain resembled Phillip II*: King of Spain (1527–1598) who reigned from 1556 to 1598, reputed to be a cruel tyrant.

ABOUT THE NORTON LIBRARY

Exciting texts you can't get anywhere else

The Norton Library is the only series that offers an inexpensive, student-friendly edition of Emily Wilson's groundbreaking version of Homer's *Odyssey*, or Carole Satyamurti's thrilling, prize-winning rendition of the *Mahabharata*, or Michael Palma's virtuoso *terza rima* translation of Dante's *Inferno*—to name just three of its unique offerings. Distinctive translations like these, exclusive to the Norton Library, are the cornerstone of the list, but even texts originally written in English offer unique distinctions. Where else, for instance, will you find an edition of John Stuart Mill's *Utilitarianism* edited and introduced by Peter Singer? Only in the Norton Library.

The Norton touch

For more than 75 years, W. W. Norton has published texts that are edited with the needs of students in mind. Volumes in the Norton Library all offer editorial features that help students read with more understanding and pleasure—to encounter the world of the work on its own terms, but also to have a trusted travel guide navigate them through that world's unfamiliar territory.

Easy to afford, a pleasure to own

Volumes in the Norton Library are inexpensive—among the most affordable texts available—but they are designed and produced with great care to be easy on the eyes, comfortable in the hand, and a pleasure to read and re-read over a lifetime.

W. W. NORTON & COMPANY

Celebrating a Century of Independent Publishing

p. 81 *in particular, of Polignac:* Jules de Polignac (1780–1847) was a French statesman and ultra-royalist politician after the Revolution.

THE NOSE

p. 87 *always called himself Major:* The rank of collegiate assessor in the civil service was equivalent to the rank of major in the army.

p. 87 *who play a game of boston very well:* Boston is a card game, a precursor of whist.

p. 89 *it was wearing buckskin trousers; there was a sword hanging at his side:* The nose is referred to as "he" when personified.

p. 104 *Khozrev Mirza:* A Persian prince who led a mission to Petersburg following the murder of the Russian ambassador to Tehran.

p. 105 *dancing barefoot a trepak:* A spirited Russian folk dance.

p. 107 *It's simply par amour:* For love (Fr.).

THE PORTRAIT

p. 122 *a portrait of the Tsarevna Miliktrisa Kirbitievna:* A beautiful but treacherous figure in Russian folklore.

p. 123 *these paintings of Yeruslan Lazarevich, or He ate and drank a great deal, Foma and Yeryoma:* Foma and Yeryoma are two brothers featured in popular prints. Yeruslan is a figure from Russian folklore.

p. 135 *dropped by somewhere else:* Most likely this indicates a visit to a brothel.

p. 147 *children of Mars:* Soldiers or warriors.

THE OVERCOAT

p. 163 *name the child after the martyr Khozdazat:* In Russian, names are traditionally chosen from the calendar of saints' lives.